Kate Solly is a writer, a mother of six and really quite good at getting the bubbles out of plastic book wrap. While most of her time is spent finding lost shoes and investigating what's making the car smell bad, Kate frequently escapes to write entertaining things. She has penned many articles, columns and reviews for various publications and is the author of *Tuesday Evenings with the Copeton Craft Resistance* and *The Paradise Heights Craft Store Stitch-Up*. When she is not writing, she enjoys starting crochet projects and never finishing them.

PRAISE FOR *THE PARADISE HEIGHTS MINIATURE RAILWAY BUST-UP*

'Clever, witty – charm for days! Reading a new Kate Solly is the literary equivalent of coming home.' – Emma Grey

'A delightful story interwoven with mystery, humour and real insight. Heartwarming and genuinely uplifting.' – Amanda Hampson

'This is the feel-good book we all need right now. Kate's stories are full of humanity, authenticity and love for humankind. Add in a mystery and railways and it's a winner.' – Josephine Moon

'Kate Solly's latest Fleck Parker mystery is as clever as it is charming – a winning, witty mix of kids, crafts, crime and quirky community antics. This series just keeps getting stronger.' – Jane Tara

'No one meddles better than Fleck Parker. If you love the cosy cleverness of an Agatha Christie, you will love this.' – Kerryn Mayne

'I devoured this book and loved every second of catching up with Fleck Parker – who, by now, feels like a dear friend.'
– Rhianna King

'A delicious, funny and warm-hearted novel from the queen of crafty clues. Friendships, family and handicrafts entwine with a mystery that only our heroine, Fleck, can unravel, along with her yarn.'
– Mary-Lou Stephens

'I didn't think I could love Fleck Parker more, but Solly has upped the charm, wit and mystery with *The Paradise Heights Miniature Railway Bust-Up* and I am so here for it.'
– Sandie Docker

PRAISE FOR *THE PARADISE HEIGHTS CRAFT STORE STITCH-UP*

'For fans of Joanna Nell's writing, with a twist of Richard Osman–style action.' – *Books+Publishing*

'This is cosy crime at its snuggliest … [Kate Solly's] writing is rooted in lived experience and drenched with light-hearted humour.'
– *The Australian Women's Weekly*

'Entertaining, clever and faultlessly constructed and paced work.'
– Living Arts Canberra

'A cosy detective story about craft and craftiness, told with heart and humour – the perfect pick-me-up and beach read all in one.'
– Sophie Green

'Warm, witty and wise – Kate Solly is the balm for a bruised world.'
– Josephine Moon

'Move over, Miss Marple. Fleck Parker is here! Be prepared to snort-laugh your way through this funny and unpredictable mystery.' – Kerryn Mayne

'Kate Solly has penned a delightful cosy crime for those who want mystery and intrigue in a feel-good package. Her main character is so relatable you'll feel like you're reading about your best friend.'
– Rachael Johns

'Kate Solly's effervescent storytelling and cast of eclectic characters kept me delighted and intrigued from the first word to the very last.'
– Rhianna King

'A delightfully modern mystery for anyone who knows what it's like to feel invisible. Once again, Kate Solly weaves serious themes into an astute tapestry of heart, humour and a cast of gloriously unique characters.'
– Jane Tara

'Kate Solly is back with a warm, funny and deliciously tangled cosy crime. I loved it to pieces!' – Emma Grey

PRAISE FOR *TUESDAY EVENINGS WITH THE COPETON CRAFT RESISTANCE*

'Joyous, warm and utterly charming – I smiled for days.' – Toni Jordan

'Warm, funny and big-hearted, Kate Solly stitches together a cast of characters here who will restore your faith in people power.' – Cate Kennedy

'Kate Solly's debut novel is certainly big-hearted feel-good fiction with larger-than-life characters.' – *The Age* and *The Sydney Morning Herald*

'This charming story is a fun read with a deeper message. Resistance has to start somewhere and small gestures can have a big impact. With engaging characters and some sharp observations about modern Australia, it's both entertaining and enlightening.' – *Good Reading*

'A sharp, witty, clever but kind observation of our society, told via the multiple points of view of an irresistibly interesting and diverse collection of characters.' – Living Arts Canberra

'If you feel in the mood for a fun bit of escapism, I highly recommend Kate Solly's debut, *Tuesday Evenings with the Copeton Craft Resistance*.' – Meredith Jaffé

'*Tuesday Evenings with the Copeton Craft Resistance* is funny, charming and will keep you turning the pages. Heck, it might even have you reaching for your crochet hook.' – *The AU Review*

'A fantastic debut novel from Kate Solly. She brings these characters together, with their intentions, flaws and insecurities, in what had me turning page after page, unable to put it down.' – Tara Marlow

KATE SOLLY

The Paradise Heights MINIATURE RAILWAY BUST-UP

affirm press

affirm press

First published in Australia in 2026 by Affirm Press, a Simon & Schuster (Australia) Pty Limited company
Wurundjeri Woiwurrung Country
Level 3, 162 Collins Street, Melbourne VIC 3000

Affirm Press is located on the unceded land of the Wurundjeri Woiwurrung peoples of the Kulin Nation. Affirm Press pays respect to their Elders past and present.

New York Amsterdam/Antwerp London Toronto Sydney/Melbourne New Delhi
Visit our website at www.simonandschuster.com.au

10 9 8 7 6 5 4 3 2 1

NATIONAL LIBRARY OF AUSTRALIA
A catalogue record for this book is available from the National Library of Australia

9781922863058 (paperback)
9781761822476 (ebook)

Cover design by Nada Backovic
Cover images by Nada Backovic (house); from iStock.com: Fourleaflover (footprints), moonnoon (needle), svetolk (ivy), tassel78 (magnifying glass), YURII ZASIMOV (signals); from Shutterstock.com: Vladimir Grigoriev (train)
Author photograph by Darren James
Typeset by Adobe Garamond Pro in 12/18
Printed and bound in Australia by Opus group

FSC www.fsc.org MIX Paper | Supporting responsible forestry FSC® C001695

For David

CHAPTER ONE

Fleck stared at the hot pink sticky note. It wasn't a square sticky note. It was cut in the shape of a duck. Fleck Parker did not know why it was shaped like a duck. Sure, duck-shaped notes were cute, but why pink? Wasn't yellow the standard colour for both ducks and Post-It notes?

Fleck uncapped a pen and continued to frown at the mallard-inspired bit of paper. Matthew had left for work early today. Norah was eating Weet-Bix in her pyjamas. Alice sat in the highchair, periodically pitching her sippy cup overboard. Sam was already wearing his red and blue school uniform and sitting at the table. They were all out of Sultana Bran. When there was no Sultana Bran, Sam liked to be informed of every breakfast option before deciding. He also liked to sound unimpressed with every option. The breakfast options remained the same every day, but every day Sam required his mother to list them for his approval.

'There's Weet-Bix and Corn Flakes,' Fleck began.

'What else is there?'

'I could make you some porridge?'

'What else is there?'

'There's toast with Vegemite or honey.'

'What else is there?'

'Oooh – you could have peanut butter and banana on toast. That's nice.'

'What else is there?'

'Um. I think that's all. Unless you want some raisin toast?'

'What else is there?'

Fleck shrugged. 'There's a bowl of last night's casserole in the fridge.'

'Meat is not a breakfast food, Mummy.'

'Don't let the casserole hear you. You'll hurt its feelings.'

Sam frowned. He picked up the box of Corn Flakes and inspected it. Fleck returned to the sticky note. It was probably a good thing it was hot pink. She needed her note to be attention-grabbing. Of course, the ducks Fleck knew in real life weren't yellow. Most of the ducks in Gardiners Creek and Paradise Lake were brown, but where's the fun in that? Whoever heard of a brown sticky note?

Her pen hovered over the note as she bit her lip. Suddenly, her phone rang. It was Trixie.

'Hiya!' As Fleck answered the phone, she peeled a note off the pad and carefully stuck it to the fridge. She didn't need to write on it. She knew what it meant.

'Have you seen this thing about a one hundred days dress-up? Is that today?'

'Oh no! One hundred days? I remember seeing something about that. Is that *today?*'

'I think it's today. But I didn't realise they were supposed to dress up. Does Sam have a costume?'

'Argh. No. I forgot it was on. He's already in his school uniform. Does Joseph have anything?'

'No! I just saw the notice now! We need to google.'

Trixie McAuley was Fleck's new best friend and the mother of

Joseph, Sam's new best friend.

Fleck put the call on speaker and opened her phone's browser. 'So they need to dress up as old people? Is that right?'

'Yes. One hundred days of school, so they need to dress up as one-hundred-year-olds. Apparently it's adorable.'

'But wait. It hasn't been one hundred days. I'm sure it hasn't. It's too early.' It was also too early to do mathematics in her head. But she was fairly certain that a one-hundred-day celebration should be occurring later in the year. It was only Term One.

'Yeah, but I think the actual date would clash with some other school events. So they rescheduled it.'

'That makes no sense.'

'None of this makes any sense. Okay. I'm seeing ideas on Pinterest. Apparently, dressing kids up as old people is a thing. Everyone is doing it. You can put flour in their hair. Girls can wear shawls. And they put their hair in old-lady buns,' Trixie said.

'But what about the boys? What do the boys do?' Fleck stared bleakly at the pile of clothes spilling from the dress-ups tub.

'Hold on, I'm checking it out. Um. Braces? And they stuff pillows in their clothes. Plus there are instructions here on how you can black out their teeth.'

'Geez. That sounds a bit harsh.' Fleck scrolled her phone. 'Oh wait. Here it's saying they can have walking sticks as part of their costume.'

'Walking sticks? Sure, let's give the kids sticks to whack each other with. What could possibly go wrong?'

Fleck and Trixie fell silent for a moment as they mused over online inspiration. Then Fleck spoke again. 'There's a website here that shows you how to make one of those walking frames out of PVC piping. Do we have time to go to Bunnings?'

'We definitely do not have time to go to Bunnings.'

'I want to go to Bunnies!' This was Norah, bouncing to her feet.

'We're not going to Bunnings, Norah. You're going to kinder, remember? Oh look, you can order an inflatable walking frame from Temu.'

'Can they deliver it in the next ten minutes? No? Then get off Temu!'

'I would if I could, but that's all the internet is these days. Just one massive collection of Temu ads.' Fleck sighed.

'Bunnies! Bunnies! SAUSAGE!' Norah bounced on the spot.

Fleck picked Norah up and danced with her on her hip. '*You're* a sausage, Norah! Can you get me the hair basket?' She put Norah back down and Norah ran off. Fleck looked at her phone. 'This one says you can put fake teeth in a glass to look like dentures. You can use those teeth lollies.'

'They don't make those teeth lollies anymore.'

'What? Since when?'

'It was a little while ago. It was on the news.'

'Oh. I liked those teeth lollies.'

'You can't have liked them that much if it took you this long to notice they're missing. Anyway, it's a moot point. Even if they did have them at the shop, you don't have time to go to the shop. You need to work with what you already have.'

Fleck strode over to the large bin full of dress-ups and started to dig through it. Norah reappeared, carrying the little basket filled with hair ties and hairbrushes above her head, like a hat. Fleck gasped. 'Hang on! I bought Sam an old man cap from the op shop a few weeks ago. I just remembered.'

'What do you mean?'

'I know I said I forgot about the one hundred days dress-up thing, but that's not entirely true. I did remember at one point; I thought about it a few weeks ago. It's only now, when I actually need to remember, that I've actually completely forgotten.'

'What's an old man cap? A fedora?'

'Nah. You know, one of those tweed flat caps you see bus drivers wear.'

'What kinds of buses are you taking? I catch buses all the time and I never see tweed caps. Only official Ventura Bus uniforms for my bus drivers.'

'Well, bus drivers in movies then. And they always say, "Right you are, guv'nor!" It's like a mandatory requirement for wearing that kind of cap.'

'Okay. Well.'

'Except I can't find it now.' Fleck's hair was in her face. She grabbed a claw clip (missing two teeth) out of the hairbrush basket and tried her best to corral her unruly red curls.

'Mu-um.' Sam was looking mildly outraged. 'Norah says she wants to dress up too, but it's not dress-up day at kinder. It's only dress-up day at school. It's only dress-up day for *me*.'

'That's okay, Sam. Any day can be dress-up day if you want it to be.' Fleck tried to infuse her tone of voice with a measure of whimsy and enthusiasm that she did not feel. 'Would you like to dress up like Sam, Norah?'

Norah nodded her head with emphasis. 'I dress up!'

'All right. Would you like me to put your hair in a bun and give you a shawl?'

'No!'

'But don't you want to dress like an old lady?'

'No!' Norah looked highly affronted. 'Batman!'

'Does Norah want to be Old Batman?' Trixie's voice chirped out of the speaker.

Fleck felt the corner of her mouth hitch up. 'How do you make Batman old?'

'He's Batman, but he's started listening to AM radio. Morning talkback with Ross and Russ.'

Fleck smiled broadly as she fished an orange feather boa from the bin. 'He's Batman, but he always has his phone torch on without realising it.'

'He's Batman, but he's really interested in documentaries about World War II.' Trixie giggled.

'He's Batman, but he's installed a rain gauge in his garden and won't stop talking about it.' Fleck cackled. They were both becoming delirious from the stress of it all. 'I love Old Batman. Do you want to be Old Batman, Norah?'

Norah shook her head, rusty curls swinging. 'Not Old Batman! Batman Caped Crusader!' She picked the soft black bat cowl up off the couch and pulled it over her head. She glared at Fleck through the eyeholes.

Fleck shrugged. 'So a normal day, then? Okay.'

The tweed cap was not in the dress-ups bin, but there was a pair of cheap plastic sunglasses with one lens missing. Fleck popped the other lens out.

'Right. So I've found spectacles, and hopefully I can find the hat here somewhere. What do you have?'

'I found a pair of braces and a cardigan. Maybe I'll give him a beanie as well. I don't want to put flour in his hair.'

'I found the tweed cap! It was down the back of the couch. Okay. I'm gonna get him dressed up. I'll see you soon.'

'Hey, Fleck?'

'Yeah?'

'He's Batman but now Robin doesn't want him to drive the

Batmobile after five pm.'

'Goodbye, Trixie.'

Fleck and Trixie stood at the edge of the school playground watching a flock of small would-be centenarians climb and swing. Trixie was wearing denim overalls over a rainbow-striped top. Her glossy turquoise hair was in two thick plaits.

'We need to make friends with a more organised school parent,' Fleck murmured to Trixie.

Sam and Joseph made a very cute pair of old men. Sam looked a little like the old man from the movie *Up*. Joseph kind of looked like the old man from the movie *Up*, too, but a West African version. Fleck had never met Joseph's dad – he had died in Ghana when Joseph was a toddler – but Fleck imagined Joseph looked a lot like him. Sam inspected Joseph's braces and Joseph adjusted Sam's tie (a last-minute addition). Fleck found it funny the way six-year-old boys were constantly in each other's space. It was like they needed to jostle and sling arms over each other's shoulders and sit on top of each other just to reassure themselves that the other was there.

Fleck looked out over the playground. Everyone else had remembered to dress their kids up. Little girls wore shawls and bead necklaces and carried baskets of knitting. Boys wore trousers hiked up to their armpits with cushions stuffed into them to mimic pot bellies. One child wore a bald cap. Another had a white-haired fright wig. The parents were laughing and taking photos.

A little boy was running down the hill towards them. It was Asher, Helen's grandson.

Helen Greythorn was the founder and chair of Many Hands

Society, a women's charity that fundraised through a local craft shop. She was one of the 'old guard', along with Bev, who often volunteered at the counter, and Douglas, who looked after the accounts. Trixie had recently been inducted as manager of the shop. While Trixie's relationship with Helen and the others had been rocky in the past – Helen's stern traditionalism clashed with Trixie's reforming zeal – they seemed to have settled upon a wary ceasefire. At least for now.

Little Asher was wearing a sparkly superhero cape, fedora, University of the Third Age brooch and aviator sunglasses. Helen strode behind him in a crisp beige suit with an upward tilt to her chin.

Asher reached the playground and struck a pose. 'I am a super senior!' he proclaimed. 'I'm not buying into all the ageist nonsense!'

Joseph and Sam were inspecting the sequins on Asher's cape as other children came across to join them. 'That Asher is a cool kid,' Trixie muttered to Fleck. 'Hi, Helen. Excellent costume. I wish I'd thought of that.'

'Me too!' Fleck gazed as Asher twirled, his spangled cape fanning out.

Helen pursed her lips, then a corner of her mouth twitched upwards. 'Well, as it happens, Bev made a few capes. The fabric was cheap and we wanted to try out different colours. We have plenty to go around.'

Trixie stared at Helen with an open-mouthed smile. 'You subversive witches! I didn't know you had it in you!'

Helen shook her head at Trixie in her usual stern manner. 'Oh, please, Trixie. You act as if you *invented* insurrection.' She strode off to the group of children, opening her shoulder bag as she did so.

'Do we need to talk about the fact that Helen only does the school run two days a week, yet was completely across this whole dress-up situation?' Fleck asked Trixie as they watched the small crowd of six-year-olds being issued with sparkly capes.

'We do not,' Trixie said. Coco Waller-Hunt came running past them, her shawl fashioned into a cape ('Super Nanna to the rescue!'), while Lexi Michaels galloped after her, swinging her string of pearls like Wonder Woman's lasso. Trixie blinked. 'I think we need to lift our game.'

'I think we need to start reading the newsletter,' Fleck replied.

It was hard to believe Fleck hadn't known Trixie before the start of this year. It felt like they had been friends for ages. When Trixie had been accused of stealing money from Many Hands, Fleck helped to investigate and clear her name. That was Fleck's first case, her first taste of detective work. And now she was hooked.

The school bell rang. Helen clipped her shoulder bag closed and straightened her blazer. 'Well, I have work to do, and so do you,' she said to Trixie. 'Would you like a lift to the shop?'

Trixie shook her head. 'I'm on my bike. I'll see you there.' She turned to Fleck. 'It's our first Monday workshop today. It's at ten thirty if you'd like to drop by.'

Fleck smiled. 'Absolutely. But I might be a little late. I'll see how long my other thing takes.'

'Other thing?'

'I have a mystery to solve!'

CHAPTER TWO

'Are you nervous?' George placed Fleck's strong latte on the table and they both looked out the cafe window. Alice slept peacefully in her pusher.

Fleck wrapped her hands around the glass, as if to anchor herself. 'I want to say I'm not nervous. I want to say I've got this. But I've got no idea what I'm doing. I'm definitely making this up as I go along.'

'Ah, you can come and join the club with the rest of us.' George picked a newspaper off a nearby table. 'Do you want to do the quiz while we're waiting?'

'Yes. Definitely.'

George stood at the table, flipping through the pages. Fleck loved the quiz. She loved every sort of brainteaser, from daily Wordles and Waffles, to the Friday cryptic in *The Age*. The challenge of puzzles soothed her brain and untangled her thoughts. In theory, she loved physical jigsaws too, even though her lifestyle didn't currently support them (Alice would surely eat the pieces). But her favourite puzzle of all was a real-life mystery.

Fleck opened her 'everything book'. On the outside, it was a very unassuming A5 exercise book; but Fleck's everything book contained all of her drafts for greeting card messages, meal plans, to-do lists and now, her detective notes. She flipped open to the page with the sticky bookmark: the Mystery of the Purple Tags.

The paint had been her first clue. Fleck had pocketed a pebble that had been covered in the paint that had been used to graffiti George's cafe. The tag, 'TACO', had been scrawled once on George's Kitchen, and several times on the shops on the other side of Highett Road.

Fleck had taken the pebble with the purple metallic paint on it to Bunnings after school, with Sam, Norah and Alice in tow. The paint section had a large rainbow wall of paint sample cards. Sam had collected thirty-seven different cards in the brightest colours he could find. Norah had amassed seventeen, all in Snorkel Sea (which she dubbed Batman Blue). She was incensed when Fleck suggested she couldn't have a whole pile all of the same colour. Sam had lots. Norah wanted lots as well. Sam, meanwhile, couldn't possibly give up any of his paint cards because they were actually all his favourites. He could never get rid of his favourites. Not any of them.

Sally the paint specialist wore a green apron covered in gold pins. She gave Fleck a conspiratorial wink and told her not to worry. Then she had told Fleck that the purple stone looked like car paint, not house paint, and that they didn't stock it in purple.

If Fleck were more creative, she would make her everything book beautiful. She had seen a lot of aspirational reels on social media of bullet journal design. They always seemed to pop up on her phone when she was feeding Alice late at night. They were all inky pens and washi tape and calligraphy and stickers. Apart from the occasional colourful title using Sam's textas, Fleck's everything book was rather plain, aesthetically speaking.

The notes Fleck made after her visit to Bunnings were in blue biro.

She supposed she could have dressed them up by cutting out little hearts from the paint sample cards – which Norah and Sam had swiftly abandoned on the car floor – and pasting them in. As it was, the only thing stuck on the page was the pink duck sticky note, and that had nothing to do with the case. It was only there because Fleck had shoved it between the pages when it had fallen off the fridge. And she still hadn't got around to chasing it up. Argh.

George frowned at the newspaper. 'I can't find the quiz.'

'Did you check the lift-out?'

'Ah!' George walked across to the bench by the window where the lifestyle supplement lay and began flipping through it.

Fleck ran her thumb over her handwriting. She didn't write in calligraphy and she didn't use decorative flourishes, but she still found this page beautiful in its own way. It was satisfying information. Delectable data. It was a record of an activity that brought her joy.

The notes for the next section were written up in green ink. Fleck had chosen a quiet time of day to visit Supercheap Auto and she hadn't brought the kids with her.

'I reckon you're looking at Daytona Violet right there.' The man in the paint section was short and stocky and his name tag read 'Phil'. He squinted at the rock a moment longer, then moved to the shelves. 'Let's see if I'm as good as I think I am.' He scanned the small pots as he spoke. 'You're not going to find many cars on the road these days that aren't white, black, silver or grey. You've got your reds and you've got your blues, but they're only maybe twenty per cent. So if you're talking about purple or green or orange, you're talking about one, maybe two per cent of cars on the road. Not each. All together those colours are two per cent.' He pulled some pots off the shelf. 'Something like this is what we call a hero colour. It's attention-grabbing, but it only ever sells in lower numbers and it'll only be available for a few years.' He held up the pots. 'So here we've got BMW Daytona Violet, Midnight Plum and Passion Berry Pearl. Let's see if I'm right.' He unscrewed each pot and painted a small stripe onto a sample strip. Then he held the strip against the rock.

'It's definitely that one.' Fleck pointed to the first streak.

Phil grinned broadly. 'What did I tell you? Daytona Violet. You'll find this one on BMW M3s and M4s.'

'Okay. I've got a weird question for you.'

'Shoot. I love weird questions.'

'Is this the sort of paint people might use to graffiti a wall?'

Phil snorted. 'Maybe if they're rich and stupid. This sort of paint costs three or four times the price of normal spray paint. I don't know why you'd use it to tag a wall. Bit of a waste if you ask me.'

Fleck had spent a lot of time looking at cars after that. She'd noticed purple cars and learned what BMW M3s and M4s looked like. But she'd never spotted a purple BMW.

George smoothed the quiz page open. 'Okay, let's look at what we got here. One-pointers. Let's go. "Which Australian animal is renowned for leaving uniquely cube-shaped droppings?"'

'Haha. Wombat!'

'Wombat is correct.'

Fleck cast another look out of the window. Not there yet. She gazed across the street at the shops on Highett Road: the cafe on the corner where Dima worked occasionally, the vacant shop, the Rotary Recycle op shop, the takeaway pizza shop and the other fish and chip shop (the good one was on Peppercorn Street). With the exception of the op shop, they all had purple graffiti on them. They all had campaign posters for the upcoming state election, too. Even the empty shop had a campaign poster in the window. And the side wall of the cafe had a large placard on it, the size of a real-estate ad. The cafe, beside a small car park and playground, was the last building of the strip. The six-foot-tall headshot with its bold writing smiled benevolently at all the city-bound traffic on Highett Road. Nathan Garland for Ashthorn.

'Right. Question two is hardly worth reading but here we go. "What kind of animal is AA Milne's Eeyore?"'

'Ugh. Too easy. Donkey. Next!'

Fleck had kept a watchful eye while she was at the train station or park or any places where graffiti tended to be. She was looking for the 'TACO' tag. It wouldn't have been hard to spot. There was something amateur about it. It seemed far too legible to be a tag. But there were no 'TACO' tags anywhere. The only place they seemed to exist was on the Highett Road shops. There were none even on Peppercorn Street, the smaller perpendicular street which hosted more shops.

'Okay. Question three is a bit trickier. "Which instrument is largest: bassoon, oboe or piccolo?"'

'Oh. That's tough. I mean, I know it's not piccolo.'

'Yeah, the clue is kind of in the name there.'

'But bassoon or oboe? Which one is the bassoon again?'

'It's the musical instrument.'

'Oh yeah. Thanks. Big help.'

'Don't look at me! I don't know this one.'

'I think the bassoon is big. It sounds big.'

'You don't know what a bassoon is, but you know what it sounds like?'

'No, I mean the name sounds big!'

'Okay. Let me check. Bassoon is right!'

Fleck looked out the window again. 'Heads up. Here he is.'

The car pulling into the space outside George's Kitchen was like a giant ad for Nathan Garland. It looked similar to the graphic on the campaign poster, with the same headshot of Garland in a suit and tie, the same bold block letters spelling 'NATHAN GARLAND, CANDIDATE FOR ASHTHORN', the same cursive font spelling 'Getting it done'. It was one of those vinyl skin decals that covered the entire car. Nathan Garland himself got out of the car, looking ruddier and more unkempt than his campaign photo. He was talking on his phone as he walked towards the cafe.

'No. No. I'm telling you, we've got to—no. No, I need you to listen. Yes, well, Head Office are a bunch of—They are. They're a bunch of—no. No. Just get it done, okay? Okay? I'm hanging up now. Goodbye. Goodbye. Get it done.'

Nathan jabbed at his phone and then looked up as if surprised to discover himself in the cafe. He blinked and put his phone in his pocket. The cafe was small, the size of one room, and Fleck and George were the only other people in it. Nathan pointed at Fleck and squinted, head tilted to the side. 'Are you Sandra from the Wattle Park Residents Association? Are you the one who emailed me to set this up?'

Fleck smiled politely. 'I am the one who emailed you.'

Nathan sat down across from Fleck. He turned to George. 'I'll have a full-cream magic. Do you know how to make a magic?'

Fleck had to credit George. He said, 'Coming right up!' with perfectly friendly intonation. There was nothing in George's smiling bearded face that betrayed what Fleck knew he must be thinking: *arrogant prat.*

Nathan turned to Fleck. 'Okay, Sandra, let's make this quick. I'm sorry I was late to get here. Musbrook Highway was down to one lane of traffic because this government insists on pouring taxpayer money into white elephant infrastructure projects in areas that are already over-serviced while neglecting growth areas and public transport deserts. Meanwhile, it's impossible to drive anywhere without sitting in gridlock for half an hour. Mismanagement is what it is. Classic mismanagement.'

'I'm not Sandra, by the way. My name is Felicity. You can call me Fleck.'

'Wait. You're not Sandra? What's going on?'

Fleck sipped her coffee. 'I wanted to talk with you about something important.'

Nathan hesitated. 'Are you affiliated with the Residents Association or are you just a crank? I have another meeting in the city that I'm already late for. Are you one of the Teals trying to wind me up?'

Fleck shook her head. 'No. I genuinely do want to talk to you about the graffiti.'

Nathan looked mildly reassured. 'That graffiti is yet another classic symptom of government mismanagement. Did you know they're planning to close the Paradise Heights police station in September? All over the place they are slashing funding and—'

Fleck cut him off. 'Yes, but I wanted to talk specifically about the purple tags down Highett Road. Those are your buildings, aren't they?'

'They are. I've been directly impacted by the government's neglect of law and order in this electorate.'

'It's a rather convenient narrative for you, wouldn't you say? George was telling me about how you had a full camera crew here with you last week filming a spot for one of the current affairs shows. It seems like that graffiti artist played right into your hands. Wouldn't you agree?'

'I wouldn't know anything about that. I was in Canberra when it happened. I came back from my trip to find my property had been vandalised. Look, I have places to be. What's this about?'

Fleck looked at him levelly. Then she looked past him out of the window. 'You have a nice car, Mr Garland. I've seen it all over the place.'

'What? Okay. Sure. It's nice.' Nathan shifted in his seat impatiently.

'Is it a BMW M3?'

'Yes.'

'And they did a good job with that ad. It covers the whole car. What do they call that? A skin?' Fleck peered at the car.

'It's a custom vinyl skin. Yes. But hold on—'

'A custom vinyl skin. So you can't see any of the car's actual paintwork with that on. That car could be any colour,' Fleck said.

'Sure. Look, if that's all we're here to talk about—'

'There's a gap, you know.'

'What?' Nathan looked disconcerted.

'There's a tiny gap. At the back. Where the number plate is.' Fleck lifted her chin. 'I took a look at it the other day when it was parked across the road. The skin doesn't run right to the edge. You can see that the car underneath is purple. Actually, it's Daytona Violet. Exactly the same colour as the tags down Highett Road.' She watched him carefully. 'It was you.'

'What are you talking about? What was me?' Nathan's forehead was shiny.

'You're the one who graffitied your own shops.'

'That's impossible. I was in Canberra,' Nathan said.

'Okay, so you got one of your lackeys to do it. But you were the one behind it all,' Fleck said.

Nathan stood up. He planted his hands on the table and loomed over Fleck. 'Who even are you? Why do you think you can just call me in here and start accusing me of things? Those are some serious allegations you are making. What – are you threatening me?' His voice was raised. His whole face gleamed with sweat and there seemed to be a rash creeping up his neck.

George materialised beside Fleck. He set Nathan's coffee on the table and remained at Fleck's right shoulder. 'How about you take a seat, mate?' His tone was feather light.

Nathan remained standing, but he eased back a little. 'I don't even understand why this is an issue for you,' he said in a sullen voice. 'It was my property that was vandalised. Why do you care?'

'Because this cafe was tagged, too. More than once.'

Nathan gave a start of surprise. 'What? That wasn't – what do you mean?'

'That purple paint of yours is a bugger to clean off.' George had not returned to his usual station behind the counter. He stood beside Fleck, watching Nathan steadily.

Nathan sat down. He seemed to have lost all of his bluster. He opened his mouth, then closed it again. Twice. After a moment, he spoke. 'I know I said I had nothing to do with it and I have no idea of where that paint came from and of course, I stand by that assertion.' Nathan put his hands face down on the table. 'Having said that, your plight has caught my attention. I have a heart for small business owners and I would like cover any cleaning costs you may have incurred as a result of this vandalism.' He paused and sipped his coffee. 'And while I know nothing of the graffiti artist involved, I get the sense that this was a mistake on their part. I don't think they realised that your shop should be off limits. I'm certain that anybody involved would want to apologise.' He drew in a long breath and exhaled. 'But this is mere conjecture on my part, of course. I want to cover your costs. I'm hoping we can say no more about it. Agreed?'

Fleck offered a smile. 'I'm so glad you have agreed to cover costs. I went to the trouble of drawing up an invoice for you.' She produced the document and handed it over.

Nathan looked at the invoice. A slight wavering at his throat was the only indication that he'd noticed the generous rate Fleck had awarded George for his labours. 'Consider it done.' He folded the invoice in half. 'And can I get this coffee put into a takeaway cup? I really do have to go.'

CHAPTER THREE

'Hey, wow! Everything's different!' Fleck stepped through the door at the Many Hands Society craft shop, setting the bell off with a jaunty tinkle.

Trixie was stationed behind the counter, holding an embroidery hoop. She looked up at Fleck and smiled broadly. 'Do you like it? I moved things around on the weekend. It's not finished yet.'

Fleck looked around the shop. 'It just seems so much *bigger*. And I can move around with the pusher without knocking shelves over.'

Trixie nodded. 'I've been reading up on the science of shop layouts and displays. How you draw the customer's attention. How you, like, manage traffic around the shop. It's my current hyperfixation. As soon as I read it, I couldn't rest. I had to come here and try it out.'

'How did Helen take it?' Fleck asked.

'Surprisingly well. I think she's on her best behaviour. I could still tell she wasn't entirely happy, but she says I'm the shop manager now and she trusts my judgement. Which is a lot coming from Helen.'

'Is she here now?'

'She's upstairs with Bev. They're talking to someone doing some work for the Society.'

Fleck nodded. Although the Many Hands shop had been a quiet presence on the Peppercorn Street strip for many years, she had only recently learned of the not-for-profit organisation it funded. The Many Hands Society was established in the 1980s by Helen Greythorn and Joan Cooper. Fleck was still learning about the different things the Society did, but she knew they had an affordable long-term rental scheme for single mothers, a drop-in centre for women in crisis, and various programs to assist asylum seekers and refugees. Helen was still a driving force of the Society, and while Joan had died many years ago, her sister, Bev, and husband, Douglas, were still very much involved.

'Who are they talking to?'

'I don't know. I didn't see them come in. But it's society business, not shop business, so I'm leaving them to it.'

'And they're leaving you to get on with shop business. Helen says she trusts your judgement?' Fleck raised her eyebrows. 'That's pretty big.'

Trixie nodded. 'And the weekend's reshuffle is only the beginning of my plans. Eventually, I want to swap these middle shelves out for ones on coasters. Then we can move them to the side when we want to do events.'

'Oooh! What kind of events?' Fleck bounced on the spot.

'I'm not sure yet. Exhibitions? Book launches? I'm thinking I'd like to have a party for us as well. Just to celebrate all of this. Like, look here.' Trixie stepped out from behind the counter to show Fleck a group of shelves to the left of the front door. 'I've corralled a lot of the really fussy lacy stuff into this section. Remember how it used to take over the shop and kind of permeate the whole place? Now, it's a feature and it's given recognition, but it's no longer creating that sort of visual noise all over the shop.'

Fleck smiled. 'You've really thought about this.'

Trixie shook her head. 'Oh, I'm just getting started! I've got this whole idea about making this display over here into a Featured Maker shelf.' She gestured to the prominent group of shelves near the front of the shop. 'So, like, every week – or maybe every month, that might be better – we use it to showcase the work of a specific maker. I've got this plan that I'll reach out to some of the really influential makers on Instagram and offer to sell their things here on consignment. This will raise the Featured Maker shelf's profile and get things rolling. Then once we've established the shelf and given it some credibility, we can start charging makers for the shop space and advertising. But first I need to get my head around endcaps and how they work.'

The shop bell jangled and Jo, a Many Hands volunteer, walked in with another woman. She was large and attractive, with an expressive face. Her straight dark hair was cut with a chunky fringe and she walked using an iridescent purple cane. Trixie introduced them. 'Fleck, you know Jo, but I don't think you've met Kerryn. Kerryn's a regular customer and is going to start coming to our workshops.'

Kerryn smiled. 'I'm an acrylic artist,' she said. 'Basically, I make jewellery out of plastic.'

'Wait until you see her work,' said Trixie. 'It's wonderful. When Bev gets back downstairs, we can start, but feel free to go in and make yourselves a cup of tea.'

'Thanks, Trixie. I'm gonna go sit,' Kerryn said. She disappeared behind the curtain into the back room with Jo.

'Anyway, enough about my current obsession,' said Trixie. 'How's your current obsession going?'

'Good! I solved the mystery!' said Fleck. 'But also bad! I solved the mystery.' She picked up a red knitted 'emotional support chicken' and turned it around in her hands. 'I'm going to miss having it to work on.'

'We'll have to find another mystery for you,' said Trixie. 'But first, tell me all about this one.'

By the time Fleck had finished updating Trixie on what had happened with Nathan Garland in George's Kitchen, Bev had appeared and taken her spot behind the register. It was time to join the others for the workshop.

Trixie slid into her usual chair. 'We're still waiting on Dima, and maybe Lynette,' she said.

'Who's Lynette?' Fleck asked.

'She's Jo's friend from church. She called the shop last week to ask about the workshops and she said she wanted to start coming along.'

Jo looked up in surprise. She seemed to be about to ask Trixie a question when the tinkle of the shop bell and Bev's greeting signalled Dima's arrival.

Jo grinned and leaned in to whisper, 'Do you think she brought cake?'

Trixie shook her head and whispered back. 'You can't ask her if she brought cake. Otherwise she'll think we only care about her for her cake. Don't ask about the cake.'

Fleck giggled. 'I really hope she brought cake.'

'Shhh!'

Dima walked through the curtain divider. She was a petite young woman, originally from Syria. She wore a loose blue headscarf over her dark hair, and a mischievous grin. Dima had started a small business making gorgeous celebration cakes. The volunteers at Many Hands often got to taste her experiments and off-cuts. Fleck noticed that she was not holding anything that could possibly be a container for cake. Sad news. Still, it was lovely to see her.

'How have you been, Dima? Have you been knitting much?' Jo said this with a significant look at Trixie. (*See? I can behave myself!*)

Dima smiled. 'I have been so good. I've been working at the refugee welcome centre. I've bought a new skein of wool on special from Lincraft and my mum looks like she'll be getting her bridging visa soon. Also, I've been binge-watching *The Family Next Door*. It's very good. Have you seen it yet?' She waited while everybody nodded and smiled and muttered pleasantries. Then she clapped her hands together, before disappearing back into the shop and reappearing with a zipped-up freezer bag. 'I have cake.'

The room seemed to erupt with enthusiasm as Dima pulled plastic containers out of the bag. Fleck hopped up to make a pot of tea. When there was cake as lovely as Dima's, you needed to enjoy it slowly and with tea. That was the rule.

'This one looks like a mess now, but it's from a cake I made for a baptism.' She held her phone out to show a photo of the finished product: a simple cylindrical cake with white icing and gold leaf detail. 'It's sticky ginger cake with finger lime pearls. You're getting the offcuts and trial batches.'

There was a bit of fussing with cups and plates and sending slices upstairs and out to Bev, but soon everyone was sitting around the table contentedly, enjoying the cake and listening to Trixie.

'Welcome to our first official workshop!' Trixie said. She smiled around at everyone in the room. 'I have been trialling different styles with Fleck, my guinea pig, but this is the first one that is open to everyone. We're still in our infancy so today, I wanted to get everyone together to have a talk about our plans for workshops and events. I'm conscious that we don't want to do too much too soon, but I also don't want us to become stagnant and lose our momentum. I'd like to discuss our wish-list classes and our practical plans for where we want to start.' Trixie gestured to the whiteboard that was affixed to the wall beside the stairwell. 'Hit me with some ideas.'

‘Beginners’ workshops!’ said Dima.

‘Sip and stitch evenings!’ said Jo.

‘Come and try mornings!’ said Fleck.

‘Knit and natter!’ Jo again.

‘Crafting for a cause!’ Dima again.

Trixie wrote these ideas onto the board. ‘I’m going to write “social crafting”, Jo, so that we’re not limiting ourselves to knitting. Anything else?’

Kerryn frowned. ‘I would love to have a workshop, or even a series of workshops, that aren’t about a specific skill, but are sort of about how you make it as a creative. Like, how do you sell your work? How do you find your market? Is it worth building a social media profile? What do you do when you feel stuck creatively? That sort of thing. Kind of like the theory side of things.’

‘I’m putting it on the board,’ Trixie said. ‘I’m loving this.’

The shop bell jingled. They could hear a woman talking loudly as she entered the shop. ‘Just through here is it? Here? Through here? I thought so. Ta!’

A woman came through the curtain with a strong waft of perfume. Fleck’s immediate impression was of a rather attractive rhinoceros. This was an unkind thought, perhaps, but the woman just seemed *formidable*. And she seemed to wear clothes and make-up like armour. Her eyebrows were perfect arches. Her jewellery was thick and gold. Even her large, flat handbag seemed like a shield. She scanned the room as she entered with a pretty smile that seemed more ornamental than genuine. ‘I’m Lynette Chester, everyone. How are you? I’m sorry I’m late. I got caught in some bad traffic. But it wasn’t too bad. I was listening to a *fascinating* podcast. I’m like that. I need to keep my mind active. I’m a bit of a nerdy girl! Do you know? I just love learning!’

Trixie welcomed Lynette and introduced the others around the table. Then she invited her to have some of Dima's cake.

Lynette looked around the group. Fleck followed her gaze. Kerryn sat with a kind of tackle box in front of her filled with jewellery-making paraphernalia. She was threading small charms that looked like pieces of fairy bread onto earring hoops. Jo was using double-pointed needles to knit a bright red cone, which Fleck knew was destined to be a gnome hat. Dima was also knitting, but it was something square-shaped and she was using traditional needles. Fleck was working away at a knobbly bit of crochet. Trixie held an embroidery hoop. In navy floss, the cross-stitched words on it read *Fight Truth Decay*.

Lynette reached into her bag and pulled out a mindful colouring book. It still had a price sticker on the front. She waved it around almost defensively, as if it were an all-access pass, then opened it to the first page and smiled.

'When Jo convinced me to join you all, I didn't know what to expect,' she said.

Fleck noticed Jo's expression shift. She shifted her position, angling slightly away from Lynette. Lynette didn't seem to notice. 'We go to church together at ChristLife. It's so nice to get a chance to *do life* together, too.'

Jo offered a tight smile and nodded.

'I think I know ChristLife,' Fleck offered. 'It's that really big church with the auditorium out past Ringwood?'

Lynette nodded and looked like she was about to launch into a response but was interrupted by footsteps on the stairs. It was Helen – and Ranveer.

Trixie gave a small start. 'Ranveer! What are you doing here?'

Ranveer was Fleck's neighbour. Before Fleck's first case, she had never even had a conversation with the serious accountant next door.

Though their relationship had once been distant and formal, Ranveer had ended up helping Fleck and Trixie to decipher doctored financial statements and suspicious bookkeeping. That said, before Fleck's first case she'd had little to do with the tall school mum with the vivid turquoise hair, either. But Trixie, Fleck and Ranveer had been pulled together by circumstance and formed an unlikely trio. Still, Ranveer didn't have anything to do with Many Hands, as far as Fleck knew. It was strange to see him in this context. Fleck looked across at Trixie. She also looked surprised, and perhaps a little self-conscious. Helen had already slipped into the shop, but Ranveer stood at the foot of the stairs.

'I have been helping Helen. Why is this room so crowded? The shop was empty when I arrived.'

'This is our Monday workshop. What do you mean, "helping Helen"? Like, as an accountant? Douglas Cooper will *not* like that!'

Ranveer shook his head. 'No. It is a new scheme for the charity. I am helping her to set it up. Microfinance.'

Trixie looked at Fleck. Fleck shrugged. She didn't know what that meant, either. The others fell into their own conversations as Trixie and Fleck spoke with Ranveer.

Trixie looked back at Ranveer. 'What's microfinance? Are you writing everything down on a little tiny ledger?'

Fleck grinned. 'And people have to keep their tiny receipts to show you in a shoebox for Barbie shoes?'

Fleck and Trixie cackled and Ranveer shook his head. 'No. It's a small loans scheme. Interest-free. A not-for-profit cooperative.'

Fleck grinned and nodded. 'Those are all definitely words. And I could definitely tell you what each of those words mean by themselves. But I'm still not following.'

Ranveer hitched his laptop bag further up his shoulder. 'Imagine you wanted to start a hairdressing business, but you needed equipment before you could start making money. Or perhaps you needed to purchase a special chair for an eyelash-extension business.'

'How do *you* know about eyelash extensions?' Trixie looked amused.

Ranveer met her look with an upward tilt of his chin. 'I am a man of the world. I know about lots of things.' He smiled. 'Also, one of the applications we got was for a special chair for eyelash extensions. Well, they call it a chair, but it looks more like a bed to me.' Ranveer seemed to relax a little as he settled into information-sharing mode. 'At any rate, a lot of the women assisted by the Society have bad credit history. Sometimes they have come from abusive relationships where the partner had a gambling problem, or sometimes they are refugees and have no credit history. It can be hard for them to access loans. So we are putting together a program to grant small business loans. I have been meeting with Helen to discuss the best practices for a scheme like this.'

If Trixie had looked self-conscious, which Fleck was now beginning to doubt, any evidence of this had now cleared. 'I like the sound of that. Would you like to join us?' she gestured to the empty seat next to Jo. 'I could teach you some micro-stitching to go with your microfinance.'

Ranveer smiled and shook his head. 'I need to get to a meeting with a client.' He disappeared out the back door.

The meeting continued, but the dynamic seemed to have shifted since Lynette arrived. She had a habit of dominating the conversation. Sometimes it was to assure the group of some fact about herself ('I'm strange like that – always wanting to learn new things!', 'I'm a bit of a hashtag girlboss', 'People think I'm weird. I'm just so friendly'). Other times she would make odd announcements to narrate what the group was doing ('Look at us! Women working together. Isn't that what it's all about? Don't you think? Don't you think?'). By themselves her words might be whimsical, but they were paired with an almost aggressive insistence that the others should agree with her, or at least respond somehow. Fleck found herself falling quickly into the role of supporting cast ('Oh yes, absolutely'). She couldn't help herself. Lynette declined the offer of cake ('I'm all about health at the moment. I'm all about healthy living'), although Fleck noticed she stirred two sugars into her coffee. She also had a tendency to hijack the conversation, interrupting Trixie in a conversational way and steering the chat away from plans for the shop, away from crafting.

Trixie was telling them about the Featured Maker shelf. 'I'm putting together a list of Melbourne-based craft influencers that we might approach. I'd love to hear your suggestions if you have any favourites.'

'Craft influencers? Is that a thing?' Lynette looked surprised.

'It's absolutely a thing. We were thinking—'

'That just goes to show, doesn't it? We can all be influencers really. Don't you think? Don't you think? I mean when you think of all the people you know in all your different circles. We really have a lot of reach. There is so much potential right there.'

'But coming back to the list—'

'But don't you think?'

'What?'

'We all have such influence in our own way. In our own circles. I think we would be surprised if we knew what we could become if we were to find an *outlet*. If we could find the right *pathway*. There is so much potential within all of us. We can be such girlbosses. Such mumpreneurs!'

'Uh. No.'

'No? No?' Lynette looked around the room with a beam of appeal. 'I think you all could be *total* girlbosses. Absolute boss babes.'

'We don't tell men that they can be dadpreneurs and boybosses though, do we?' Trixie kept her tone light, but Fleck could see that Lynette's manner was beginning to grate on her. Chatting with Lynette wasn't a relaxing experience. Chatting with Lynette felt more like a tug-of-war.

Fleck's eyes met Trixie's involuntarily. An unspoken query: what was Lynette's *deal*?

CHAPTER FOUR

Fleck pulled the car out of Trixie's driveway and turned onto the street. 'I know you could probably have walked there from home,' she said, 'but if I drive you to parkrun it means I have to go too. I'd be letting you down if I didn't go. If I didn't have you relying on me, I'd just stay in bed.'

'It works for me too. It forced me out of bed, knowing you were coming to pick me up.' Trixie rubbed her eyes and yawned. 'What happened to Ranveer? I thought you were giving him a lift too?'

'He's going to *run* all of the way there. He says it's a warm-up. Ridiculous.'

'At least if we go to parkrun once, we can tell Ranveer we gave it a try,' Trixie said.

'Yes. We can tell him we tried it and it wasn't for us. Then he can stop asking us.' Fleck turned onto Musbrook Highway.

'How long has Ranveer been into running, anyway? Is this a new thing?' Trixie asked.

'I honestly don't know. I didn't know a single thing about Ranveer before this year. But I think it's new. He has all the zeal of a convert.'

‘And he did say we don’t have to run the whole way? He did say that, right? We could walk bits if we need to?’

‘He said we could walk the whole way if we liked.’ Fleck turned the car through the large double gates of Paradise Lake Park and drove up the sweeping drive.

‘What if we want to lie down in the middle of the course and have a quick nap? Is that allowed too?’ said Trixie.

Fleck parked the car and the two of them walked up to the meeting spot. The Paradise Lake parkrun started at 8am every Saturday. The starting line was at the barbecue area near the miniature railway. Fleck tugged at the hem of her brand-new running top. She was wearing two different sports bras and anti-chafe shorts. This was necessary. Fleck had discovered that if she were to be successful in running any sort of distance, she needed to firmly immobilise all the parts of her that jiggled.

They tentatively approached the crowd. Fleck had expected a league of lithe bodies, all tall and toned and in their twenties. She had thought she’d be the only one who was short and, well, *abundantly* built. Instead, an eclectic bunch of people milled around the rotunda: seniors, kids, people with prams, people with dogs, people with every possible body type.

Ranveer spotted them as they approached, and ran towards them.

‘Don’t run now, Ranveer!’ Trixie said to Fleck. ‘He should save all his running for the actual run.’

Fleck nodded. ‘He’s going to run out of running!’

Ranveer smiled. ‘I’m glad you came. I’ll show you where to go for the first-timer’s briefing.’ He led them to a lady with a broad smile and a slim clipboard. While they listened to the briefing, Fleck cast looks across at Ranveer as he stretched and talked with two other men. When the clipboard lady was done, Fleck turned back to Trixie.

'Has Ranveer always looked that *athletic* or is this a new development?' They both looked in his direction. 'I mean, is it just that this is the first time we are seeing him in shorts and a singlet or has he somehow grown biceps overnight?'

Trixie shrugged. 'It's a mystery.'

'Maybe his muscles are like the stars in the night sky. They are still there during the day, even when you can't see them.'

Trixie was peering at a dog that was rolling in the grass. 'I can't say I've noticed.'

Fleck grinned. 'Oh, you've *noticed*.'

Now a different lady was standing on the picnic table, wearing a vest and wielding a megaphone. As she spoke about dogs on short, hand-held leads and the importance of keeping to the left of the path, and as everybody clapped a lady in her seventies who was celebrating her fiftieth parkrun, Fleck took a look at the race route map, a laminated card propped up on the barbecue bench. They would run around the lake and then up the hill to the manor house. Then they'd come back down the hill and run around the outside of the miniature railway, past the small playground and back to the barbecue area for the finish line. She was not looking forward to that hill.

They shuffled to the starting line. Ranveer stood towards the front of the pack, while Trixie and Fleck moved themselves determinedly to the back.

They set off around Paradise Lake. It was a very picturesque route, or it would be if every fibre of Fleck's being wasn't burning with pain. Running was *hard*. In the past, Fleck had considered 'lake' to be a rather generous description of the ornamental body of water in the park. Today, though, the lake seemed enormous and the track around it never-ending. They plodded along. Fleck tried to remember to breathe.

'Do you want to walk for a bit?' Trixie was loping along beside her.

It wasn't fair: one of Trixie's long-legged steps was worth two of Fleck's, she was sure of it.

Fleck shook her head and managed to cough out a response. 'Let's get to the bridge first. Then we can walk.'

The fastest runners had looped the manor house and were coming back down the hill. Fleck waved to Ranveer, but his face was set in a frown as he powered along. He didn't see her.

They managed to run and walk in stints around the rest of the lake. When they reached the foot of the big hill, they decided to walk the whole way up. Fleck looked over as Trixie pulled an inhaler from her pocket and took a puff. 'I didn't know you had asthma.'

Trixie shook her head, slowly exhaling, and put her puffer away. 'I don't really. I just get it sometimes when I'm running. Or maybe if there's a lot of dust.'

Fleck nodded. 'That's like Matthew. He has a puffer but he hardly ever uses it now. But sometimes cats set him off.'

The manor house stood at the top of the hill. 'Why does it seem to be getting further away and not closer?' Trixie grumbled.

'Because that house is haunted. I am convinced.'

'Really? I think it's charming, like a storybook cottage. I like the dormer windows.'

'Which ones are the dormer windows?' Fleck squinted at the house.

'The ones that poke up through the roof. And they have their own little roofs on them. They're adorable. And look at those pretty wrought-iron grilles. Why do they curve out like that at the bottom?'

'I dunno. Maybe to fit flower boxes in? Dormer windows look pretty from the outside, but it would be annoying on the inside.'

'What do you mean?'

'Well, you'd have to deal with all that slopey ceiling in your room. I know I'd keep banging my head on it.'

'Hmmm. Yeah. I hadn't thought about it. But why do you think the house is haunted?'

'Have you ever seen it up close? It's definitely giving creepy vibes.'

When they reached the top of the hill, Fleck and Trixie decided it was really important that they pause and read the historical information board next to the creepy manor house. For education. Not because the hill had literally almost killed them.

> 'Paradise Lost'
>
> The original manor house was built by Bradford Mann in 1924. Mann, a great admirer of the works of John Milton, named the house and estate 'Paradise Lost' after the work which he considered to be Milton's greatest achievement. Surrounding suburbs, Paradise Heights and Paradise South, take their names from the original Paradise Lost estate.
>
> The house passed through other private owners, including the Walter family (1948–1961) and Rohan Neeson (1961–1979). In 1979, the entire estate was sold to the Melbourne and Metropolitan Board of Works. Today, the building operates under the administration of Parks Victoria.

A black-and-white photograph showed the manor house in the 1950s. Trixie peered at it and then at the house itself. 'It hasn't changed much. I don't know why they don't do more with this place. They could have events here. Wedding receptions maybe. It's a pretty building. That ballroom is so pretty. Do you think it's still like that inside?'

'I suspect it's not up to code,' Fleck said as they wandered closer to the building. 'A lot of these old places don't fit today's standards for things like fire safety and, I don't know, structural integrity, that kind of thing. Maybe it would be more expensive to fix it up than any benefit they might get from it. I think there used to be an information centre here or something. But it's been closed for so long. Maybe the hill puts people off.'

Fleck peered into the front window. There was no furniture inside; at least, there was nothing in the part of room visible from the window.

'I can see why you think it's haunted,' said Trixie. 'I usually find these sort of old houses charming. But now that I'm up close, this one seems creepy. I don't know what it is. I don't know if it's just because it's been empty for so long, but there just seems to be bad energy around this house. Let's keep walking.'

The side of the house was overgrown with greenery. 'I think that's a bay window behind there; it's hard to tell,' said Trixie.

'Are you the window expert? You know about – what was it? – *dormer* windows and now you're going on about *bay* windows. How do you know so much about windows?'

'You don't need to be a window expert to know what a bay window is. Do you think we could just roll down the hill? It would save time.

They started jogging again as the path finished its loop around the manor house and began retracing their steps down the hill. It was a relief to see that there were still plenty of people behind them on the course. Ranveer had assured them that it would be impossible to finish last; there was a volunteer whose job was to literally finish last. But it was still reassuring.

Soon they were back on flat ground, running around the lake again. Fleck swiped a rogue curl out of her eyes. 'Okay, let's talk about something. I need something to distract me from the pain in my legs.'

'Let's talk about your next case.'

'I don't have a next case. That's the problem.'

'That's what we need to talk about. How do we find you another case?'

Fleck groaned. 'I don't *know.* I've really been missing having a mystery to work on, but I don't know how to find another one.'

'I suppose you could ask around,' Trixie mused.

'Like what? Go to the school office and ask if they want me to chase up items in the lost property box?'

'Or maybe you could advertise? Careful of the root here.' Trixie dodged an uneven part of the trail and kept running.

'I could go on Marketplace, maybe. Or the Paradise Heights and Surrounds Community Page.' Fleck gasped out the words.

'For sale: Detective skills. All problems solved. Big and small.' Trixie was puffing a bit too.

'Especially small. Small problems a speciality. Send me your small problems. I could be like one of those Hire a Hubby franchises. Are they still a thing?' Fleck peered out over the lake.

'I think they're still a thing. They have those little trailers they cart around. What would you call it, though?'

'Hire a Mummy?'

'Nah. Hire a Crack Detective!' Trixie neatly dodged an overhanging branch.

'That doesn't have the same ring to it.' Fleck dodged it too, but not as neatly.

'Jim's Sleuthing?'

'That's it!'

Morning light dappled the lake's surface. Trixie pointed and called out the names of all the waterfowl they passed. They were running to a rhythm.

'I think you are in your slog era. That's what this is.' Trixie didn't even seem to be puffing all that much now.

'My slog era?' Fleck gasped. 'Are we talking about running?'

'No. I mean with your detective work. Look at the Wiggles. Not just the one with the nice arms. I'm talking about the original Wiggles. They weren't always selling out massive stadiums. They spent ages carting their equipment around to shopping centres and performing to small audiences.' Trixie reached back and tightened her ponytail without breaking her stride. 'You're in your slog era, too. You might have to take on boring jobs that aren't exactly what you want to do. But one day people will see how brilliant you are.'

'Technically, all audiences for the Wiggles are small, just saying.' Fleck's voice was strangled.

'Yeah, yeah, yeah. But the Wiggles weren't always this big. They were just a bunch of guys playing in community centres at the start. Did you know they didn't even have a Captain Feathersword to begin with? Captain Feathersword was just Anthony in a hat.' Trixie slowed her steps a little. 'Should we walk for a bit?'

Fleck nodded gratefully. When she got her breath back she spoke again. 'You sure know a lot about the Wiggles.'

'I watched a documentary about them.'

'You watched a *documentary* about them? You did a deep-dive on the Big Red Car?'

'What? It was interesting. Joseph used to be big into the old-school Wiggles. We watched the same DVD so many times. I think in the end I started to identify with them in some sort of Stockholm-syndrome way. That DVD travelled with us everywhere. And Anthony is a bit hot.'

'Anthony? No, he isn't! Anyway, this new purple Wiggle is a lot hot. Have you seen him?'

'The boy band one? I mean, he is, but he's kind of hot on purpose. He is *meant* to be hot. Anthony isn't meant to be hot. He is hot by accident. I like it much better when someone is accidentally hot.'

'Accidentally hot?'

'Yeah. Like when a newsreader is hot. It's better than when, like, a Marvel superhero is hot.'

'Nerdy hot?' Fleck said.

'Nerdy hot is the best kind of hot.'

'Yeah. I *like* nerdy hot. Oh yeah, baby, gimme some of that sweet, sweet nerdy action!'

'Gross, Fleck. Nobody wants to hear that. And Matthew isn't nerdy hot. He's just Matthew,' Trixie said

'No. Matthew is hot on purpose.'

'Vomit.'

Fleck looked out across the lake. A Pacific black duck had its wings extended, showing off the bright teal patch underneath. 'The thought of saying "I'm a detective" out loud to people makes me cringe to my very core. I don't think I could do it. How do I find more mysteries to solve if I can't call myself a detective?'

Trixie shook her head. 'I don't see why you shouldn't call yourself a detective. You've solved two cases so far and done a brilliant job both times. You managed to clear my name and find out who was exploiting Many Hands and you discovered who had vandalised George's Kitchen. Enough with the imposter thoughts. You've got to claim it. No one else will do that for you.'

'You should be a motivational speaker.'

'I really should.'

They started running again. Fleck looked longingly at the finish line, but they were supposed to go past the barbecues towards the playground, then loop all the way around the miniature railway before they could cross the line. Ranveer had already finished. He was waiting to get his token scanned. He waved as they passed.

They trudged ahead in silence, thumping down the trail. They didn't stop running until they reached the railway. Then they slowed to walk again.

'I keep meaning to bring Joseph here,' Trixie said as they passed the large station and ticket sales booth. 'You're here most Sundays, aren't you?'

'Yeah. You should come sometime.'

'I should. It's funny. I know people always say autistic kids love trains, but Joseph doesn't really fit the stereotype. He can take them or leave them. But if Sam was here, he'd like it.'

'I don't think you have to be into trains to enjoy it. It's just good wholesome fun. And there's a big festival coming up. You should definitely come to that.'

'It's bigger than I thought it would be too. The whole thing, I mean. Not the size of the trains.'

'Yeah, it covers a lot of ground. And there are a few different loops. One train ride takes about fifteen minutes.'

'Oof. I wish we could catch a little train for the rest of parkrun. We could choof on through the finish line. Come on. Let's run the last bit. People are passing us.'

CHAPTER FIVE

'The Daddy-mountain goes up! All the way up high! All the way up to the sky! And Norah says—'

'Bye bye!'

Norah was sitting on top of Matthew's knees as they bent to form a rising 'mountain' under the covers of the big bed. At Norah's word ('bye bye'), Matthew's legs suddenly flattened, sending Norah tumbling off her perch, giggling maniacally.

'My turn!' Sam had been curled, warm and deliciously sleepy, in the space between Fleck and Matthew. When Fleck came home from parkrun everyone was still in bed. Matthew had taken the night shift with Alice and was loath to get up. He was trying to coax a few more minutes of sleep-in out of the children by inviting them into the big bed. Fleck showered and put her pyjamas back on, sliding in beside them. The sleepiness was wearing off now, though. They would need to get up soon.

Sam was getting a bit heavy for Daddy-mountain, but Matthew still managed to hoist him on his knees. Fleck lay watching them. She hated to admit it, but Ranveer had been right. She felt really good after her run.

After a few more rounds of Daddy-mountain, Sam and Norah climbed under the doona at the opposite end of the bed to play caves. Fleck curled against Matthew. He was nice and warm.

'So what time do you need to be at the railway today?' Matthew volunteered at the Paradise Heights Miniature Railway, where Fleck had just been running, one Saturday a month. This week was his Saturday.

'Not till eleven. Do you want pancakes for breakfast? I think we've got all the toppings.'

'Mmm.' Fleck made a non-committal sound, half thinking, half sleeping. Then, 'Yeah. Let's do it.'

'And next week I've got the kids and you're going out. Have you worked out what you want to do with your time?' Matthew rolled onto his side.

Fleck groaned. 'No! I wanted to do some detective work. But I don't have a case anymore! And I have no idea how I can find another one. I need a new project.'

Matthew was quiet for a while. Fleck wondered if he had been listening or if he'd fallen back asleep. Finally he spoke. 'I might have one for you.'

'Have one what?'

'A mystery. At least, I think it is. There's something I need someone to investigate for me. It might be nothing, but it would really help if somebody looked into it. Someone from outside.'

'What do you mean? Something at work?' Fleck said.

'No. Something at the railway.' Matthew rolled over to face her. 'You know how I've taken on the role of quartermaster? I can't get the supplies to reconcile. It could be nothing, but it could be that someone is stealing things. I don't want to say anything about it until I'm sure of what's going on. It would really help if I could have someone from outside the railway have a look at it.'

Fleck rolled back and gazed at the ceiling. The doona inched lower as Sam pulled on it from under the end of the bed. She turned back to look at Matthew. 'Are you doing this just to humour me?' she said in a small voice. 'Because you feel sorry for me?'

Matthew frowned. 'I don't get it. You said you were looking for a mystery to solve ...'

Fleck huffed. 'Yes, but it needs to be a real mystery. I don't want some pity mystery.'

Matthew tugged the doona back up the bed. Sam yelped. 'It *is* a real mystery. I couldn't work out how to solve it and when you said you were looking to investigate something the solution presented itself. It needs to be somebody from outside the railway investigating. That's you. It wouldn't be strange for you to be there asking questions. You'd blend right in.'

Fleck pursed her lips. In the room across the hall, Alice began to grizzle. Matthew got out of bed, and returned with Alice in his arms. Fleck sat up and pulled the cushion onto her lap. Matthew passed Alice to her, went to the ensuite and returned with a glass of water, which he also handed to Fleck. 'Come on, kids. Breakfast time!' he said. Then he turned to Fleck. 'Think about it. I can show you around the railway today maybe. I'll call Mum and see if she's free to watch the kids.'

Fleck usually visited the railway with the children on Sunday. The railway didn't run on Saturday, but the volunteers still met there to set things up and do maintenance. As Fleck and Matthew approached from the car park she spotted a plain engine towing a carriage full of garden cuttings around to the second shed.

'I spend most of my time in the signal box. I'll show you that part last,' Matthew said. 'Let's look at the engine sheds first.'

'So up until recently, who managed the supplies inventory?'

'Well, we've never really been strict on managing our supplies at the railway. Technically, it has been up to Dennis Ray, but he's been out of action for a few years now, with bad health.'

'And you've taken it on?'

'For now. It's unofficial. I don't really have time to be the quartermaster, and I don't want to step on Dennis's toes – not that I think he'd mind – but I want to find out how we're losing so much money. Maybe it's a cost-of-living thing but we seem to be pouring money into buying new things and yet never have enough of what we need.'

'So it could just be a matter of bad housekeeping.'

Matthew sighed. 'I mean, it could be. That's why I don't want to make a big thing of it. I don't want to make Dennis look bad. But I can't get it to make any sense. I've started taking copies of the delivery slips when supplies arrive.'

'Does anybody know you have been trying to audit it?'

'Not yet. Like I said, I don't want to stand on any toes.'

'Keep it like that. We don't want to tip off the thief. If there is a thief.'

'We don't know that there's a thief.'

'If things have been mismanaged for a while, that could attract a thief.'

Matthew rubbed the back of his neck. 'I hate suspecting people.'

'Don't worry. That's my job. So take me over it again.'

'We got three big boxes of toilet paper delivered last Saturday. And fifteen sacks of expensive fertiliser for the grounds. I know because I saw it all in the back room of the engine sheds,' Matthew told her. 'But when I went in on the Sunday, a week later, there was only one box of toilet paper and three bags of fertiliser. I checked the gardens and couldn't see any fertiliser had been put down. We'd never go through thirteen bags of it, anyway. And we only stock toilet paper for our clubhouse toilets, not the whole park. There is no way we would have gone through two large boxes in eight days.'

Fleck chewed her lip and looked across the park. Then she looked at Matthew.

Matthew gestured to the path, and they fell into step. 'Oh, and here's a weird thing. The Thomas livery has gone missing. The Percy livery too.'

'You've lost me. The Thomas what?'

'It's like a costume for the steam engines to wear. You know, when we dress the engines as characters from Thomas the Tank Engine? But nobody can find them anywhere. And they'll be expensive to replace. They're the proper licenced characters.'

They were walking towards the engine sheds. Tall gum trees rustled overhead, and the creek honked softly with the sound of frogs.

'Diesel is the other thing,' Matthew continued. 'I haven't been monitoring the diesel supplies, but I feel like we've really been going through it lately.'

Fleck frowned. 'It's weird. If it were any one of those things, it could be that someone is stealing them for personal use. But if somebody's stealing fertiliser and toilet paper and diesel fuel – what ties them together? And what does that have to do with Thomas cosplay?'

'"Livery" is the word you are looking for. And I have no idea how it's linked.'

They arrived at the engine sheds. Fleck always imagined this building as a little dorm bedroom for the locomotives. The tracks radiated out from the turntable at the front like spokes from a wheel. The engine sheds were curved in a concave shape to hug the turntable wheel. There were twelve little doors set into this curved wall, with a track running up to each.

'The engine sheds are so cute. I love seeing the trains go through their own little door when they need to go home for a nap.'

Matthew shook his head, smiling. 'It's built to imitate the traditional roundhouse design, at half scale. The turntable out the front feeds all of the interior tracks, but unlike the classic American semicircle design, our tracks eventually resolve into parallel within the shed, to fit the rectangular shape of the shed. We can fit more engines in that way.'

Fleck nodded. 'Okay, sure, but to me, it just looks like the toy at home that we keep all the Thomas trains in.'

Matthew grimaced. 'But that's *because* Tidmouth Sheds from Thomas the Tank Engine is modelled on the HO Scale Vollmer Roundhouse building, which is in turn a replica of a prototypical German roundhouse. Honestly! I can't take you anywhere!'

Fleck had never been inside the engine sheds before. It was hard to know what to look at first. The first room was a storage shed for the carriages; they moved through this quickly to get to the larger engine shed: the locomotives' bedroom.

There were many engines, some exposed, some covered in cloth. Fleck could see that the tracks that led up to the little doors on the outside extended inside with enough space for each track to hold a full train of carriages. The floor around the tracks was sunken, allowing workers to stand with the trains on the track at chest height. There was a pungent smell of diesel oil, and the benchtops against the workshop walls were covered in tools and rags and rinsed-out yoghurt tubs full of metal bits.

A young man emerged from one of the side rooms. He was holding something metal with wheels on it.

'Fleck, this is Quinn. He's one of our engineers. He's been volunteering for a couple of months now. He knows everything there is to know about trains. Quinn, this is my wife, Fleck.'

Quinn nodded. 'Good to meet you.' He said it quickly. Then he hesitated, nodded, and disappeared back into the room he'd emerged from.

'He's a good kid.' Matthew spoke in an undertone. 'Not a fan of small talk, but get him talking about trains and he can hold court with the best of them.'

'So he works on maintaining the engines?' Fleck asked.

'He's studying mechanical engineering at Monash Uni, so he knows his way around a bogie,' Matthew said. Then, seeing Fleck's blank face, added, 'A bogie is the running track you build an engine around.'

One of the small doors opened and an engine appeared. Fleck recognised it as the one she had seen earlier, pulling a carriage of garden clippings. The carriage was now empty.

The man driving the train pulled it slowly up to the end and carefully climbed out. Matthew introduced him. 'Fleck, this is Top – er – Sydney Tozer. He's one of the longstanding members of the railway.'

'Topham Tozer,' the man corrected Matthew and moved in to offer Fleck a firm, vigorous handshake. He was rather tall, with a shiny bald head, and had a voice like a radio announcer. 'My nickname around here is "Topham". I don't suppose you can guess why?'

Fleck hesitated and offered a confused smile.

Topham turned sideways and patted his protruding round belly. He grinned broadly. 'Are you familiar with Sir Topham Hatt?'

Fleck nodded. 'The Fat Controller.' Thomas the Tank Engine books were on high rotation in Fleck and Matthew's home.

Topham chuckled. 'Yes, well, some say I bear a passing resemblance to that man. And I am in charge of a lot of things around here. Some might say I'm a bit controlling but then, you know what they say about Mussolini.'

Fleck hesitated and cast an appealing look at Matthew.

Matthew gave a wry smile. 'He made the trains run on time.'

Topham smiled. 'That's right. Which is why I don't mind being a bit of a Fat Controller sometimes. Railways need it.'

Fleck nodded, though she wasn't sure what she was agreeing to. As soon as Matthew spoke the quote about Mussolini, she remembered it. Privately, she had always thought the reason Mussolini was famous for efficient railways was because he controlled the press and anybody who dared complain about it did not live long to tell the tale. But now wasn't the time to quibble over Italian fascist dictators.

'I hope you've put the Sunday of the long weekend in your diary. You do know it's our festival day with the night train?'

Fleck nodded. Topham smiled. 'We've purchased the rights to dress up one of the trains as Thomas the Tank Engine and I am going to dress as the Fat Controller. I have the top hat and tails already.'

Matthew grinned. 'And Topham has been helping me with the plans to duplicate the outer loop.'

'Yes. I was here when the original outer loop was added in the eighties. Nineteen eighty-seven to be precise. Before that, the railway was much smaller: just a simple loop around the station. The outer loop allowed us to make the ride more interesting. A bridge across the creek; picnic areas inside the loop. Plus, it made the railway visible to the cars going past the park on Musbrook Highway.' He paused. 'Duplicating the track will be a huge endeavour.'

Matthew nodded. 'Yes, but it'll be worth it. We've applied for several grants to fund it. With a double track, we'll be able to run more services, and cut down on wait times. We can vary the routes in all sorts of new and interesting ways. We could even have a race!'

Fleck smiled as they exited the sheds and walked back up the path towards the clubrooms. She'd heard all of this before, many times.

His plans for the new outer loop line was one of Matthew's favourite conversation topics. It was the sort of thing he could talk about at length with very little input from her. He could, in fact, talk about the loop on a loop.

She looked out across the park as Matthew and Topham continued to enthuse about tracks and signals. A section of park not far from the engine sheds looked like it had been cleared and levelled. Red and white fencing tape on poles surrounded it.

'What's that over there?' Fleck pointed to the small piece of land, surrounded by tracks.

Topham looked across to where she was pointing. 'Ah. That's a new development. We have a local artist building a little fairy garden there. A spot of interest, you know? And something to show the girls in the family, eh?'

Fleck nodded. She didn't know this man well enough to bother schooling him in gender stereotypes. Plenty of girls loved trains. Plenty of boys loved fairy gardens. But that was a whole other conversation.

A petite young woman with short, spiky black hair was pulling a wagon full of materials to the patch of land. 'Is that the artist?' Fleck asked.

'Yes,' said Topham. 'Let's go over. I'll introduce you.'

Fleck found it a little amusing that Topham had taken over Matthew's role as tour guide. Perhaps his reputation as controller was valid.

As they approached the artist, Topham seemed to have realised his mistake. It was clear he did not know her name. 'Hello there. Here we have – well – we have our famous young artist! It's good to see you again, dear. I wanted to introduce you to – well, ah – to Mrs Flanagan here.'

Fleck smiled brightly and raised her hand in a wave. 'I'm Fleck

Parker.' She turned to Topham in explanation. 'I kept my name when I married Matthew.'

The young woman smiled. 'I'm Ruby Chen. I am a miniatures artist. I'm creating a village display.' She looked as if she might elaborate, but Topham stepped in.

'Yes. Ruby is making a fairy garden that will be visible from the trains as they go past,' he mansplained. 'It was commissioned by—'

'It's not a fairy garden,' Ruby interjected. She turned to Fleck to reiterate her point. 'It is *not* a fairy garden. There are no fairies involved at all. It's not for fairies. It's a miniature village.'

'A miniature village,' Fleck repeated, with a smile of encouragement.

'Well, you know what I mean,' said Topham. 'It's basically a fairy garden. The point is—'

Ruby looked distressed. 'There are no fairies. It's built to the same scale as the trains. It's a miniature village.'

'Ah, now you raise an excellent point,' Topham interjected. 'The engines on this railway are all built to scale – at least up to a point. But this is not a model railway, it's a miniature railway. In order to operate effectively as a passenger-carrying service, certain exceptions need to be in place. For example …'

Topham continued to talk on this point as he led them away from Ruby and towards the clubhouse. It was a large building with a wraparound veranda. Downstairs featured another workshop. 'For track works and points,' Topham explained. The upstairs room had the feel of a sporting club room. A polished wooden board, with names and dates inscribed in gold, dominated one wall. There was a large kitchen, with signs on the fridge and microwave and a collection of coffee mugs. A whiteboard featured a roster. There was a boardroom-style table at one end and a cluster of armchairs at the other.

Back out on the veranda, most of the volunteers were sitting on the many chairs looking out over the railway. Topham finished his tour here, as he fell into conversation with a couple of the other volunteers. Fleck and Matthew crept downstairs while Topham held forth on the incompetence and his suspected corruption of local government officials.

In the downstairs workshop, a central bench was covered with metal strips and jars filled with rivets and screws. Walls were covered in pegboards, with tools neatly outlined. 'This is where all the work is done on the tracks,' Matthew said. 'And there is some additional engine storage at the side there.'

'What's this?' They'd approached a small room, not much larger than a cupboard, with a window in the door. She could see rows of small square images glowing within.

'Oh, this is the security room,' Matthew said as he pushed the door open. 'It's all very high-tech.' The room wasn't really big enough for them both to stand inside, so Matthew hovered by the door. There was a swivel desk chair facing a wall with a computer and five monitors, each showing four black-and-white video feeds in split-screen view.

'Does this footage get saved?' Fleck peered at a screen labelled 'Ticket Booth 1' where she could see a large black raven strutting across the footpath.

Matthew nodded. 'It's all digital, but each day's footage goes into a file saved in the cloud.'

'Can we access it?'

'I think so. What's the plan?'

'If we can get the footage on the engine sheds for the time between when you counted the supplies and when you noticed the supplies were depleted, we can narrow our pool of suspects to people who visited the shed. And we can see if anyone unusual is finding their way in. Oh, and if there's footage of the car park, maybe we can see if there's someone smuggling things out to their car?'

'Like a big round Thomas face?' Matthew grinned.

'Exactly!'

Matthew squeezed past her and sat down in the desk chair. He fiddled with the keyboard and mouse. One of the monitors displayed a catalogue of files. The other monitors adjusted to accommodate the extra screens that had just disappeared from the one Matthew was working on. 'They're sorted by date,' Matthew said. 'Which files would you like?'

Fleck bounced on the balls of her feet. 'Give me all of that week.' She leaned over his shoulder to point to the folders. 'Everything from the Saturday when you took inventory to the Sunday a week later when you noticed that things were missing.'

Matthew scrolled through the folders of files. He opened the desk drawer and pulled out a thumb drive. A minute later, he unplugged the stick and put it in Fleck's hand. 'All yours, m'lady! Now, can I show you Minihan Junction?'

There were two signal boxes that served the railway, but Minihan Junction was Matthew's favourite. It was patterned after the historic Ringwood signal box, built at half scale. It was very cool. It had a lot of antique fittings from the old Victorian Railways board. You could see the different routes lit up across a display running along the length of wall above the window. Matthew spoke with such enthusiasm about the levers, which were operational, though a digital option was also available. Fleck rolled the memory stick in her fingers, then slid it into her pocket as Matthew invited her to switch the track.

'The full-size version has levers that come up through the floor and are almost as tall as the person operating them. This is an eighty-lever interlocked frame built along the same lines, but in miniature. And it's set in a bench, not the floor.'

Fleck pulled the lever Matthew was pointing to and watched the light change on the map above the window. She smiled and nodded and made enthusiastic noises.

But her mind was on the clue in her left pocket.

After they got home, thanked Marian, ate lunch and fed Alice, Fleck decided it was time to sneak off for some detective work. This was a trick she had learnt. She used to ask Matthew to take the kids out so she could have some time to herself. He would do it, but it would take him forever to get organised. She'd only ask for this favour when she was feeling completely spent, so his deliberation would drive her up the wall. *Please just go! I need to think my own thoughts for a change!* Plus, it was always such a jolt when they arrived home again and disturbed her peace. But now she knew: it was so much easier if *she* left the house. There was no waiting around and no interruptions. Fleck kissed Matthew, hugged the kids, grabbed her laptop and left the house.

George was busy with customers as Fleck arrived, but he called out a greeting. She set herself up on a small table and opened the laptop and her everything book. She set to work reviewing the footage.

It took her a little while to get her bearings, but the recording files were clearly labelled and systematically filed, which made things a lot easier. Fleck concentrated her efforts on the camera above the door to the engine sheds, which showed people entering and leaving, and the camera showing the car park and main entrance. There was another camera covering a side door to the engine sheds, but this door was not used at all for the whole eight days.

George put a strong latte on the table in front of Fleck. 'Are you looking at surveillance footage?' he said.

Fleck nodded. 'It's my new case. The great trainyard robbery. Somebody has been stealing supplies from the miniature railway. I'm looking to see who is going in and out of this shed.'

'Who needs Netflix?' George deadpanned.

'Yeah, well, I narrowed the timeframe down to an eight-day window. I've only watched the first two days so far, but there are a few different people coming in and out. I've noted down the timestamps. But then I realised I should be focusing on people carrying large things in and out.'

'And did you see anyone who did?' George asked, peering at her screen.

'Yes. Two so far: an artist who is creating a miniature village at the site, and an engineering student who volunteers there. I'm pretty sure their names were Ruby and Quinn. They both had good reason to be carrying large bags and wheelbarrows in and out of the sheds, but still, it's a good starting place.'

George moved back behind the counter. 'I have an update on the Nathan Garland graffiti situation.'

Fleck looked up. 'Really? What's the latest?'

'He paid the invoice. In full. I was surprised. I thought he was going to dodge it for sure. But he's coming here to do a listening post next week.'

'What's a listening post?' Fleck asked.

George shrugged. 'I'm not sure. Something involving card tables and matching T-shirts. I think he paid the invoice because he doesn't want me to come across the road shaking a broom at him when he's busy trying to charm the neighbourhood.'

'That's a pity. I'd buy tickets to that show!'

CHAPTER SIX

Fleck returned to the railway the following day. It was Sunday morning, and Matthew had taken the children to the playground near the barbecue area to have a play before the engines started running. Fleck was hoping to talk to Quinn, the engineering student, while he was in the clubhouse.

Quinn was standing at the 'control centre' section of the clubhouse, checking the schedule for the day. Fleck sidled up beside him and gazed at the whiteboard on the wall. Volunteer names were printed on magnetic labels. She spotted 'M Flanagan' and 'S Tozer'.

'Hey, where's your name?' she asked Quinn. She couldn't see a 'Q' anywhere.

'I'm here.' Quinn pulled a magnet off the board labelled 'T Tait'. Then, seeing her confusion, added, 'Quinn is short for Tarquin.' He put the magnet back on the board. He was tall in a way that gave the impression that the rest of his body was still catching up. A confusion of jutting shoulders and knees and wrists and elbows. His face might be handsome one day, but right now it just looked scared. Fleck remained standing beside him. She had read somewhere that men often feel more comfortable communicating this way, side by side instead of face to face. She wanted to make this as easy as possible for Quinn, who seemed almost panicked after this brief exchange of words.

Fleck had decided the night before to write a feature article on the Paradise Heights Miniature Railway. It was her cover story, but it was also the truth. Of course, it would be simpler to just *say* she was working on an article, without actually writing it. Fleck was pretty sure that's what most detectives did when they needed a cover story. But Fleck knew she wasn't a good liar. She would get flustered and confused and would give the game away. Better to make the lie true. She had started a document to plan out the sections and everything. It didn't have to be any good. It didn't have to get published. But it was definitely true.

Fleck knew from her conversation with Matthew that Quinn was shy, but he warmed up when talking about trains. She told Quinn about her article. 'I'm thinking I'd like to include some interesting facts on railways in general. Matthew says you might be a good person to talk to. Do you have some colourful railway facts I could use to dress up my story?'

Quinn visibly relaxed once he started talking. He spouted interesting train facts and little-known snippets of Melbourne transit history. He had a great skill for zeroing in on the best information. By the end of the conversation, Fleck had made little progress investigating Quinn, but had learnt much about the Fawkner hearse train, the Eltham trestle bridge, and that time in the nineties when an empty metropolitan train accidentally rolled downhill along an entire train line, all the way from Broadmeadows to Flinders Street Station.

'You should start your own podcast,' Fleck said. By now they had moved across to the kitchen area and were sitting on the stools by the bench.

Quinn gave a small smile. 'That's what my girlfriend says,' he said.

'She thinks it would be really good. She might even go on it with me.'

The careful way he spoke. The way he paused for a fraction of a second before and after 'girlfriend'. Fleck could tell this was a new relationship, and possibly his first. 'I was originally going to do a podcast with my housemate. Well, I say he's my housemate, but he was also my friend in high school. We were going to make a podcast together. We had the name picked out and everything, but that's not … We're not …' Quinn left his sentence unfinished. He looked away.

'What's your girlfriend's name?' Fleck asked.

A blush crept up Quinn's neck. 'Gwendoline,' he said, brightening. 'She's great. She lives in Swan Hill, but she's going to move up to Melbourne soon. We message each other all the time.'

'She sounds lovely,' Fleck ventured.

'She is. She's actually really cool. And she's a great listener. Plus she's really beautiful. Not that … I mean, that's not the only reason I like her.'

Fleck nodded and they sat quietly for a moment. When Fleck spoke again, her voice was gentle. 'Are you still going to make the podcast with your housemate?'

Quinn winced. He made a drawn-out noise like an old man grunting to get out of a chair. 'I don't know. We were going to once, but – I don't know. I don't think so.'

'What changed?' Fleck asked.

Quinn frowned. 'Liam got a girlfriend. It just meant that everything changed.'

'That sounds hard,' Fleck offered.

Quinn shrugged. 'It is. But I've got Gwendoline to talk to about it. We might move in together when she comes to Melbourne. I can't wait.'

Fleck nodded. She was keen to ask Quinn about the missing

equipment, but it was already time for him to start work in the engine sheds. At any rate, it seemed important to draw him out slowly. Afterwards, Fleck met Matthew and the children at the end of the winding queue, ready to catch the first train of the day. Sam and Norah chattered happily about their time on the flying fox. Fleck half-listened as her mind whirred over her conversation with Quinn. She looked out over the line of people queueing. An engine had pulled to the platform and the line shuffled forwards and then stopped as the carriages filled with passengers. The man taking tickets closed the gate and the engine took off.

The ticket collector was large and bear-like, wearing a Paradise Heights Miniature Railway hat and a brightly coloured T-shirt emblazoned with the words: 'Nathan Garland for Ashthorn'. He smiled broadly at each person as they approached the front of the queue.

'Matthew,' Fleck said slowly. 'What is Nathan Garland doing here?'

'So you're telling me that Nathan Garland has been volunteering at the railway for the past few weeks? And stuff has been going missing for the past few weeks?' Fleck pulled a tiny singlet out of the washing basket, folded it and put it in the 'Alice' pile on the table.

'Just because somebody is a politician doesn't mean he's a crook.'

'Yeah, well, it doesn't mean he *isn't* a crook,' she said. It was a pity she hadn't been able to confront him at the miniature railway. By the time they had reached the front of the queue, Nathan had left and there was another person checking tickets. 'He's just such a charmer. He doesn't seem the type to be into trains.'

Matthew paused in his Vegemite spreading to quirk a single eyebrow at her assessment. 'What are you saying about train enthusiasts? Are you saying we can't be smooth and socially ept?'

Fleck smiled and shook her head. 'You are ept. You are very ept. But this guy is just so *polished*. I'm not sure I trust him.'

'Do you have any hard evidence against him?'

'No.' Fleck folded one of Sam's T-shirts.

'So the only thing you have on him is that he is too charming?'

'That's the only thing.'

'Okay, then. Good luck with that.' Matthew pulled more bread out of the bag. 'Do you think you might be a little prejudiced? Because of the sort of man he is?'

Fleck paused in her folding. 'What do you mean?'

'Well, he is wealthy and personable …'

Fleck pulled another onesie out of the basket. 'So you think I have a thing against rich, white, charming men? I don't think that's a bad thing. I think that's a healthy prejudice. If I'm going to be bigoted against someone, make it rich, white, charming men.'

'Okay, but why would he be stealing random things?'

Fleck paused and frowned. 'Maybe it's the same as the graffiti. He wants to make it look like there is more crime in the area because he's running on a law-and-order platform.'

Matthew tore open the second bag of cheese slices in the tub. 'But if that were the case wouldn't he make it more public? Nobody would have noticed the things going missing if I wasn't keeping tabs on supplies. Actually, so far, nobody *has* noticed the things going missing!'

'I don't know why you're so keen to defend the man.' Fleck rolled a navy bath towel into a neat cylinder.

'I'm not defending him. I just don't think he's had much to do with the engine sheds since he started. He's been mostly in ticket sales and marshalling. And I think he's looking to get his driver's licence.'

'That would get him into the engine sheds.'

'Yes, but he hasn't started on that yet.' Matthew placed another sandwich on the stack. 'What is it they say? Means before motive? And you didn't see him in the surveillance videos, did you?'

Fleck groaned. 'You're right. But he seems like such a villain. He's already shown himself to be untrustworthy.'

Matthew put the sandwiches in the bread bag and put the bread bag in the freezer. He cast an eye over the pantry contents as he put the Vegemite back in its place. 'Are you planning a big shop soon?' he said. 'I think we're running out of a few staples.'

Fleck swallowed and placed the *To the Batmobile!* T-shirt on Norah's pile. Meal plans were supposed to be her thing. Fleck prided herself on the sensible, nutritious and economical meal plans she wrote up in her everything book. She wasn't usually an organised person, but the meal plans were different: they were a thing of beauty. And, in turn, they informed a detailed shopping list that Fleck ordered to match the layout of the supermarket. Fleck might not be currently earning an income, but she felt good that she could save the family money by being on top of the grocery spend.

At least, this had been the case until recently. They had reached the end of the last meal plan and Fleck hadn't made up a new one. Fleck usually shopped on Thursdays or Fridays, but it had been a few weeks now since she'd done a big shop. They'd been relying on the top-up shops Matthew did on his way home from work.

Everything was chaotic without a meal plan. It meant scrabbling about every afternoon, desperately trying to think of something to feed everyone. Fleck definitely needed to go to the supermarket. And she would. She'd even written the meal plan now. She'd written a few, actually, moving the pink duck sticky note aside so that she could write on the page. But she hadn't managed to actually go to an actual supermarket. Just like she hadn't dealt with the pink duck sticky note. She just kept forgetting.

At the Flanagans' Sunday night dinner, the kitchen was an explosion of noise and industry. Marian was pulling a large casserole dish out of the oven, which she quickly set down when Fleck and Matthew arrived, so that she could rush across to hug them. Matthew's older brother, Frank, sat on a stool at the bench, slicing lettuce, while his older sister, Aggie, emptied potato chips into a bowl. She also stopped what she was doing to greet them and offer them snacks.

'Yeah, okay, Aggie, just let me get in the door!' Matthew grinned as he kissed his older sister and she scooped Alice out of his arms. Two teenage girls were playing some sort of Uno variation at the table. The older one was Ruth, Matthew's much-younger sister. She was playing with Lily, Aggie's eldest.

'We are fourteen tonight,' Marian announced as she spooned some tinned corn into a little bowl and stirred the rest into the mince casserole. 'Agnes-Mary is husband-free, aren't you, Aggie? Diego's working, so it's just Agnes-Mary and her four. Your brother, Xavier, is not flying all the way back from Cambodia to see us for dinner, which I think is incredibly rude. Therese called to say that she was bringing someone, but that she was running late. Where's Norah?'

Norah and Sam had made their way into the kitchen and were busy greeting everyone in the room. 'Thank you, Nanna!' Norah exclaimed as she grabbed the small bowl filled with corn.

'So is Therese bringing someone or Bringing Someone?' Aggie said. She was a younger, larger version of her mother. She shot a look out to the backyard, where her twins were hitting each other with garden stakes 'Daniel! Miguel! I SAID NO STICKS!'

'Who can tell with Therese? He might be a friend she made at the bus stop for all I know. Fourteen. Have I got that right?'

Fleck frowned in concentration. 'Marian is one. Plus Aggie, and four kids is six. Plus Frank is seven. Plus Matthew, me and three kids is twelve. Plus Therese and friend is fourteen. Plus no Xavier. Plus Ruth is fifteen. I count fifteen. Did you remember to count yourself?'

Marian laughed. 'I always forget to count myself. Fifteen. You're right, Fleck.'

Fleck looked at Matthew. 'We are fifteen tonight. Do we have enough chairs?'

Matthew had already positioned the large trestle table at the end of the already-large kitchen table. 'I can get some from the study if I need them, but I think I have enough. Wait. You counted Alice. She doesn't need a chair. She has her highchair.'

'I might put another can of beans in,' Marian mused, half to herself. 'Oh no. Wait. I have some cooked rice in the fridge. That'll do the trick.'

Norah sat at the table, a cushion on her chair, eating corn with a spoon complacently. 'We are fifteen,' she announced. 'Fifteen. Fifteen.'

'You're making it too hard on yourself, counting it that way,' said Frank, who had finished slicing the lettuce and was now dicing tomatoes. 'All of us, when we are all here, are sixteen. Sixteen is the magic number. Two missing tonight and one extra, so that's one less and that's fifteen. Bang. Easy.'

Fleck cast a quick glance at Marian. Sixteen should not be the magic number. It should be seventeen. Marian was digging through the fridge, so her expression was impossible to read.

It was almost four years now since Gerard, Matthew's father, a man full of warmth and sincerity, died of a heart attack on his morning walk. He had only been sixty-two. Fleck opened a box of taco shells and began arranging them on the oven tray.

It was a lot when they were all around the table, eating and chatting. Therese was filling her taco shell with the vegetarian bean mix and chatting to Daniel and Miguel. Matthew and Frank were loudly arguing about something to do with privatisation. Norah and Sam were at the end of the table, giggling at their big cousin Carlos who was showing off and making a mess, tipping lettuce in his glass and drinking it.

There was so much going at once, Fleck found it hard to keep up. She marvelled at Aggie's ability to maintain several conversations at the same time, contributing regularly to all of them and never losing the thread. Occasionally, Marian would call everyone's attention to announce 'news'. This 'news' was always some small achievement of one of her children or grandchildren.

'Fleck, Matthew mentioned you did a big run yesterday. Five kilometres!' Marian said.

Fleck smiled. 'Yes, it was a bit of a slog, but we managed it. It was at the park with the miniature railway.'

Aggie clasped her hands together. 'Oh, I love the little trains! All my kids have had birthday parties there. And Lily had more than one. I became an expert at making the *Women's Weekly* train cake. The trick is to skip the baking and just use store-bought madeira loaves and swiss rolls and stick icing on them.'

'We used to take all of you kids there when you were small,' Marian said from across the table. 'Though nobody loved it quite as much as Matthew.'

'Except maybe Dad,' volunteered Frank.

'Of course. Your father loved it too. But it was the model trains that were his favourite. Do you remember the train set he had in the rumpus room? He had it on the underside of the table-tennis table.

We still have that somewhere.'

'Does Ruby Chen volunteer there?' Therese called from across from the island bench, where she was getting seconds. 'I went to art school with her. Well, for one semester anyway.'

'She's just started,' said Matthew. 'I forgot you went to art school.'

Therese grinned. 'I think the semester of art school came between the semester of social work and the semester of town planning. Ruby dropped out too. They were a pretty toxic group. Not Ruby, but some of the others.'

'What was Ruby like?' Fleck asked.

Therese pursed her lips, thinking. 'She was pretty quiet. A bit sensitive. I still see the stuff she puts up on social media even though I don't really see her much these days. The algorithm seems to think I want to see tiny things, and to be fair, it's not wrong.'

'Tiny things?'

'Yeah. Have you seen her grid? She's a miniatures artist. She makes tiny everything.'

'Like doll houses?' asked Aggie.

'Sort of. She makes lots of things. And she has a whole series on YouTube of stop-motion videos. She has a pretty decent following, actually.'

'I always thought that manor house – you know, the one at the train park? The one on the top of the hill? I always thought that manor house would make a pretty doll house. Don't you think?' This was Marian.

'No way, Mum!' Therese exclaimed. 'I always thought that house was haunted. Can you imagine how much worse it would be if you populated it with scary dolls?'

'I went past it on Saturday and it definitely gave off creepy vibes,' Fleck said.

'Nonsense,' Marian said. 'It's just a very old building. Your father mentioned it was one of the few houses around when he came out to Paradise as a boy. It used to be seen as a trip to the country to come out here, you know. It was all orchards and farms. Gerry would come to stay with the aunties on their poultry farm. When he passed the Paradise estate, with its big house on the hill, he would know he was almost there.'

'I'm surprised they just let it sit there empty. They should do something with it.' Aggie, having removed Carlos's lettuce soup-in-a-cup, returned to the table.

'There were some women who wanted to do something with the house, back in the eighties,' Marian said. 'They wanted to convert the house into an art gallery and cafe. And they said "cafe" too. Back then we would be more likely to say "coffee shop" or "tea room" but they said "cafe". They were arty types, I suppose.' Marian used her fork to pick some dropped lettuce off her plate and lever it back into her taco shell. 'But that would have been nice, don't you think? They've used the house as an information centre in the past – you know, with pamphlets and maps – but I think a cafe and a gallery would have been so lovely to have there. I wonder why it never got up and running. Of course, one of the women left her husband and moved away, so that probably put a stop to things. She was married to that fellow at the railway. You know who I mean. The main fellow.'

'The main fellow?' Fleck asked.

Marian flapped her hand. 'Oh, you know. Bald.'

Therese had an impish grin on her face. 'Aren't they all bald? Did he have a Santa beard as well? You're not narrowing it down, Mum.'

'They are not all bald!' Matthew was indignant. 'I'm not bald! And I don't have a Santa beard.'

'You will one day. It's only a matter of time, Matthew. Embrace your destiny.' Therese was enjoying this conversation.

Fleck frowned in thought. 'Do you mean Sydney Tozer? The one they call Topham?'

Marian nodded. 'Yes, yes. I told you that already. He's the main one. Well it was his wife who left him. Just got up one day and walked out on him. They say she got sick of all the train business. Well, I know the man is obsessed, but is that a good reason to break your vows? I do not think so. For better or for worse. Those words mean just what they say. For better or for worse.'

'For richer or poorer,' Therese continued in a pious tone. 'In normality and in weird train fixation.'

'For tolerable and for completely insufferable,' Matthew added, looking pointedly at Therese.

'For ordinary in-laws and for completely bonkers in-laws,' Fleck muttered under her breath.

CHAPTER SEVEN

Fleck and Trixie were in the back room at Many Hands, setting things up for the Monday morning workshop.

Trixie was counting the plates on the bench. 'So, we're expecting Dima and Kerryn today. Also Jo, but she says she might be a little late.'

'What about Jo's friend? What was her name? Lynette?'

'Lynette hasn't responded. I'm not sure if she's coming or not. I get the feeling she would rather make a surprise entrance than let me know in advance. But maybe I'm being unfair.'

The shop bell jingled and Dima walked through the door, holding insulated grocery bags in each hand. 'I've brought a variety of delicious things today,' she announced. 'I have both cake and yarn donations!'

Trixie helped Dima bring the bags to the workshop table and the three of them set to work unpacking them. 'It's Persian love cake,' Dima explained. 'I'm still experimenting with the recipe to get the proportions just right. These are my rejects.'

'That's a lot of rejects! I'm not complaining, mind.' Trixie lifted the lid on one of the boxes and peered at the wedges of cake.

'I may be a little obsessed with finding the perfect mix.'

Fleck opened the cabinet door to find a platter to serve the cake on. Trixie rinsed out the large metal teapot.

Kerryn arrived. 'Hi, party people! I'm so keen to get started today,' she said. 'Is Jo here yet? I've got some supplies for her.'

'She's going to be late,' Trixie said. 'It's just us for now, and possibly Lynette, the lady who came last time. Are you working on your earrings today?'

'Nah, today is brooches.' Kerryn lowered herself into a chair and started unpacking her bag. 'Oh, do you have new yarn in? Let me see!'

Fleck passed the bag of yarn donations to Kerryn. Kerryn peered in the bag and pulled balls out, lining up her favourite colours. 'I never got the hang of knitting or crochet, but I'll never get tired of playing with yarn.'

'It's the squish factor,' Trixie said, picking up a ball and squeezing it.

Kerryn smiled. 'That's exactly what it is!'

Jo emerged through the curtain into the back room. She smiled as she put her bag down and sat. 'I thought I was going to be really late, but I ended up getting a good run down the Eastern. Oh, is that new yarn?'

It was nice chatting in a group, but Fleck found it hard sometimes to keep up with the conversation. This larger group felt different to when it was just Trixie and Ranveer. Fleck was sometimes focusing so hard on making eye contact at the correct frequency and duration and performing an interested facial expression while also not fidgeting that she forgot to contribute to the chatter. It wasn't a bad thing, she supposed. Detectives were supposed to sit back and observe.

When there was a break in conversation, Fleck spoke up. 'I wanted to ask you all something,' she said. 'So many of you have creative things that you love to do and you've managed to build your life around it, sometimes even make a business of it. How do you do it? How do you get from “I like making jewellery” to “I am a jewellery maker and it’s my business”? How do you make your thing a Thing?’

There was a brief chuckle at her earnest wording, but the others seemed to be genuinely considering her question. At last, Kerryn spoke.

‘I suppose there were lots of little steps. But there’s definitely something to be said for saying it out loud. Telling people you are the thing. And not waiting in hope for somebody else to give you that title.’

Dima nodded. ‘Yes. Like, a writer doesn’t need to be published to be a writer. A musician doesn’t need a record deal to be a musician. You can give yourself the title. You don’t need external validation.’

Fleck frowned. ‘But there has to be more to it than just giving yourself the title.’

Kerryn nodded. ‘Perhaps. But it is a big part of it. Also, I know people talk about vision boards and manifesting and it sounds all woo-woo. But it’s actually really practical.’ She lowered her jewellery pliers and looked at Fleck. ‘If you keep what you want from the universe at the front of your mind and keep talking about it to your hairdresser and the man at the petrol station, you’re more likely to get solutions to your problems. Nobody’s going to help you get what you want if you don’t even know what that is. And once you start saying it out loud, you connect with a wider network of people.’

Jo leaned back in her chair. ‘Yeah. And people are generally nice. They want to help you succeed.’

Kerryn paused in her unpacking. ‘And one more thing: you need to be prepared when it does take off that this will come with its own set of challenges. You don’t want to lose the joy of creative work. It can’t just be a business. I didn’t get into this so that I’d have a business to run. That’s part of it now, but I mustn’t lose sight of why I do it in the first place. Otherwise I’d just start making earrings that are BAS forms and grant applications.’

Jo looked at Fleck in an assessing sort of way. 'You're not talking about crochet, though, are you? It's detective work you mean, isn't it?'

Fleck swallowed and nodded. 'I love doing it, but I don't know how to take it seriously. Like, how to *be* a detective. I know it's not the same thing as creative work.'

Dima smiled. 'I think solving mysteries is a form of creative work. It all comes down to creative problem solving, really.'

The shop bell jangled and soon Lynette appeared at the curtain. She was holding a large Tupperware container in front of her. 'Hi, everyone! I made my famous mini muffins! They're so good. You'll have to try one.'

Trixie gave her a welcoming smile. 'That's so generous of you, Lynette! We have some Persian love cake from Dima as well. Here next to the tea things is good.' She gestured to a space on the bench near the urn and cups.

Lynette was looking at Dima's cake. The platter was in pride of place, in the centre of the table. 'Persian love cake. That has quite a bit of sugar in it, doesn't it?'

Dima grinned. 'There is a lemon rosewater syrup poured over it, so it's fairly sweet, yes. But it also has almond meal and pistachios, which are almost healthy. And the rose petals could be counted as a vegetable, maybe?'

Lynette pressed her lips together. She didn't put the Tupperware container on the bench beside the cups and urn. Instead, she shifted the platter of cake to the side to make room on the table for her rectangular plastic box, then peeled the lid off to reveal neat rows of small brown cakes in patty pans. 'That's what I love about my mini muffins. They taste really naughty, but they are actually good for you. They can actually *help* you lose weight.' She gave an encouraging smile to Fleck as she made this last comment. Fleck returned the smile, a little uncertainly, and tugged at the hem of her T-shirt.

'I can't believe this is your reject cake, Dima! It's so good!' Kerryn was pressing her fingers into the crumbs of cake left on her plate.

Jo laughed and shook her head. 'No! Shush! It's terrible! I think you need to keep experimenting, Dima. Further research is required. Lots and lots of research! We are willing to eat the failures, if that helps.'

'Absolutely,' said Kerryn. 'Sign me up for cake disposal service.'

'The thing about the mini muffins is that I made them with this awesome supplement.' Lynette was talking in a loud voice, as if announcing to the group. 'It's full of vitamins and all sorts of trace minerals. They make you lose weight, but they taste sinfully good. These ones are chocolate, but I put some freeze-dried strawberries in, just to make it *fun*.'

Fleck nodded politely, then turned back to Dima. 'So is it almond meal you use for flour, or do you—'

'Most people know GelVita for our gels and supplements, but they don't know you can also use them in your cooking. I make these mini muffins all the time. They can go in the freezer, they're great for school lunches and just the best guilt-free snack.' Lynette beamed at the group. She could have been presenting an infomercial.

'Why should I feel guilty about snacking?' Kerryn had a look of challenge in her eyes. 'Food is fuel. It's morally neutral.'

'Well, I can tell you, you don't need to feel guilty about these mini muffins. They are magic. Eating them makes me want to eat more healthy food and exercise and then I lose so much weight.'

'So you don't think it's the eating healthy food and exercising that makes you lose weight?' Trixie asked sceptically. 'It seems like the cupcakes are incidental to that. Like a placebo, maybe.'

'Oh no. No. It's not just that. There's something *in* the GelVita. It turns your fat cells to water and they wash away.' Lynette indicated ‘water splashing off hips’ with her fingers outstretched.

Trixie narrowed her eyes. ‘That doesn’t sound right. Are you weeing fat? Are you gonna go to the bathroom after this and flush away a dress size?’

‘The science is complicated. All I can tell you is that when I’m taking GelVita every day, the weight just falls off me. And I don’t even want to eat bad foods.’ She gestured towards the glistening slices of love cake.

Kerryn’s eyes flashed with anger. ‘Maybe we should eat what we want to fuel our bodies. Maybe we should eat what makes us feel good and not see food as the enemy. Maybe you shouldn’t be policing other people’s eating with your toxic diet culture propaganda.’

Jo got up abruptly and started making herself an instant coffee.

‘It’s not about *diet.* I hate the idea of diets and weighing myself. It’s about a total metabolism makeover. It’s about lifestyle. My skin and hair glow. I’m alert and—’

‘Yeah. Okay.’ Trixie cut Lynette off. ‘We’ve been discussing getting started with a creative venture. What do you do when you’ve found the thing that you want to do and you want to do more of it?’

Dima piped up. ‘I think part of it has to do with getting comfortable with a portmanteau career. You might need to patch together different sources of income when you’re a creative. And hustle is part of it. You can’t just go from no career as a creative to one hundred per cent full-time creative income. The main thing is—’

‘I’m so lucky that I can make all the money I want from home, working my own hours in a job that I love,’ Lynette interjected. ‘It gives me time to be with my kids, and heaps of time for all the hobbies and pastimes I like. I bet this sort of lifestyle would really suit everyone here. I mean – who doesn’t want a bit of extra cash, am I right?’

Trixie ignored Lynette’s question and turned back to Dima. ‘I suppose the real question is, how do you get started in your creative pursuit? Not so much how to juggle it once you've already got started. What's the first step?'

'Start by doing,' said Dima promptly. 'I made heaps of cakes as gifts for friends and family and it helped me to find my style.'

Kerryn nodded. 'And it's also about how you identify yourself. It took me ages to be able to say "I'm an acrylic artist".'

'What would you say instead?' Jo was intrigued.

Kerryn put on a high-pitched girlish voice. 'Ohhh, I like playing with jewellery. It's silly! It's silly!'

Dima grinned. 'Yes! I would say it was silly too. Then I'd get mad when people didn't take me seriously!'

Lynette beamed. 'That's like me with GelVita! I say it's a bit of fun, but it's also serious. I've been making serious money!'

'I think part of it is has to do with how we view traditionally feminine forms of creativity.' Trixie pressed on with the conversation as if Lynette hadn't spoken. 'The tendency to downplay the artistic merit of women's creations is misogyny in action. When a man creates a sculpture, it's high art. When a woman creates a tapestry, it's cute craft.'

As Trixie talked, Lynette watched her with narrowed eyes. There was a lull in the conversation. Fleck could sense the tension in the room. Which was probably why she smiled brightly and picked up a mini muffin. 'I'm feeling so spoilt with all these lovely treats,' she said. (Who *was* she?) 'Thank you, Dima and Lynette!'

Fleck pulled back the mini muffin wrapper and took a bite. To call it 'dessert' was a bit generous. Fleck nodded dutifully as she chewed the rather dry cupcake. It tasted like chemicals. The chocolate seemed more like the flavouring you might get in a chocolate yoghurt, more like the description of chocolate than actual cocoa. There was the odd tang of olive oil. Fleck smiled and nodded as she chewed. When she swallowed, the aftertaste of artificial sweetener lingered on her tongue.

Lynette smiled gratefully at Fleck. 'Right? I made them with chocolate GelVita. It's available in Dutch Cocoa, Berry Bliss, Vanilla, Cookies and Cream and Tropical Dream. It's just a healthier option than eating cake all the time. Perfect if you're trying to slim down. You know what they say: a moment on the lips, a lifetime on the hips!' Lynette tapped at her phone and continued talking. 'The best way to get the products is to become a consultant. That's the smartest way to do it. You get a big discount on the products and you get the chance to make a bit of extra money selling to your family and friends. Is this you on Facebook?' Lynette held up her phone, displaying Fleck's Facebook profile. Fleck nodded, speechless. 'Good. Well, we should be friends anyway. I sent you a request. Did that come through?'

Fleck pulled out her phone and nodded. She clicked 'accept' on the request as Lynette watched. She didn't know what else to do.

'Look, Lynette, can we can the diet talk while we're in the shop?' Trixie's tone was firm. 'I really want these workshops to be a place where people can relax and be themselves. We're not counting calories when we're at Many Hands, okay?'

'Oh I agree. I'm not about counting calories at all! I'm all about wellness.'

'You can call it what you like, but if it has to do with overthinking eating in order to change your shape, that's not a discussion for this room. Okay?'

Someone was coming down the stairs. It was Ranveer.

Trixie smiled warmly and gestured to the table. 'Hi Ranveer! Why don't you help us eat some of this food?'

Ranveer looked at Trixie and then at the table. Apart from the muffin Fleck had eaten and the two Lynette had taken, the Tupperware container remained largely untouched. There were also a couple of pieces of Dima's cake left, though the supply was much depleted. His hand hovered over the offerings, then he hesitated and asked Trixie, 'Which one tastes better?'

Another man might have said this in a teasing tone. Another man might have made a joke of it. Ranveer was simply seeking information. He was cheerfully oblivious of the hornet's nest he had managed to step into.

Dima smiled broadly and said nothing. It was not a competition for her. Lynette's eyes darted around the room. She had lost a little bit of the bravado she had arrived with, but she still had plenty to spare. 'I haven't tried Dima's cake, but I can tell you the mini muffins are super healthy. They are so good for you. I made them with—'

'You probably should try the cake.' Trixie's tone was conversational and encouraging. You could hardly hear the steeliness underneath. 'Dima made it and Dima's cakes are incredible.'

'The mini muffins are the healthier option, but they also taste delicious.' Lynette seemed to have made it her mission to win Ranveer's heart and mind. 'They are sinfully good. They're made—'

'I always think when people say that something tastes sinful it might taste really gross,' Trixie interrupted. 'I mean, what sins are we talking about here? Murder? Manslaughter? Regicide? Does the cupcake taste like actual gore? I don't think I would enjoy it if the cupcake tasted like actual gore.'

Lynette frowned and gave Trixie a sidelong glance. Trixie smiled and took a sip of her tea. Lynette tried again. 'The thing that makes the mini muffins different is that they are really healthy too. I made them myself with GelVita. They have basically negative calories. They are perfect for the health-conscious.'

Ranveer smiled and nodded and took a large piece of Dima's cake. He looked surprised by Trixie's explosive giggle, then looked about the room for clarification. It seemed to be only just dawning on him that there might be subtext he was missing.

Lynette cleared her throat. 'I thought you would have chosen the mini muffin. You look like a health-conscious sort of person.'

Ranveer offered another small smile and shook his head. 'I exercise so that I can eat whatever I want. I don't like diet food.'

Lynette frowned. 'I never said they were diet food. GelVita isn't a diet food. It's not. It's a holistic health solution. There are all sorts of miracle benefits to these health gels. They can help with psoriasis, IBS, migraines, PMT and autism.'

Trixie set her mug of tea firmly back on the table. 'Wait. Did you say autism? How does your chocolate gel help with autism? Do you mean you have a gel that helps people to not be autistic?'

Lynette nodded enthusiastically. 'Yes, absolutely. Used long-term, it can actually cure autism. It can completely fix it.'

Trixie curled her lip in disgust. 'What on earth are you talking about?'

Lynette's voice had taken on a teacher-like tone. 'I don't know what the science is exactly, but it's cutting edge. It's absolutely cutting edge. They are going to publish their studies on it soon, I think. I'm not sure. But anyway, I know one lady whose son started out with autism. Full-blown autism. He would, like' – she leaned in and dropped her voice to a whisper – '*flap* his hands and sort of *rock* his body.' She shook her head, eyes wide, then resumed her normal volume. 'And his mum started giving him milkshakes with GelVita mixed in. She gave them to him every day after school. And he's not even *on* the spectrum anymore. He doesn't flap his hands *at all*. She got him to stop doing it *completely*.'

Trixie's eyes flashed. 'That's not how autism works, you ninny. The diet talk is one thing, but this is next level. Cure autism? Cure *aut*ism? Can it cure Helen of being a full-blown Catholic? Can it cure Ranveer of being an accountant? There is no cure for autism, because autism isn't a disease. So you managed to compel some poor kid to mask his autism and repress his stims. Great job. I'm sure that will work out splendidly for him long-term. While you're at it, teach him to never be sad or angry and just smile all the time in every possible situation. Honestly. You are dangerous. The minute someone claims they have something that cures autism is the minute I know they're selling snake oil. What. Rot.'

Lynette made a face. She held her hands up in front of her in a 'surrender' gesture. Then she packed up her things. She paused as she got to the still-almost-full container of mini muffins and began to offer them around. 'Everyone needs to take a couple home with them. Don't be shy. I don't want them to go to waste.'

Trixie stood up. 'You'll be okay. They freeze well, remember?' Then she started to clear the table.

Lynette narrowed her eyes at Trixie for a fraction of a second. Then she replaced the lid on the container and was gone.

Fleck lingered after the others had left. She could tell Trixie was feeling rattled.

'Just what is her deal, anyway?' Trixie shoved a pile of clean dishes back into the cupboard. 'I'm trying to create a community of crafters, not a recruitment ground for the convenience of local *mumpreneurs*.'

Fleck was drying cutlery and slotting it back into the drawer. 'She is very one-note about it all. What are you going to do?'

Trixie straightened up. 'I don't know. "All welcome" means "All welcome". But I don't think I can bear much more of her diet talk. And as for her apple cider vinegar "We can cure autism" rubbish – she can take her ableist brain rot and shove it up her—'

The shop bell jangled. 'I need to look after the shop,' Trixie said. They both stepped through the curtain.

A man had entered Many Hands. He was neatly dressed and solidly built, with tattoos on his forearms.

'Max!' Fleck exclaimed. 'What are you doing here?' Fleck had got to know Max when she was investigating the Many Hands mystery. They had been through a lot together, had even survived being held at gunpoint and trapped in an industrial refrigerator together, and had now formed a friendship of sorts.

'I almost didn't recognise you,' said Trixie. 'You have hair now!'

Max smiled and ran his hand over his very short dark hair. He was also sporting the beginnings of a beard. 'Yeah. It was time for a change. It looks like you've changed the shop a bit too. I wanted to look for a present for my mum.'

'So not official business, then?' Trixie asked.

Max shook his head. 'Nah, I'm off duty.'

Another customer entered the shop and began asking Trixie questions. Fleck fell into conversation with Max. She told him about her success with the graffiti case and her latest investigations of the miniature railway. Fleck liked Max. He took her seriously.

'But I know once I find out who has been stealing the supplies, I'll be back to having no case to work on. I enjoy detective work, but I don't know how to get cases. I don't know what the next step should be.'

Max rubbed his chin. 'Would you consider joining the force? You have good instincts and excellent intuition.'

Fleck's face warmed. 'You're kind. No, I think I want to work as an amateur. At least for now.'

Max nodded. 'That's fair. Look, let me think on it. In the meantime, have you made that phone call?'

Fleck looked away. 'Not yet. But I'm going to.'

'You still have her number?'

Fleck nodded.

Max peered at her. 'I strongly recommend that you do. She's one of the best and she doesn't usually take on new clients.'

Fleck nodded. 'Yep.'

Max maintained his piercing stare. 'This isn't a little thing. It's a big thing. It's big for both of us, but it's harder for you because you don't have my training.'

Fleck gave a reluctant smile. 'I know. I've made a note of it. Now, have you seen these fingerless gloves? I don't know your mum, but I still think she would love them.'

CHAPTER EIGHT

Fleck handed her reuseable takeaway cup to George. 'Has he been set up there long?' she said, indicating the group of people in matching T-shirts and caps standing outside the playground on the other side of Highett Road.

George grinned. 'About twenty minutes. They've mostly been handing out shopping bags, but I think he's had a few conversations. No aggro ranters yet, but I live in hope.'

Fleck gazed out the window as George prepared her coffee. Nathan Garland stood beaming in his campaign T-shirt alongside a sign that said 'Listening Post'. Soon Fleck would give him something to listen to. She drew a fortifying breath and turned back to George.

'I'm going to confront him about the missing supplies at the railway,' Fleck said.

'Confront him?'

'Okay. Maybe not confront him. But definitely make some inquiries.'

'What sort of inquiries?'

'I don't know yet. But they will be sternly worded.'

George handed her the travel mug. 'Good luck.'

Nathan Garland smiled broadly at Fleck as she approached. He offered her a branded shopping bag, squinting slightly as he looked at her, as if trying to picture where he'd seen her face before. A flicker of displeasure, or possibly embarrassment, passed across his face, but his smile never faltered. 'I've met you before, I think. You're George's friend. We met at the cafe.'

Fleck was surprised. She had expected Nathan to be evasive, to pretend he didn't recognise her, or to *actually* not recognise her.

'I must say, George makes an excellent coffee. I can get really fussy about coffee, especially first thing in the morning, but George's are consistently lovely.'

Fleck nodded. George did make great coffee, but she wondered if Nathan was just saying this in an attempt to win her over. 'Yes. George works hard. It's not easy running your own business.' *Especially when sleazy would-be politicians vandalise that business to garner publicity.* If she were Trixie, she would have said this out loud. But she wasn't Trixie, so she communicated it with her eyebrows.

Nathan drew a breath. 'I don't feel like we got off to a good start. You got me on a bad morning and then I was thrown off guard about the whole graffiti mix-up. I'm sorry. Can we start over?'

Fleck peered at him. 'I hear you've started volunteering at the miniature railway. My husband volunteers there too.'

Nathan nodded, eagerly seizing what he perceived to be an olive branch. 'It's a brilliant organisation, don't you think? I'm really enjoying spending time there.'

'I'm curious as to why you've decided to start volunteering there. Is this part of some scheme to give your image a glow-up?'

'You make it sound so exploitative,' Nathan replied. 'I'm in a unique position to shine a light on the excellent work the organisation does. It's not just about providing a fun activity on a Sunday afternoon. The railway gives connection and meaning to a group of men who might never allow themselves to seek counselling or mental health support.'

'There are plenty of women who volunteer there,' Fleck retorted.

'There are,' said Nathan, unruffled, 'but I think the railway is especially well placed to serve a particular section of the community that might be reluctant to seek help otherwise.'

Fleck opened her mouth and then closed it again. She wanted to argue with him, but couldn't. She tried another tack. 'You're shining a light? You're not using their good name to make yourself look virtuous?'

'Well, can't it be both?' He twinkled at her. 'But seriously, I have a lot of time for the Paradise Miniature Railway. I owe it a debt of gratitude. And you would have to be a deeply cynical individual to not find joy in those little trains.'

'What do you mean when you say you owe—' Fleck broke off. Something had caught her attention. On the other side of Highett Road, in matching T-shirts, two more Nathan Garland volunteers were heading towards the pedestrian crossing. One of them was Quinn Tait. He waved at Nathan, who waved back.

Fleck looked at Nathan. 'Quinn is on your campaign team?'

'Quinn's one of my staffers, actually. I'd be lost without his help.'

'And you both volunteer at the railway?'

'Yes. Though he's been at it for longer than me.'

'Sorry I'm late,' Quinn said as he reached them. 'Where do you want me?' For someone who was usually so shy, Quinn seemed very relaxed around Nathan. He smiled at Fleck. 'Oh hello, Fleck. I didn't see you.'

Nathan looked from Quinn to Fleck. 'Do you two know each other already?'

Quinn smiled. 'Yeah. Fleck is a reporter. I was talking to her on Sunday. Do you want me to hand out bags outside the IGA?'

Nathan nodded. When Quinn disappeared with the bags, he turned back to Fleck. 'You should have disclosed the fact that you are a reporter before we started talking. Look, these listening posts are for the community. They aren't really designed for press interviews.' It took Fleck a moment to realise he was talking about her. He thought she was the press! She considered stepping in to correct him, but he was still talking. 'What are you planning to write about our meeting at George's? About the graffiti? None of that was on the record. You never told me you were a reporter.' He raked his hand through his hair. His face was grey.

Fleck bit her lip. 'How about we make an appointment and we can talk everything over properly? You can tell me things from your point of view. Thursdays are good for me.'

Fleck sat perched on an armchair gazing at the large map of the Ashthorn electorate that covered most of the wall. Fleck loved a good map. Her eyes roamed over the neatly labelled streets, locating her home, the school, Paradise Lake Park, the library, the shops on Peppercorn Street.

The door opened and Nathan Garland walked in, carrying his jacket and a grocery bag. He handed the bag to the bright-faced young woman sitting at the reception desk. 'Thanks, Hayley. I got some snacks for the mail-out party.' Then he turned to Fleck. 'Sorry I'm late. Let's go through to my office.'

Nathan's office was fairly nondescript, with a desk and computer at the side and a larger table in the middle. Fleck sat at the table. Nathan moved a stack of papers aside and sat also. He looked, if not exactly nervous, a shade less confident than his usual full-force bluster.

'Thanks for taking the time to talk to me.' Fleck couldn't help it. Despite her distaste for this man, her manners were deeply ingrained.

Nathan nodded. 'Thanks for coming. I was hoping I could talk to you about my plans for Ashthorn.'

Fleck nodded. 'I'd be very interested to hear of your plans for Ashthorn if you tell me first about the graffiti. I'd like to know about how Quinn is involved in all this.'

Nathan's face fell. 'Quinn?'

Fleck smiled. 'He's the one who painted the graffiti, isn't he? While you were in Canberra?'

Fleck had figured it out when she'd been washing Norah's hair. Not because massaging conditioner into a small head of bouncy red curls had anything to do with the case, but because it was a boring job, and boring jobs were good for breakthroughs.

She might have been wrong, but it made the most sense. Nathan would have delegated the job to somebody, probably someone young, while he was in Canberra. Quinn already worked for Nathan and they seemed to have a good relationship. As well as that – and Fleck had felt really clever when she worked this out – 'Taco' was probably short for 'Tarquin'.

Looking at Nathan's reaction now, she knew she'd hit the nail on the head. He looked properly flustered. He shook his head with his hands up in front of him. 'I don't want Quinn to get implicated in any of this. He's a good kid.'

'But he was the one to do the graffiti?' Fleck's tone was encouraging and matter-of-fact.

Nathan hesitated. Fleck pressed on. 'I'm not going to write about the graffiti. But I need to know the facts on that if you want me to report on your other issues.'

Nathan expelled a long sigh and paused for a moment. Then he looked up at Fleck. 'Off the record?'

Fleck made a show of pushing her notebook away. 'Off the record,' she confirmed.

Nathan ran his hand over his face. Then he started talking. 'I was horrified when I discovered George's cafe was tagged. That was never part of the plan. There was a clear breakdown of communication on that front.'

'But there was a plan?'

Nathan sighed. 'There was a plan. When I was in Canberra, Quinn was going to get the spray paint out of my garage and graffiti the shops on Highett Road. I only meant for him to graffiti the small strip on the north side of the road – the buildings I own. I'm sure I told him that. But he crossed the road and did the cafe as well. That was a mistake.'

'Why did he use car paint? And not just regular spray paint?'

Nathan groaned. 'That was the other thing. I told him to use the spray paint in my garage. He already had a key to the garage because he mows my lawns. I'd bought three cans of red paint and had them there for him in a bag, just inside the garage door. But he missed it and ended up grabbing the touch-up paint for my car instead.'

'But why do it in the first place? I understand you didn't mean to vandalise George's Kitchen. But why did you want to graffiti your own shops?' Fleck said.

Nathan sighed. 'I suppose the short version of the story is it was an elaborately staged photo opportunity.' He ran his thumb across the woodgrain of the table. 'Our police are dangerously underfunded. It's shameful. But the issue goes ignored unless there is some sort of narrative the press can get hold of. Waving around a balance sheet and saying "Look at these figures" or quoting rising crime statistics isn't newsworthy. But if I point to a set of shops covered in graffiti and with a broken window, I am providing a visual representation of an abstract problem. We scheduled it for a time when I wouldn't be in Melbourne, so that I could have some distance from it. We cleaned it all up afterwards.'

'And Quinn was happy to do this for you?'

'Quinn has been desperate to pick up more work lately. And I pay him for his time. So, yes, he was keen to take this on.'

'What do you mean, *desperate*?' Fleck could almost feel her ears pricking up.

'He's just been asking for more jobs, I guess. It's not like he doesn't have enough work. I'm surprised he has enough time to study. He was already working at a supermarket when I got him the job at the office, and he hasn't given the supermarket job away. None of it seems enough for him.'

'Wait, if you got him the job here, does that mean you knew him before he started working for you?' Fleck said.

Nathan looked self-conscious. 'Ah. Yeah. I try to keep that quiet, but Quinn's actually my nephew.'

'Your nephew?'

'Yeah. His mum is my older sister. His dad's not around and she has her hands full. I promised her I'd keep an eye out while he was in Melbourne, but I didn't want to be accused of nepotism when I gave him a job as a staffer. We have different last names so I can get away with it,' Nathan said.

'And you think he's desperate for money?'

'Yeah, it's a bit strange. Firstly, he was working the two jobs, plus mowing my lawn whenever he could. Then I discovered he was looking into those dodgy payday lenders. I told him I'd loan him money if he needed it, but he must not, under any circumstances, do business with those predatory cowboys. But then he clammed up and didn't want to talk about it. Anyway, I'm getting off topic. I wanted to talk to you about my five-point plan for law and order in Ashthorn.'

Fleck ended up staying for another fifteen minutes listening to Nathan talk at length about his proposed plans for Ashthorn and other campaign promises. She took random, flimsy notes. Her mind buzzed.

CHAPTER NINE

Fleck had set up her laundry wall with notes for this new case, but she didn't have much information up yet. Fleck used her laundry as a control room for her detective cases. Brightly coloured notes were often stuck all over the wall. There were questions and pictures and occasionally a map. Fleck loved it if she could get a map up on the wall for a case. It made everything seem more official. The wall currently had a map of the miniature railway, unfolded from the tourist brochure and Blu Tacked to the wall beside the ironing board, but apart from that, there weren't many notes. Fleck gazed at her list of suspects as she pulled wet clothes from the machine into the basket. She'd seen both Quinn and Ruby on the security footage taking things out of the sheds. Nathan was a suspicious character, but she was yet to find evidence against him. Nothing made sense in terms of a motive. Why would somebody want to steal such random supplies?

Fleck had asked Marian for the name of Topham's ex-wife. Marian couldn't remember if it was Julie or Julia. Fleck had tried to find social media profiles for Julie Tozer or Julia Tozer. She had sent a message to someone named Jules Tozer but hadn't heard back. Of course, it was likely the ex-Mrs Tozer had gone back to her maiden name. It would be worth finding that out and tracking her down, Fleck thought. Ex-spouses could be great sources of unfiltered information.

Fleck lugged the basket of wet washing outside and propped it on the table near the washing line. Norah was ignoring the picnic rug where Alice sat with a scattering of toys and instead made a beeline for her mother – specifically, for her mother's basket of clothes pegs.

'Peg shop! Peg shop!' Norah seized the basket, spilling a few colourful pegs onto the grass.

Fleck suppressed a groan. 'Hello, peg shop lady, may I buy two pegs, please?'

'Two dollars!'

'Here you are.' If Fleck were feeling virtuous, she might have said, 'Here is five dollars, may I have three dollars change?' But today she just wanted to put the washing on the line.

Norah dispensed two pegs for her immediate use. They were not the pegs Fleck would have chosen. One of them was a flimsy el-cheapo peg with a tiny spiderweb in the crevice that Fleck never used if she could help it. She needed to let this go. They were just pegs. She shook out Sam's school uniform shirt, applied the sub-par pegs and turned back to the basket. She fished out an Alice-sized singlet. 'May I buy one more peg, please?'

'Yes! Two dollars!' The peg Norah handed her was sturdy and heavy-duty. Fleck usually liked to save these for bulky towels or jeans. Alice's delicate little singlet did not need a heavy-duty peg. Should she ask to speak to the peg shop manager? No. She smiled brightly and pegged the singlet on the line. She pegged it in a different section to Sam's school shirt. This was her new 'sort as you go' technique. She was still getting the hang of it, but she had mentally assigned different sections of the clothesline to different members of the family. This was supposed to save time sorting the clothes later. It didn't work so well when the clothes were all pulled in higgledy-piggledy at the onset of rain.

She needed to get the laundry room in better order so that she could finish setting it up for the new case. Of course, she needed to get the laundry room in order to ensure a smooth and efficiently running household, but that never seemed enough of a motivating factor to get her to work.

Right now, Quinn was looking like her main suspect. She hadn't ruled out the idea of Nathan being involved somehow, but that had more to do with her general mistrust of Nathan than any actual evidence. Quinn, on the other hand, appeared in the video footage leaving the engine sheds with a large bag, plus it seemed like he was desperate for money. Might he be helping himself to supplies to save money at home? Might he be selling them online? Would it be worth investigating his online profiles to see if she could spot anything?

'Come and buy the pegs for sale! Come and buy the PEGS FOR SALE!'

'Oh. Whoops. Right.' Fleck snatched up a pair of Sam's tracksuit pants. 'Two pegs, please.'

Norah beamed. 'Forty million dollars!'

Fleck feigned shock and rage. 'Forty million dollars? *Forty million dollars?* I can't pay forty million dollars!'

Norah cackled. Anybody would think that this was new. Anybody would think that they hadn't played this game in exactly this way seventeen times before. 'Forty million dollars! Forty million dollars, please!'

'That's too expensive! I'll need to get a loan!'

'Give me money!'

'This is price gouging!'

'I need – you need, um – you need to pay the money, please!' Norah held her small hand out, smiling. Alice, meanwhile, was investigating the contents of a plastic bucket on her rug. It was filled with Duplo bricks.

Fleck grumbled as she searched the back pocket of her jeans for forty million imaginary dollars. 'Here you go. I needed to get a bank loan for that!'

Fleck took the proffered pegs, turned aside and pegged the tracksuit pants to the line. What if it was a loan? What if Quinn had taken out a loan with an unscrupulous lender and was scrabbling to pay it back? She pulled a Batman-branded onesie from the basket. 'Two pegs, please.'

'Forty-forty-forty-forty-forty-million-million-forty dollars!'

That's not how numbers work, Norah. Norah didn't care. She was drunk on power and wheezing with laughter.

'What? You said they were two dollars before! Forty million billion dollars is too much! Too much!'

'You have to pay! PAY THE MONEY!' Norah was gasping. Alice banged two plastic bricks together, frowning with concentration.

Fleck checked all of her pockets. 'Where will I find forty million billion dollars?' She dug through the basket of washing and extracted a pair of jeans. 'Here we are!' She reached into the soggy jeans pocket and pulled her hand out with a flourish. 'Forty million billion dollars for you!'

'One peg!' Norah handed over one of the steel pegs. The steel pegs were okay, but they weren't Fleck's favourite. Surely, if she were paying a premium, she should be allowed to choose her own peg?

'Wait! I need two pegs!'

Norah's face broke into another smile. She held out her hand. 'A million, a million, a million, a million, a million, a million, a million DOLLARS!'

Fleck sighed inwardly. She should love peg shop. She should relish this chance to bond with her little girl. But peg shop messed with her rhythm. Couldn't Norah just let her peg out the clothes in peace? On the other hand, while peg shop felt like an exercise in inefficiency, Fleck knew that it was the lesser of two evils. The moment Fleck turned her back and became absorbed in the sheer indulgence of a solo peg-out would be the moment Norah climbed the pantry shelves or painted the kitchen with Vegemite or dismantled the lounge room bookcase. One day, Norah would be a great scientist or engineer or medical researcher, or, indeed, a price-gouging retailer. Right now, though, her relentless curiosity and constant demands for autonomy were exhausting.

Fleck smiled weakly and hunted for some more imaginary cash.

The playground on Highett Road, opposite George's Kitchen, had a section underneath the slide tower designed to mimic a house or shop. It was just a panel with a window cut out at the top and a little bench to rest things on. For Norah, it was always her cafe. Fleck sat on the park bench with her back to the road. Unlike the other bench, this one was in the sunshine and thus was dry of morning dew. While she fed Alice and awaited service from Norah's cafe, she continued her investigation of Quinn's online presence.

Fleck was getting better at navigating the different platforms. Quinn had a Facebook profile, but was more active on Discord and Reddit. Fleck knew from her conversations with Lily and Ruth that kids their age tended to keep Facebook profiles only to stay in touch with their grandparents. Fleck had used her suite of false profiles to shadow Quinn, infiltrating interest groups and channels and servers. Now, as she watched Norah prepare her a woodchip cappuccino, she snuck looks at Quinn's posts and thought longingly of the real cappuccinos being made in the building across the road.

As well as many railway enthusiast groups, Quinn had an interest in the music of Neil Young, and the *Legend of Zelda* video game. She found a page where he had listed items for sale. There were some collectible figurines, a fitness watch and, more recently, a Nintendo Switch with extra controllers. Fleck took screenshots of these postings and moved on.

Quinn's 'Trainboy' Reddit profile had a lot of postings on 'r/steamengines', 'r/locomotives' and 'r/trains', plus a single posting on 'r/aita'. Fleck clicked on the post.

> **AITA for shouting at my housemate's girlfriend**
> I (20m) moved out of home last year to go to university. My best friend from school became my housemate and I think this might have been the biggest mistake of my life.
>
> It started out really great. The house is a two-bedroom unit in Mount Waverley, and just the right size for two people. It isn't far from where we both study and there is a bus stop right out the front that goes straight to uni. My friend and I could hang out and game on my console when we needed a break from study.
>
> Everything changed when my friend got a girlfriend. I don't begrudge my friend for finding someone. We are getting older, it's going to happen, I get it. But this girlfriend is impossible to be around.
>
> To begin with, she is just always there. She is always in the house, to the point that I've started to wonder if she even has a home of her own. She's slept over more nights than she hasn't, and even when she's not there, the bathroom is full of her toiletries and the fridge is full of her food.

> Also, her standards of cleanliness are a lot higher than what we had been happy with. She just seems to be cleaning all the time. Like, angry cleaning. And then she puts these sarcastic notes on the fridge. Pretending to be nice, but telling me off for every little thing. One time she wrote a numbered list of things I did wrong. There were fifteen things.
>
> But the worst thing is she's jealous of any time my friend spends with me. We used to spend the evenings sitting on the couch gaming or even just scrolling our own stuff but in the same room. It was nice. But now when I enter the room she makes it clear that she wishes I wasn't there. And it's had an effect on my relationship with my friend as well. It's like she's turned him against me. I walk into the room and they stop talking. I can't relax at home anymore. I just go straight to my room when I'm there. Then we ended up having this big argument all about a loaf of bread, if you can believe it. I ended up shouting that I wished she had never met my friend. I know I shouldn't have shouted, but I was upset. Now my friend is demanding that I apologise to his girlfriend. AITA?

Norah was sprinkling small gumnuts over her little pile of woodchips. She picked her creation up and carried it to Fleck. Alice had finished feeding and was looking at the playground with interest. Fleck purchased her 'coffee' with some gum leaves and Norah deposited it on the bench beside her.

Fleck looked back at Quinn's posting for the sale of his gaming console. The date of this posting was more recent than the AITA post. It seemed to take on a poignant significance now. Fleck looked more closely at the photo. There was a hand holding up one of the extra controllers. Fleck could see a window in the background. It was golden yellow, made of that old-fashioned glass that was all the rage in the seventies – the sort that looked like a lot of circles in rows. When Fleck was a child, her parents used to rent a holiday house in Rosebud that had glass like this. Fleck would press her face against the bumpy circles and look out to the front yard, where her two brothers were wrestling among the twisted tea trees. They'd looked like they were floating in beer.

Fleck purchased another pile of tanbark from Norah. She was craving an actual coffee. 'Five more minutes, Norah!'

When Fleck arrived at George's Kitchen, she spotted Trixie sitting at an inside table with Helen and Bev. It looked like they were having a planning meeting.

Fleck pushed through the plastic strips in the doorway with Norah and Alice. Norah balanced one strip on her face for as long as possible as she moved inside until it slid off the top of her head and swung back to the doorway.

They approached Trixie's table and Fleck greeted them. 'Are you having a meeting? I haven't seen you in here before, Bev.'

'We used to meet at the cafe next door to the shop, but they play their music so loud it's hard to hear what anyone is saying,' Bev replied. 'Trixie suggested we come here instead.'

'Have you been working on the case, Fleck?' This was Trixie. In front of her was a notebook, patterned with characters from *My Neighbour Totoro*, and she held a black texta in her hand. Her pencil case was crocheted in textured mosaic stitch.

'I have, actually. I was looking at the online profile of a person of interest. I managed to gain some insight with a post he made on Reddit. It was one of those AITA posts.'

'What's an AITA post?' Helen asked.

Fleck faltered. She looked at the faces of the two respectable elderly women, and at Trixie who was smiling broadly. She sensed George was listening from behind the counter.

'It's – er – it's a place where you can ask a question to see if you were in the right. It's kind of like a modern-day agony aunt, except that anyone can post a response.'

Trixie's eyes flashed with false innocence. 'Oh, but I think Helen was asking what the actual letters stand for. Can you tell us what AITA actually means?'

Fleck felt herself blush. 'It stands for "Am I the", er, "Am I the *Antagonist*".'

Trixie and George started coughing at the same time. Fleck ignored them and turned to Helen. 'Actually, maybe you can help me with something.' She showed Helen the photo that had the golden window in the background. 'Do you know what this kind of glass is called?'

Bev looked at the picture too. She laughed. 'Oh Joan used to have that, remember? That sort of glass was everywhere.'

'Do you remember what it was called?' Fleck asked.

'I think we called it bottle-bottom glass,' Helen said. 'You can't buy it anymore, though. Our old holiday house in Blairgowrie had that kind of glass. We weren't able to replace it when it broke.' She closed her large diary and put it into her bag. 'Anyway, we need to get back to the shop.'

Helen stood up to pay for the coffees. Trixie stood up, too, pulling her card out of her purse. Bev chuckled. 'Good luck, Trixie. Helen always pays. I've learned not to argue.'

As it was, Helen conducted the transaction so swiftly that it would have been impossible for Trixie to raise an objection. A moment later, she returned to the table, swinging her handbag onto her shoulder. The three women bid goodbye to Fleck and the children. Fleck turned to George. She still hadn't ordered her coffee.

George was already making her strong latte. He shook his head when she took out her phone to pay. 'Helen paid for yours as well.'

It was spaghetti bolognese for dinner that night. Fleck parked herself in the kitchen with two saucepans on the stove: the big one with water heating for the spaghetti, the smaller one for the sauce. Fleck loved making spaghetti bolognese. It required her to be in the kitchen, undisturbed, but it did not require her to think. Fleck poured boiling water from the kettle into the big saucepan, then refilled it at the tap. She emptied the frozen brick of leftover taco mince into the smaller saucepan, added a tin of tomato soup and poked it with a spoon. Then she leaned back against the bench, pulled out her phone and began to scroll.

Marian always sent Fleck home with a large rinsed-out margarine container full of taco mince after family night. It was good for a whole other meal. Sam was always a little suspicious of the meat mix when making his taco ('I just want cheese and lettuce, Mummy') but as soon as it was poured over spaghetti, he couldn't get enough of it.

Now that Lynette was her friend on Facebook, Fleck was seeing a whole lot of her posts in her newsfeed. Facebook even took it upon itself to inform Fleck in her notifications every time Lynette posted something new. Why did Facebook do this? That was not news, Facebook!

Lynette's posts all seemed to be variations on a theme: Lynette's life was awesome; Lynette was so healthy; Lynette had the secret and she was willing to share.

Here was an artfully angled close-up of two milkshakes.

> Loving my morning shake. Dutch Cocoa or Berry Bliss? Decisions, decisions!
> Are you looking to
> ⏰Wake up feeling refreshed?
> 💰Make your own money?
> 🥊Work for yourself?
> 🤸Have more energy?
> 💆Enjoy clear skin and thick hair?
> ⚽Have more time to PLAY with your kids?
> 💪Be a total girlboss?
> DM me for more information! @everyone

Next was an old photo of a larger, tired-looking Lynette holding a baby and frowning alongside a photo of Lynette beaming in gym gear. The second photo was taken from an angle that made Lynette look even leaner than she did in real life.

> Me before – and me now! Loving feeling healthier and happier the GelVita way.

Then there was a photo of some sort of paper report. A plate with a mini muffin sat on the table beside it. The caption read:

> Have a look at Amyxia's Naplan results! Band 5 in Conventions of Language! Thank you #gelvita!

And another:

> At the beach with my girl – because I can! Loving the #gelvita life!

Lynette didn't seem to post anything that wasn't #gelvita. Fleck stirred the sauce as the meat iceberg softened. She tipped the second kettle of water into the big saucepan. Then she saw she had a direct message from Lynette. She had shared a meme of baby Yoda gazing winsomely at the viewer with the caption 'Of course I talk to myself. Sometimes I need expert advice!'

Underneath this, Lynette's message read:

> Hey hun,
> I saw this meme and it made me think of you! Don't forget to DM me if you'd like to know more about becoming a GelVita consultant.
> L

Fleck frowned. She wasn't sure what it was about Lynette that she found so off-putting. Usually Fleck liked it when people talked about things they were passionate about. She didn't mind at all when Kerryn went into great detail about acrylic mouldings or when Matthew got excited about setting track routes, because even though Fleck wasn't interested in the subject, she was attracted to their passion and enthusiasm. But she didn't feel that way about Lynette. Every time Lynette started talking about GelVita, Fleck wished she would change the subject.

Fleck stirred the sauce and flipped the small piece that was still frozen over to its other side. She put salt into the pasta water.

Perhaps it was because Lynette was not passionate about GelVita, despite her claims. It didn't feel like passion. It didn't have the same texture. It was desperation. Lynette would say she was 'excited' and 'obsessed', but to Fleck it felt more like despair.

Another message arrived from Lynette.

> Hey hun,
> I just wanted to say I think you would be so well-suited to join the GelVita team. You really have the leadership qualities and girlboss energy that make a great GelVita consultant. Have you been thinking about it? I could get you started whenever you're ready. It's easy to start. Let me know when you're ready to start earning more money for yourself and living the GelVita life!
> L

Fleck cringed and put her phone away.

CHAPTER TEN

Fleck wasn't a stalker, but she was almost certain she could figure out where Quinn Tait lived. She wasn't sure what she would do with that information once she had it, but it was a fun puzzle to figure out. She was learning that a lot of detective work was about following random threads and seeing what came of them.

So far she knew:

1. Quinn lived in a two-bedroom unit in Mount Waverley.
2. This unit featured gold bottle-bottom glass, probably in the front door panel. Such glass was in dwindling supply in Melbourne, as it no longer fit safety standards.
3. The unit was close to a bus stop on a route that ran directly to Monash University.

This was plenty of information. Fleck had downloaded a map of the bus route (there were two routes that travelled through Mount Waverley, but only one went to Monash University), and used Google Street View to look for houses small enough and old enough to be Quinn's share unit. Then she looked at their windows for the telltale gold glass.

There were some houses that were old enough to have the bottle-bottom glass, but the front windows were shrouded by trees and not visible from the street. After she had finished analysing the entire Mount Waverley leg of the bus route, she had a shortlist of five likely houses. This list could be made shorter once she investigated the houses where she couldn't see the windows online.

Fleck was getting a little obsessed with bottle-bottomed windows, truth be told. Since seeing Quinn's photo, she was seeing the glass everywhere. When Fleck blinked, the inside of her eyelids were patterned with a matrix of circles.

Marian had arrived to look after Norah and Alice, so Fleck took the chance to jump in the car and head to Mount Waverley to investigate the situation further. She wore a pink polo top, a pink baseball cap, and a lanyard she found on a shelf in the laundry. She also held a clipboard. She had managed to rule out three of the houses on the list on closer inspection. Two did not have the bottle-bottom glass, and one had been demolished and was now a building site.

This left two houses. Fleck chose the one that didn't have garden ornaments (*Grandkids spoilt here!*). It was in a set of three units on the same block, but was the only house with the bottle-bottom glass. She parked the car and waited. This was her plan. People rarely opened the door to canvassers these days and often had signs warning them away. Fleck would wait in the car for thirty minutes. If anyone were to leave the house during that time, she would stage a coincidental meeting. If nobody came out after thirty minutes, she would knock on the door.

She was in luck. After ten minutes, a young woman with her hair in a ponytail walked out of the front door holding what looked like a white plastic bag full of rubbish. She dropped the bag in the wheelie bin that was standing on the nature strip, then started pulling the bin back to the house. By the time she had parked it back in its spot, Fleck was ready.

'Hello! How has your morning been?'

The woman looked at her warily, but politeness seemed to compel her to say, 'Fine. And you?'

Fleck smiled. 'You look like exactly the person I need to talk to. I'm conducting a study into the interplay of gender roles in household maintenance. And then I see you with the bins, which so often is seen as a male job, and I knew you could give me some really good insights.'

The woman hesitated.

'My name is Felicity. I want to show in my study that despite the changes in work, women still take on more of the household chores than men. They are doing more work out of home, but are still expected to take on the lion's share of household maintenance tasks.' Fleck was parroting an article she had read over breakfast. She really didn't know where she was going with this, but the woman was nodding slightly.

'The thing I find interesting is that you are taking the rubbish out. This role is traditionally masculine. One of the things I want to explore in my study is the ways in which the breakdown of traditional gender roles in housework result in women taking on more work, not less. In fact, we have found that a lot of the invisible, incidental labour is ignored by males and that, while men tend to believe they take on a fair share of the housework, the reality is that there is a gulf in understanding between perception and reality. Half the time they have no idea what they need to do to keep a household running because their mums always did it for them. So they think they've taken on a fair share, when in reality it equates to thirty-four per cent of the total labour load.'

'Ha! Thirty-four per cent! I wish they did thirty-four per cent!'

Fleck allowed her face to look intrigued, as if she were fascinated by the girl standing in front of her. 'I would love to hear your story. It's so hard to get accurate data on the gender bias situation in households. You can imagine, if we get the data from men who are reporting on how much they do, they tend to overstate their estimations and that skews our findings.'

The woman gave a small smile. 'I bet they do.' She walked to the garden tap and washed her hands. 'My name is Jess, by the way. I'm just out here cutting some roses to put in vases inside. I bought some cute vases from Kmart yesterday. Do you mind if I work while we chat?' Jess picked up a bucket with secateurs and gardening gloves in it and carried it to the rose bushes that were lining the fence.

Fleck followed her and clicked her pen in what she hoped was an official-sounding way. 'So, what is your living situation here?'

'I live here with my boyfriend, pretty much. His name is Liam. He's studying mechanical engineering and I'm studying sociology. We met at uni. It's pretty serious. I can definitely see myself settling down with him one day.'

'And the house? Do you own or rent?'

'It belongs to Liam's grandma. She's moved into nursing care, but his parents don't want to sell the house or rent it out because that could affect his Nanna's pension. So he rents it informally. He just pays cash. And he has a housemate who pays rent with cash too.'

'Oh, there's a housemate too? Is the housemate male or female?'

'Oh, he's male.' Jess sounded reluctant. 'It would be better if it were just the two of us. I'm hoping he moves out soon. It's not really working out. Quinn seems to think that housework just happens. Like, when I first started seeing Liam, the place was a mess. Pizza boxes everywhere, dirty socks, and the two of them just sitting among it all, gaming. They're both really bad at doing housework, but especially Quinn. And especially lately. He's always desperate to go off to work or talk with his girlfriend. Cleaning up after himself is last on his list of priorities. It's like he thinks if he doesn't do it, it just happens magically. I feel like I'm the only one who ever does any cleaning.' Jess had the gloves on her hands now. She cut a peach rose, leaving a long stem.

'And when did you move in officially?' Fleck watched as Jess used the secateurs to snap off the thorns.

Jess hesitated. 'I mean, I haven't moved in officially yet. Technically I'm still living at Mannix. You know, the student accommodation college near Monash? But I stay over heaps. I keep telling Liam it would make more sense if Quinn were to move out and we just start living together. But Liam says Quinn won't have it. He says he can't do it to Quinn, that Quinn couldn't afford to live anywhere else. But that's ridiculous. Quinn works all the time. He has a job at Aldi and a job with his uncle and he's so tight. He hardly buys anything.' She placed the rose into the bucket, then selected another one.

Fleck nodded and pretended to take a note on her clipboard.

Jess cut the second rose and continued. 'One time, I went to a farmers' market with Liam. We bought a really special loaf of sourdough and left it on the bench. We'd only eaten about half of it. Anyway, the next day it was all gone. Quinn had come home from work late and was really hungry so he ate the whole thing. I was so mad. That was really nice bread. Artisan bread. And he said he was sorry, he was just so hungry, but it was okay, he would replace it. Anyway, he went and got another loaf of bread – and it was Tip Top Wonder White. Not the same. Definitely not the same bread.'

'Is that a common thing? Has he always been tight with money?'

'I don't know. He's always been, like, a bit poor. Like, I know he went to the same school as Liam, but Quinn was there on a scholarship. He definitely wasn't as well-off as the others. His mum is a single mum. His sisters both have disabilities. You know what I mean. But lately, he just seems to be obsessed with money. Like, desperate. I don't know what's changed.'

'Does Quinn have a girlfriend?'

'He does. But it's not like he's taking her on dates. She lives in Swan Hill. It's all long distance at the moment. It's all—' Jess stopped. She focused her attention on stripping the thorns and leaves from the stem.

'All what?' Fleck prompted.

Jess hesitated. She put the rose into the bucket and moved along to the next bush, which was crowded with deep-red blooms. 'I don't know. There's something weird about that relationship. At first I thought he was making her up. Like he was jealous that Liam had a girlfriend so he invented one too. Or maybe he wanted somebody to take his side on arguments or he wanted – I don't know – positive aura points. There is something about that relationship that just doesn't seem authentic. She just seems to worship him and never challenges him. She's like his manic pixie dream girl. But, it's funny, now that you mention it, he has only been stressing out about money since he's been going out with her. Oh, and that's the other thing. He has a GoFundMe page!'

'Really? What's it for?'

'I'm not sure. Liam heard him talking to someone about it and I've tried to look it up, but I couldn't find it. But Liam and I joke that it's for his toothpaste fund. He never seems to have his own toothpaste. He's always stealing ours. "Donate today and save Quinn's teeth from devastation!"' She chuckled and then fell silent, eyeing the rose bush in front of her analytically.

Fleck allowed the silence to sit for a little bit, and then she spoke. 'I don't think your problem is with Quinn. I think your problem is with Liam. But you don't want to have a hard conversation with your boyfriend because you think it means you don't have the perfect relationship if you argue. So you argue with Quinn instead.'

Jess swallowed. 'I know I shouldn't be so mean to Quinn. I can't help it sometimes. I suppose part of it is that I never know where I stand with Liam. Like, I don't know how serious he is. I want to get married young. I want to have kids. I can never tell, like, what Liam wants in his life long-term. Like, I think we're serious, because I've pretty much moved in. But it's not like we've properly moved in together because Quinn is still here. Like, I don't know. It's not official. And I think I sometimes resent Quinn for that.'

Fleck watched as Jess cut two more roses and put them in her bucket. Then she put her clipboard under her arm. 'Well, I should probably get going. Thank you so much for talking with me.'

Jess looked up. 'When you do the study, like, when you write it, can you – can you not make it sound like it's the girl's fault that things are this way?'

Fleck cocked her head. 'What do you mean?'

Jess bit her lip. 'Like, I read reports like this sometimes and they always, like, hint that, I don't know. They act like men can't help it. That women are their own worst enemies. I mean, it's bad enough that we have to take on more than what's fair when it comes to housework. But on top of that, we're expected to take on the responsibility of changing the system. Like, when they talk about the problem, it's all about what women are doing wrong. Because, I don't know, because they know the only people who are going to bother to read their study is women. I just don't want another study telling me I'm irresponsible for not training my boyfriend to do housework. I have enough going on.' Jess cut a red rose from the bush.

Fleck nodded slowly. 'I promise I won't write anything like that. Take care of yourself, Jess.'

Fleck stood in the kitchen, slicing carrot sticks. Outside, Sam and Joseph took turns kicking a football at the clothesline, where Fleck had pegged out an old bedsheet with AFL goalposts painted on it. Norah raced in laps around them.

There was nothing better than doing someone a favour that actually benefits you too. For the first few weeks of the year, the preps didn't go to school on Wednesdays, but that had finished now. Now, Wednesdays and Fridays, Joseph came home from school with Sam, giving Trixie time to close up the shop. It was actually easier to pick up Joseph than not. It wasn't as hard to drag Sam away from school when he knew he would have Joseph to play with, and he and Norah seemed to get along better when they had Joseph with them. A few times, Fleck had taken the kids to the shop to meet Trixie, but lately Ranveer had offered to drive Trixie to Fleck's as he was going in that direction anyway.

Fleck heard the front door open. 'Hellooooo!' Trixie's voice sang down the hall.

'Come in!' Fleck shouted.

After a little bit of bustle – in which Trixie took the carrot sticks to the outside table for the three older kids, Ranveer made tea and Fleck cleared the table and buckled Alice into her highchair – the three adults were sitting inside, enjoying afternoon tea and talking about Many Hands.

'I've been thinking about a relaunch party,' Trixie said, toying with a Jaffa Cake biscuit. 'I want it to be something that says, "We are here, we have new things to offer, come and see."'

'We definitely need to do a relaunch party!' said Fleck. 'It could show off the newly designed space. People could see the way the shelves move back now and they might consider booking it as a function space.'

'And I want to get the word out about our new workshop program,' said Trixie. 'Plus we always need new volunteers in the shop.'

'What about the microfinancing scheme you've been figuring out with Helen? Should we talk about that at the relaunch too?' Fleck looked at Ranveer, who was sitting opposite her.

Ranveer chewed his biscuit slowly, then swallowed. He took a sip of tea. 'I don't know. This is an important celebration for Trixie and the shop. I don't want to overshadow that in any way.'

Trixie, who was sitting at the table beside Ranveer, reached across to give his wrist a squeeze. 'Aww, you're so thoughtful, Ranveer. But I think it's a good idea.' She stood up to close the sliding door behind Joseph, who had run inside to use the bathroom. 'The whole point of the shop is to support the Society and the work they do. It would be good to be able to showcase some of the new programs. And microfinance is something we can talk about without compromising the safety or privacy of the women we assist. I say we do it.'

Alice was fed up with the highchair. She wriggled and banged her hands on the tray and started to grizzle. Fleck got up to pull her out and sat her on her knee.

'I've been meaning to ask, Ranveer, when did you start going to parkrun? You must have been going for ages to get that good.' Fleck extricated one of her curls from Alice's grip. 'Ranveer?'

Ranveer looked up. Fleck repeated her question.

'Oh, no. I've only been going to parkrun for a little while. Before that I would run on my treadmill at home.' He sipped his tea. 'So, do you think you might come to parkrun tomorrow?' He looked at Trixie. 'You did well the last time you came. You both did.'

'Ranveer. It almost killed us,' Trixie said. 'It's easy enough for you, Mr Elite Athlete. Since when were you so sporty?'

Ranveer shrugged. 'I'm not sporty. I just like to run. I've always liked running.'

Joseph reappeared from the bathroom. He stopped by Ranveer's chair on his way to the back sliding door.

Ranveer regarded him. He folded his paper towel napkin in half.

'I have learnt some new tawny frogmouth facts,' he offered.

Joseph considered this. 'I still like tawny frogmouths, but now I really like gang-gang cockatoos. I want to know all the facts about gang-gang cockatoos. But I still like tawny frogmouths.'

Ranveer nodded. 'I will try to find some facts about gang-gang cockatoos for next time.'

Joseph gazed at him for a moment longer, shifting from foot to foot. 'Would you tell me anyway? The fact about tawny frogmouths? Would you tell me anyway?'

Ranveer poured a new cup of tea from the pot. Then he looked at Joseph. 'Tawny frogmouths have a third eyelid. It is semi-transparent. It helps them to moisten and protect their eyes while still maintaining vision.'

Joseph nodded, as if reassured. 'I already know that fact,' he said, then, catching his mother's eye, added, 'And it is a good fact, thank you very much.' Then he was gone.

Trixie closed the door after Joseph and fetched the kettle. 'How is the case going, Fleck?'

Fleck groaned. 'I don't know what I'm doing!'

Trixie poured hot water into the teapot. 'You always say that. But you always figure it out.'

Fleck sighed. 'I'm just struggling to get my head around it. Things have definitely gone missing, so I'm fairly convinced that an actual crime has taken place. I have a few suspects. I just can't get it all to fit. The people who I suspect the most don't have evidence against them. And the people with evidence don't seem suspicious to me.'

'Have you done up the laundry wall yet? And do you have a dossier? You always say everything is better when you have a dossier!' Trixie was pouring herself another cup of tea from the freshened pot.

'I haven't really done the laundry wall properly, except for a few notes. The laundry's a disaster zone. I do have some spreadsheets that Matthew printed out for me. He was trying to work out what was going on before I was.'

'Well, go get them!'

'They're just here.' Fleck leaned over and levered the envelope of documents out of the pile at the other end of the table.

'Are they accounts? Show them to Ranveer. He'll make sense of them.'

'Oh, it's okay. I don't want to—'

Trixie interrupted. 'Fleck. He already has his nice highlighter pen out, you'd better give him something. The man needs to annotate.'

Fleck handed the envelope to Ranveer, who had indeed pulled the slim highlighter pen from his breast pocket and uncapped it. He unsheathed the document and began poring over the pages.

'I don't like imposing on you all the time,' Fleck mumbled to Ranveer. Nobody responded. Trixie was watching the children; Ranveer was absorbed in his work.

Outside, Norah had confiscated the football and was gearing up for a battle. Sam and Joseph seemed unperturbed and drifted off to the trampoline, leaving Norah alone to enjoy her hollow victory. Trixie turned back to Fleck. 'So, take me over your suspects.'

Fleck sighed. 'It's tricky. There are a whole lot of volunteers who work on the railway. I used security footage to find out which volunteers were working in the engine sheds, where the supplies were kept, between when the goods arrived and when they went missing. The footage covers the front and side doors. There were five people who used the shed during that time, but only two of them can be seen carrying large bags out of there.

'I don't trust Nathan Garland. He's already shown himself to be untrustworthy. But he's not one of the volunteers on the footage. And I can't work out how else he would have accessed the shed.'

'What would his motive be?'

'I don't know. But he's a dodgy man,' said Fleck.

'Maybe that's just because he's a politician. All politicians seem dodgy to me.'

'Maybe.'

'So who else is there?' said Trixie.

'Well, there's Quinn, one of the younger volunteers. Actually, I've discovered that Quinn is connected to Nathan. Quinn's an engineering student who's really into trains. And he seems to be in need of money.' Fleck told Trixie and Ranveer about her trip to Mount Waverley masquerading as a social researcher, and about her conversation with Jess.

'The other suspect is Ruby, the artist who is working on site,' Fleck continued. 'I don't know too much about her, but Matthew's sister went to art school with her so I'm going to see if she knows anything more. Oh, and there's one more thing. Jess said that Quinn had a GoFundMe page. I'd like to know what it's for but I couldn't find it.'

Trixie nodded. 'That could be a good clue. But are you sure it was GoFundMe specifically? Maybe it's on a different crowdfunding platform.'

Fleck grabbed the tablet from its charger, and soon had tabs open for several different crowdfunding platforms which she began to search.

Ranveer put the cap back on his highlighter. 'There are definitely some anomalies in the spending patterns here. As a rule, there is a rhythm to ingoings and outgoings, but there are a few sections where there is a spike in spending that doesn't correspond to a delay in the next purchase. I've highlighted the dates for you.'

Fleck took the papers from Ranveer. 'This is amazing! Thank you so much!'

The trio was disturbed by a wailing noise outside. Joseph had attempted to climb a tree, but was now stuck. Trixie went outside to help him back down. Ranveer watched her go, then turned to Fleck. 'You often worry and apologise about asking me to help,' he said.

Fleck shrugged. 'We're always asking for your help. We're always leaning on you. I worry that we're overstepping sometimes.'

'You don't need to.' He said it so quickly, he almost cut her off. Fleck looked at him in surprise. 'You don't need to worry,' he repeated. He looked out the window at Trixie, standing under the tree, pointing to footholds for Joseph to lower himself onto. 'Before I met you both, my life was – well, I was stuck in a rut I guess. All of my days looked the same. I was feeling trapped, maybe.' Ranveer looked intensely uncomfortable saying so many words in a row. But he ploughed on. 'But now, I have more courage to go out into the community. I don't just run on my treadmill. I've joined parkrun. I volunteer for a worthy charity. I have you to thank for that. And – and Trixie.' He looked down.

Outside Joseph was clinging to the tree and yelling out in fear. He was only a few feet from the ground. Trixie was laughing and coaxing him.

Ranveer gestured towards the melodrama in the back yard. 'I will always find this chaos to be a bit alien. It's different to what I'm used to.' He put his pen in his pocket. 'But I will always be grateful to be invited.'

Fleck smiled and muttered some pleasantry. They sipped their tea and sat in companionable silence. After a moment, Ranveer spoke again. 'You can tell Trixie that too.'

CHAPTER ELEVEN

Quinn was a suspect, and he seemed desperate for money. Fleck decided it would be a good idea to have a look around his workbench for clues. Matthew was home with the kids. He had told her that Quinn was not expected to be at the railway today, so it was the perfect time to snoop.

When Fleck had arrived half an hour earlier, Ruby had been sitting at a desk inside the engine sheds with an older lady. As she approached them, Fleck heard them discussing architecture. The woman, who introduced herself as Margaret, had a pile of books in front of her.

Fleck had taken one of the books off the pile, a glossy coffee table book, and flipped through it. It featured various mansions and old houses of Melbourne. Fleck saw Ripponlea, Schramm's Cottage, Amberley, Como House, Miller's Homestead, Raheen and Odyssey House. The section on Paradise Lost Manor House included large pictures of the exterior and some inset pictures of the interior, including an entrance way that looked more like a ballroom, with a sweeping staircase and tall windows that looked out over the lake. As Fleck returned the book to Margaret, she noticed the names on the cover. 'Margaret O'Dowd – is that you? Are you one of the authors?'

Margaret had offered a smile. 'Yes, all of these are my books.' She had gestured at the small pile. 'I'm a local historian.'

'Margaret is helping me,' Ruby had said. 'I want my village to be historically accurate. Some of my buildings will be authentic replicas of local buildings.'

Now, Fleck sat in the small room within the engine sheds where Quinn usually worked. She opened her everything book on the workbench and put a pen beside it. If anyone asked, she was working on her feature article.

It was funny, for someone who was apparently such a slob at home, Quinn kept a very tidy workspace. Jars were lined up along the wall with various screws, bolts and rivets, all neatly labelled. Tools were hung on a pegboard on the side wall. Fleck sat on the stool and tried to find something out of place.

She gazed through the door's window, out to the side shed. Ruby was now sitting by herself, but it looked as if Margaret had only left briefly. Her blazer and large handbag were still draped over the back of her chair. Perhaps Margaret had gone to the bathroom?

There was a small forty-eight-page exercise book wedged between two of the jars on the workbench. Fleck pulled it out and opened it. Inside was a neat table hand-ruled in black ink. There were rows of dates and figures. It was hard to know what she was looking at, but then she saw the title of the table: *Diesel usage*. Was this a normal part of Quinn's job? Or was he keeping records to cover his tracks? Fleck pulled out her phone and took photos of the pages.

When Fleck turned back to look through the window, Ruby had pulled Margaret's bag onto the desk. Fleck held her breath and watched. Ruby removed a leather-bound portfolio and unzipped it. Inside was what looked like a letter-writing kit. Ruby glanced up, then quickly removed an envelope and inspected it. She flipped it over and checked the sealing flap. Then she zipped the envelope into a pocket in her own bag, closed the portfolio and put it carefully back into Margaret's bag. She put the bag back on the seat, jumping at the sound of the exterior door opening. She resumed an attitude of working as Margaret approached and they settled back into work as if nothing had happened.

Fleck continued to look around Quinn's workspace, but there was nothing relevant to see. She could hear movement in the larger room next door where the engines were stored and maintained. She slipped through the door into the large workshop. A bright yellow diesel engine was pulling into the sheds. Topham was driving it.

'How goes the work on the feature article, Mrs Flanagan?' Topham boomed. Hail fellow well met.

Fleck hesitated, trying to think of a good response. She needn't have worried. Topham only meant the question as a social pleasantry. He immediately launched into a monologue about the uselessness of grant applications and the incompetence of government bureaucracy. He continued talking as they returned through a doorway into the side shed where Ruby and Margaret were working. 'Hello, ladies!' Topham said. 'Good to see you hard at work. I must say I'm looking forward to seeing the fairy garden when it's built.'

Margaret, who had already packed up all of her bags, stood up. 'I'm leaving,' she said to Ruby. Then she looked at Topham. The expression on her face was unambiguous. It wasn't scorn or dislike; it was unadulterated contempt.

Topham hesitated, then made his excuses and returned to the main engine shed. Fleck was still watching Margaret as she walked out the door, shoulder bag swinging.

Trixie and Fleck stood on either side of the counter at Many Hands. They held Fleck's crochet work between them.

'You see here?' Trixie said. 'You've skipped a corner. You need to work two shells into every corner. That's what's given it that odd shape. And I don't know what you've done wrong here. Oh wait. Yes I do. You've started going backwards on yourself. You're going to need to frog back until this point.'

Trixie handed back Fleck's attempt at a granny square and Fleck started to pull the work apart, undoing her mistakes.

The shop bell chimed and Bev bustled inside. She inspected Fleck's crochet work and suggested she might benefit from using stitch markers. 'They can help you keep track of what you're doing,' she said. 'Anyway, I've got the shop covered now. You two can go back and set up for the workshop.'

Trixie and Fleck ducked out the back, then Fleck heard the bell tinkle again as Jo entered and greeted Bev. She poked her head through the curtain a moment later. 'Am I the first one here? Oh, hi Fleck!'

Trixie smiled. 'You're pretty much the first. We're expecting a few others. Is your BFF Lynette coming again?'

Jo's smile faded. 'Oh yeah. Lynette, my bestie. I'm not sure if she's coming. She's not—' She looked back over her shoulder to check for any listeners, then crept inside the room and sat at the table. 'She's not exactly my friend,' she explained in a subdued tone. 'We go to the same church, but it's a really big church. She overheard me talking about this workshop to another person and just invited herself along.' Jo darted another anxious glance at the doorway. 'The business she's involved in is *all over* my church. Everyone is becoming a distributor. Some of the people are saying the company is, like, a gift from God. Like it makes you a good Christian to be involved. All about how the gels help you look after your body and your body is a temple of the Holy Spirit and stuff. It's pretty intense.' Fleck exchanged glances with Trixie and then looked back to Jo, who seemed to be rallying her thoughts. 'But that's the thing: it's everywhere now. It's like the church population has reached peak capacity when it comes to recruiting new distributors. There's nobody left to invite. They all keep trying to invite each other. So I think that's part of why Lynette latched on to this group. You are fresh meat for her. Sorry. That sounds harsh. But they've taken over my church and I'm sick of it.'

Jo suddenly fell silent as the shop bell rang again. Kerryn arrived, closely followed by Dima, and then Lynette.

Lynette sat beside Fleck and seemed to be making an extra effort to be nice to her. There was a lull in the conversation. Fleck stifled a small yawn.

'Are you all right?' Lynette placed a hand on Fleck's arm.

Fleck smiled. 'Of course! Just, you know, a bit tired.'

Lynette nodded sagely. 'I used to get tired all the time as well.'

Fleck smiled vaguely and picked up her work.

Lynette tried again. 'Not anymore, though. I don't get tired during the day anymore at all.' The pause was right there, hanging, waiting for Fleck to ask the question.

Instead, Fleck asked, 'What colour are you going to stitch next?'

Lynette looked momentarily baffled. 'Er – green. But what I was saying was, we really need to get you onto GelVita Morning Blast. It's packed full of vitamins and trace minerals. I swear, it's a total game changer.'

Fleck stretched her mouth into a smile and nodded.

Lynette pressed on. 'I'm *serious*. You really must try it. Now that I take Morning Blast, I find I just don't get tired anymore. It's magic. You should really give it a go. I'm happy to fix you up with some sample packs, but if you really want to save money, I can set you up as a consultant. Consultants get the *best* discounts.'

Fleck held her smile in place and nodded again. 'I don't know that it would help my specific situation. Unless your Morning Blast can be used to convince babies to sleep through the night, I think I'll still be just as tired.'

Lynette nodded shrewdly. 'What you need is the Sleepytime Lavender Mist gel. You take a tiny drop of it and rub it on your bubba's chest half an hour before they are supposed to go to bed. I'm telling you – I don't know what the science is, but it just works. It settles them right down. I wish I had it when Amyxia was a baby. These gels are great for everyone in the family. But I find it benefits me most of all. I don't get headaches anymore. I have more energy. Plus I've lost heaps of weight. It just falls off me!' Lynette eyed Fleck. Fleck found herself sucking in her soft midsection.

The workshop continued. Fleck noticed that Lynette preferred to discuss her chosen topics than join an existing conversation. Sometimes she would position herself at Fleck's elbow, waiting until Fleck felt compelled to acknowledge her. Then Lynette would draw her in to a sidebar conversation, pinioning Fleck with her eyes, gradually engaging others until she had taken over the whole conversation.

Lynette also used her phone photos to hijack the conversation. You could be listening to an amusing anecdote about Dima's mum when suddenly Lynette would thrust her phone under your nose. 'You know what I was talking about before? Here's a picture. Here's Amyxia in her callisthenics costume. Look.' After this, it would impossible to return to the previous conversation. Fleck didn't know how not to acknowledge something that was, quite literally, being shoved in her face.

When Lynette went to the bathroom, the conversation turned to Fleck's case. Fleck filled them in on all her suspects and theories.

'The time period I'm looking at is eight days. There's the Saturday when the supplies were definitely present and accounted for and the Sunday, a week later, when they were definitely missing. I asked Ranveer to look at the accounts and he said there was a possibility that this has been going on for quite some time. But I'm getting ahead of myself. The eight days is the magic window. When I looked at the security videos—'

'Oooh, security videos!' exclaimed Jo. 'Look at you! This is awesome. Proper detective work.'

Fleck smiled. 'It did feel pretty cool when I was going through the footage. Even though it was mostly boring.'

Kerryn looked at her appraisingly. 'We need to get you a proper hat. All the great detectives have a distinctive hat. What should it be? Deer stalker? Fedora? Bowler?'

'Yes, but you only need to wear it in Term One and Term Four,' said Trixie. 'No hat, no play, no fun today, Fleck!'

'What kind of hat does Phryne Fisher wear? You should get a hat like Phryne Fisher wears.'

'Oh stop talking about hats, you lot! I want to hear about the case.' Dima turned back to Fleck. 'So you were saying there were two main suspects.'

Fleck nodded. 'Yes. That's what the security footage told me. Quinn works in the engine sheds and seems desperate for money. I've also recently discovered he has a connection with Nathan Garland, who seems super-dodgy, so it's possible Quinn is working for Nathan to steal goods.'

Dima frowned. 'Who's Nathan Garland?'

'Dima!' Jo exclaimed. 'How can you not know who Nathan Garland is? He has a massive photo plastered over the side of your workplace!' Dima worked part-time at the cafe across the road from George's on Highett Road.

'Oh! That guy! Yeah. I know him. He was giving out shopping bags last week. I grabbed five. They're good bags.'

'Who is your other suspect, Fleck?' Kerryn cast a nervous glance at the stairwell. It was only a matter of time before Lynette reappeared and hijacked the conversation.

'Ruby Chen. She was the other one who came out of the shed with a big bag during the time stuff went missing. She's making a little village at the site – like, all in miniature. She was talking to a historian about it the last time I was there.'

'She was talking to a historian?' Trixie said.

'Yes, a local historian who writes all about buildings, I think. Ruby wants her village to be historically accurate. She's making a replica of the manor house.'

'I wonder if it will be haunted by miniature ghosts.' Dima smiled impishly.

'Yeah, I'm not sure how you replicate "creepy" in miniature. But I'll tell you something weird.' Fleck told the group about Ruby taking the letter-writing set out of Margaret's bag and removing the envelope.

Trixie frowned. 'She stole an envelope? Maybe she just needed an envelope.'

'Maybe. But why wouldn't she have asked Margaret for it? Why the need for secrecy?'

Jo pursed her lips. 'I don't know. But it's just one envelope. That doesn't seem like stealing. It's just weird.'

Fleck nodded. 'Exactly! What if the other stealing is just weird too? What if this is all just Ruby being weird?'

'Maybe,' said Kerryn. 'But she must have some motivation. What if it's some sort of performance art?'

'I don't think she's that sort of artist.' Fleck grinned.

'This is like some sort of puzzle,' said Trixie. 'What could Ruby be doing that requires fertiliser, diesel fuel, toilet paper and a single envelope?'

'And don't forget the Thomas dress-up kit,' Fleck added.

Dima chuckled. 'I'm convinced that Kerryn's right. This is performance art. Maybe she dresses as Thomas and rolls about in fertiliser. It's a searing critique of consumerism and mass transit. Oh, and that part with the envelope! It's inspired!'

When they had finished laughing, Fleck paused in thought. 'Ruby didn't just grab the envelope without looking at it. Like, you know how a shoplifter might steal something just for the rush and it doesn't matter what it is? This wasn't like that. She was looking at it as if she were checking it was the right kind of envelope first.'

'Ooh. I like that,' said Trixie. 'Furtive but not compulsive. So do you think she could have been stealing other things in a way that is furtive but not compulsive?'

'I don't know. Further investigation is required,' Fleck said. 'Oh. And there was one more thing. Margaret.'

'Who's Margaret?' asked Jo.

'She was the historian talking with Ruby. Anyway, she gave Topham the dirtiest look. She full-on snubbed him. It was like she completely hates his guts.'

'What do you think that was about?' asked Trixie.

'I don't know. Topham is a bit full of himself but it was more than just her being annoyed with him.' Fleck rubbed her chin.

'Maybe they're ex-lovers?' Kerryn raised her eyebrows.

'Maybe. But she's a good ten years older than him. Topham strikes me as someone who would like to be the older one in a relationship. And I couldn't sense any chemistry there.'

'Is Topham single?' Trixie asked.

'I don't know. I think so. I know he was married once. His wife left him because she couldn't stand all of the train stuff. But he never remarried, as far as I know. I wondered if Margaret was just mad at him for getting it wrong and saying they were building a fairy garden, but she fully turned her back on him and walked off. That seems a bit extreme for a simple error. I don't know. I'm a bit stuck.'

Lynette appeared at the foot of the stairs. 'Is that so? It sounds like *somebody* needs a brain power boost! We need to have a conversation about the Precious Perspicacity gel. I can get you a really good deal!'

CHAPTER TWELVE

It was time to investigate Ruby Chen. The weather was forecast to be clear all week. Fleck planned to eat a picnic lunch in the park every day until she encountered Ruby. This was partly a detective decision, but it was mostly because she was feeling bored out of her skull in a house full of clothes horses. She needed to get out, to spend time somewhere that didn't look like a failed theme park called Laundry Land.

'Packing a picnic lunch' was a concept Fleck was yet to master. There were just so many elements involved; so much thinking ahead required. It was completely overwhelming. The food needed to be able to travel. You needed to remember to pack all of the parts. There was cutlery and crockery involved, and rugs and seating. And what if you wanted to go next level with thermoses and little snacks and impressive, home-made slice in a tin lined with baking paper? The idea of it made Fleck panic.

Matthew always organised the picnic when they went out as a family. For Matthew, packing a picnic was a single, simple task. For Fleck, it was one thousand overwhelming tasks rolled into one.

But she would get better at this. She was a mum, for heaven's sake. Mums were supposed to be good at packing picnics and taking care of everyone. This week would be a good chance for her to improve. This week, she would learn to flex her picnic-packing muscle.

Fleck stared into the pantry. The problem was, she really needed to do a proper grocery shop. What was she going to eat? Nothing looked appealing. It needed to be something portable. This was too confusing. There was a tin of baked beans on the bottom shelf. But she didn't want cold baked beans in a tin. She wanted hot baked beans on toast with cheese. This was painful. She definitely did not want to go to the shops today. She was running out of time. Alice would wake up soon and it would be time to go. Fleck sighed. She grabbed a sandwich out of the freezer for Norah and a couple of baby food pouches for Alice and put them in a shopping bag. She threw in some fruit and lunchbox snacks and a half-empty packet of barbecue shapes. She would have her own lunch later.

The main rotunda at the park was decorated with balloons and a large group was unpacking hampers and plastic containers. Fleck took Norah and Alice to the small playground beside the railway. From here she could see the building site of Ruby's miniature village. She settled on the bench seat as Norah ran to the playground. For now, Alice was happy to sit watching the birds from her pusher. Fleck pulled out her everything book and a pen. She really needed to plan a big grocery shop. It had been too long. She would do it properly, with a meal plan and shopping list. She had started writing a plan on the back of an envelope a few days ago, but then she lost the envelope. This plan would be better. It would go for two weeks.

Fleck wrote the days of the week neatly down the left-hand side of the right-hand page of her everything book. She listed the dates and checked her calendar on her phone to see if there were any dinner events coming up. She wrote 'Flanagans' Tacos' on the lines for Sunday dinners. Now she had to think up meals for the other days.

Norah had the whole playground to herself for now. She tested out the slide and the climbing frame. She avoided the steep little rockclimbing wall. This playground didn't have a set of swings and Fleck was glad. She didn't want to spend the whole time standing up while counting gentle shoves. She had work to do.

Spaghetti bolognese, baked potatoes, chicken stir-fry, bacon fried rice. As she wrote the meals into the plan, she added ingredients to the shopping list on the left-hand page. She was going to need to do a *big* shop. A massive one.

It wasn't long before both girls were hungry. Norah was now sitting beside Fleck, eating her sandwich. Alice was investigating a cold toast finger and Fleck was spoon-feeding her some yoghurt from a pouch.

Saturday's dinner would be Surprise Chicken and glass potatoes. It was about time she made Surprise Chicken. She got the idea from a Southern lady on the internet who also had ideas on how to keep a tidy house. You clear out the fridge and make a marinade out of all of the sauces and condiments in the house that have almost run out. Worcester sauce? Peanut butter? Apricot jam? Soy sauce? Maple syrup? Vegemite? It didn't matter. You tipped it in the jug. Then you took a bag of chicken drumsticks, soaked them in the frankensauce, and then baked them in the oven. It tasted different every time. Dinner – but make it risky!

Fleck looked over at the railway. She could see Ruby pushing a wheelbarrow to her building site and unpacking materials. Bingo.

'We're going to go for a walk soon, Norah. Five minutes.' Norah always needed a bit of lead time before changing modes. But it was okay. Ruby looked like she was settling in for a long stint.

The miniature village was nestled inside a curve of track just before the beginning of the outer loop line. Ruby was designing the village to stand at one-sixth the size of the original buildings, like the trains themselves.

It looked like Ruby was poring over a large, fat scrapbook of some kind. It almost seemed like an ancient book of spells, the way Ruby reached right across to turn a page. She was writing carefully into the book and frowning at the space in front of her. After a few minutes, she moved her book to the side and started to work with a measuring tape and spirit level. By the time Fleck had corralled Norah and Alice and packed up their picnic, Ruby was again frowning into her scrapbook.

A low metal garden fence surrounded the railway. As Fleck eased the pusher through the little gate on the east side, Ruby looked up. Realising they were approaching her, she quickly closed her book. She slid it into her bag and zipped it shut. Then she moved the bag behind her. It all seemed rather *furtive.*

'Hello, Ruby! I don't know if you remember me …' Fleck re-introduced herself and introduced Norah and Alice as well. 'How is work going on the miniature village?'

Ruby's expression seemed to relax a little. Fleck suspected that she appreciated that Fleck didn't call it a fairy garden. 'I'm feeling a little stuck today,' she said. 'I'm not used to making miniatures for outdoor environments. I'm trying to get a handle on the terrain. I don't have to do that sort of thing usually.'

Fleck looked at the markings on the patch of ground and tried to picture the village. 'So I know you will be making a replica of the manor house in this village, but what will the other buildings be?'

'I'm putting a replica of the original Paradise Heights post office up the hill here. And the old All Saints Church will be over here. None of it will be geographically accurate – that would be too difficult to replicate. But the buildings will be fairly accurate miniatures. So, if you wanted to know what the old Paradise Heights milk bar looked like, you could see it here in the village – even if it hadn't been next to the post office in real life.'

Fleck nodded. 'I like how you have incorporated history into the build – that it will be educational as well as beautiful.'

Ruby smiled. 'That was part of what helped me get the grant. It's not just an art project, it's local history.'

Norah was trotting about picking flowers from the weeds that grew along the sides of the path and delivering them to Alice. Alice would probably have shoved the flowerheads straight into her mouth if she'd had better dexterity. Instead, she swiped at the flimsy stems and they fell to the ground.

'I was talking to your husband about it actually,' Ruby said. 'He's been applying for grants and not getting anywhere. I was going to give him some advice about how to do it, but it looks like his last one got through, so he might not need my help anymore.'

'Oh, that's good news!' said Fleck. 'I didn't realise he'd got through to the next stage. He had been waiting on that and not hearing anything.'

'Yeah, they're on the shortlist now. I think he got through a couple of weeks ago.'

'I'm surprised he hasn't told me. He's was tearing his hair out about that,' Fleck said. 'Oh, and I wanted to tell you: I've seen your videos online. The stop-motion ones with Ruby Ringtail. They are really special.' Fleck had binged the little videos while sitting on the bathroom bench as Norah splashed in the tub. Ruby Ringtail was an anthropomorphised possum with large black eyes who wore an olive green parka and spent her day doing cosy things. There was no dialogue in the videos. They were simple and soothing, featuring tiny cups and saucers, handkerchief tablecloths, and pie tins made of beer bottle caps. Fleck watched 'Ruby makes a blackberry pie', 'Ruby wraps a birthday present', 'Ruby reads the paper in bed' and 'Cleaning day for Ruby'.

The non-marsupial version of Ruby smiled brightly. 'You've seen my videos? Really? You like them?'

Fleck nodded emphatically. 'I loved them. The details are so beautiful. *We* loved them, didn't we, Norah? The Ruby Ringtail videos?'

Norah blinked. 'I like Bluey.'

'Haha!' Fleck felt her face become hot. 'Oh yes, I know you like Bluey. But we also liked the possum videos. Don't you remember Ruby the possum?'

Norah surveyed her mother. 'Ruby's boring.'

Fleck was sweating, but Ruby chuckled. 'Don't worry about it,' she assured Fleck. 'It's refreshing how honest she is. And I like how she's telling me directly instead of hiding behind some keyboard.' She turned to Norah. 'Ruby *is* a little bit boring. I think that's one of the things she likes about herself.'

Norah nodded, then put her finger in her nose. Fleck turned back to Ruby. 'Surely you don't get many haters in your comments? How miserable would a person have to be to hate on a felt possum who drinks tea out of a thimble?'

Ruby's face clouded over. 'People are always writing comments. And some of them are really mean. Maybe they think I don't read the comments? Of course I read the comments. I read all the comments. But they still say mean things. Sometimes it's just a throwaway line, people saying I'm not as good as some other animator. They compare Ruby Ringtail to Tiny Chef or Mini Kitchen or Frog and Toad. But I'm not trying to be those creators. I admire them, of course I admire them, but Ruby Ringtail is different. She's different.'

Fleck nodded. 'Absolutely, she's different.' Fleck had no idea who those other creators were, but she agreed with the *spirit* of what Ruby was saying.

Ruby swallowed and continued. 'And there are people who tell me I should be doing it differently. That I should use computer animation instead of stop motion, or I should make Ruby talk. And so many people want Ruby to get a boyfriend. It's weird.'

'Really?' Fleck was stunned.

'Oh, it's a whole thing. They are missing the point. Ruby is single. She lives by herself. She is happy. Her life is small, but it is beautiful. That is the whole point.' Norah was no longer picking flowers. She was uprooting them. Fleck darted over to intervene before Norah delivered a dandelion with a massive clump of dirt hanging off the roots to Alice's pusher. Alice barked a note of protest.

When Fleck had successfully redirected Norah with the help of a fluffy dandelion seed head, Ruby continued. 'I tell these people that maybe they could make their own character. Maybe they could make their own character who has a boyfriend. They could tell those stories with that character and she could have a boyfriend, not Ruby. But they don't listen. And now a lot of them are trying to make fan art of Ruby and her boyfriend and they make the boyfriend some completely different animal, too, like a wombat or a koala. Ruby doesn't have a boyfriend! And if she did, he would be another ringtail possum. It doesn't make sense for her to have a boyfriend who is a completely different species. But that's irrelevant anyway because she doesn't have a boyfriend. She is happy being single. That's kind of the point of the whole series.'

Norah was warming to her surroundings. She spotted Ruby's measuring tape and pounced on it. Fleck remonstrated with her but Ruby intervened. 'It's fine, I don't mind.' She spent a few minutes showing Norah how the measuring tape worked, then returned to the conversation.

'And then there are other people who get angry with the fan art and say people are trying to force Ruby to be heteronormative and then *they* make pictures of Ruby with her *girlfriend* and they're getting married or something. I wish they'd all leave Ruby alone. When I see all their manga-style pictures where Ruby has massive eyes and is going on dates and wearing an evening dress instead of her parka, I just tell myself it's not Ruby. I need to tell myself it's not Ruby. It's a different possum who looks like Ruby, but who isn't Ruby. Otherwise I just feel sad.'

They looked out to the rotunda where the large group was now playing lively music. Smoke puffed from some sort of cooker they had set up and children chased each other and squealed. 'That must be hard when everyone has an opinion on what you're doing,' Fleck said.

Ruby nodded. 'Yes, but they aren't the worst people. There are some people who are much worse than that. They are relentless. They say the most awful things. I think they got the idea that I'm anti-men because I keep insisting that Ruby is single. I think once you do something on the internet that makes you look like you are against men, there are people who see that as permission to write awful things. And they don't stop. They keep coming back and saying awful things. I argue with them, but they don't listen. I block them, but they come back with new profiles. I hate it. They get in my head and stop me from being able to create.'

'That's horrible!'

'Yes. And there's also this one woman. Because I made a mistake, you see. I made a mistake and wrote an angry comment on one of the fan art pictures that showed Ruby in a wedding with her kangaroo girlfriend. I said to stop drawing Ruby getting married. Ruby is not getting married! She is never getting married! This woman got really angry with me and called me a homophobe and wanted me to get cancelled. I took my comment down – I didn't mean it like that – but she won't stop. She comments on other people's comments telling them to boycott me. One time she told me I should die.'

'What? That's awful! Is there anything you can do?'

Ruby looked at her bag, the one with the big scrapbook in it. Then she looked back at Fleck. 'I mean, I can block them and report them, but it doesn't stop them coming back in other ways. I delete their comments, but sometimes I get tired and just leave them. I just want to make my art. I don't want to be a moderator.'

Norah pulled out a small length of measuring tape. Then she released it, and jumped and cackled with glee when it zipped back into the plastic container. Alice watched with fascination from the pusher.

Ruby smiled faintly at their antics. 'Sometimes I think I should turn comments off. I should make it so that nobody can comment. I shouldn't have any comments at all. But I can't do it. Because then I wouldn't know. They would still be thinking those things and I would have no way of knowing. I don't think I could bear it.'

As they talked, Ruby continued to cast looks at her bag, as if checking that the book was still there – or perhaps because it held the answers to unasked questions.

Fleck watched Norah as she attempted to unspool more tape. She was trying to pull out a long section, but she hadn't mastered the auto-retraction mechanism. Every time she tried to reach for more tape, the part she had pulled out zipped back. Her little brow furrowed in consternation.

Fleck looked back to Ruby. 'But are there nice comments too, right? You must have a lot of fans saying they love Ruby Ringtail.'

Ruby gave a little shrug. 'I do. I get lots more nice comments than mean ones. But it's the mean ones that get in my head. Still,' she added, brightening a little, 'there are some comments that are really special. One woman said she loves my videos because she feels represented by Ruby. She said it felt like I was telling her it's okay to live a quiet life filled with small joys. And another woman said my videos made her chemotherapy treatment more bearable. I write the best comments out onto little pieces of paper and put them into a jar. When I'm having a bad day, I read them again.'

Ruby cast yet another lingering glance at the bag with the book. Fleck couldn't resist. 'Is that what's in your big book?'

Ruby gave a start. 'What big book?'

Fleck pointed at the bag. 'The – the big book. You had it out before I arrived. You were looking at it.'

Ruby looked at the bag, then back at Fleck.

There are a periods of time in every conversation, little windows after your conversation partner has spoken, in which it is possible to respond normally without sounding strange. In the very moment *after* this time period had elapsed, Ruby said, 'It's a scrapbook.' The words seemed to erupt from her like an inadvertent cough. She looked intensely uncomfortable.

'Does it have your plans in it?' Fleck asked.

Ruby stared at Fleck, her eyes wide.

'… for the miniature village?' Fleck continued.

'Oh! Yes! Yes!' Another eruption. This one seemed to come with a measure of relief.

'I wonder, could I have a look at your book? Could I see the plans?' A thought had occurred to Fleck. Perhaps the missing goods hadn't been stolen at all. Perhaps Ruby was just using them for her project. Perhaps this had all been a complete misunderstanding. That would be a nice outcome. Nobody to blame, just some mix-up with supplies. Suddenly, Fleck really wanted for that to be the case. The railway was such a wholesome place. She didn't want for it to have been exploited by people who wished it ill. The big book of plans might tell her everything she needed to know.

Ruby's face fell. Again, that too-long pause. Then, 'I have to go!' The words burst out of her. 'I'm sorry. I just remembered I have to go!' She grabbed the book bag and scurried to the engine sheds, leaving all of the equipment behind. Fleck stared after her. Norah released the measuring tape with a zipping sound.

The group at the rotunda were cooking something deliciously aromatic over a charcoal fire. Fleck's stomach growled. She really wished she'd packed a proper picnic lunch.

CHAPTER THIRTEEN

'Oh no! Not the pink ones! You've gotta get the blue ones!' Fleck stared in dismay at the three plastic pouches. The three *pink* plastic pouches. They were the right brand. They were the right size. But they were *fragranced.*

Fleck had a horror of perfumed wipes. She hated anything with a fake, synthetic fragrance, but wipes were the worst. Nobody asked for your nasty fragrance, wipes! Stop getting above yourself. You have one job, wipes, and it's not a glamorous one. You do not need to be wearing perfume. Begone with you and your terrible cheap, cloying smell!

'I'm sorry,' Matthew said. 'I couldn't see the blue ones anywhere. And we need more wipes.'

Fleck said it was fine, she said it didn't matter. Even though the pink wipes would make her hands smell like pink-wipe-smell for the whole day.

But Fleck would be doing a big shop soon. She had her list and she had her meal plan. She would get proper, fragrance-free wipes when she did the big shop. She would get lots of them.

Fleck lifted the milk cartons out of the blue shopping bag and delivered them to the fridge. She would also get the roasted sesame dressing when she did the shop. Not the spicy one, which looked almost exactly the same. She wanted the non-spicy Kewpie roast sesame dressing. It was too complicated to describe it for Matthew to get, especially as it wasn't in the mayonnaise section. It was in the Asian foods section. And he wasn't doing a full shop, anyway; just a top-up shop. Fleck would get it this week when she did the big shop.

'Mum's coming to the railway on Sunday,' Matthew said, as he pulled a couple of loaves of multigrain bread out of a green bag.

'Oh good. I want to do some more investigating. I'm still trying to get a handle on Ruby Chen. Wait, that reminds me. Did you hear back about that grant you applied for? Ruby said you've got through to the next stage.'

'What's that?' Matthew was stacking a box of chicken nuggets on top of two frozen pizzas to take into the laundry freezer.

'Ruby said she was going to give you advice on the grants process, but you didn't need it anymore. You got through to the next round.'

'Ha! I wish!' Matthew disappeared into the laundry. Fleck could hear the chest freezer opening and shutting. He reappeared empty-handed. 'Unless Ruby knows something I don't know. There's been nothing but crickets.'

Fleck frowned. 'That's weird. She seemed convinced. And she said it was a couple of weeks ago too.'

Matthew shook his head emphatically. 'In that case, she's definitely mistaken. I thought maybe she'd seen an email about it before I did, but there's no way I would have missed it if it's been that long.'

Fleck stuffed three of the empty shopping bags into the zip-up freezer one. 'Wait, how would Ruby have seen your email?'

'Oh, we use the generic railway email address. So pretty much anyone can access it. Anyone at the railway, I mean. Ruby would have access too. But I've been checking it regularly, and checking the spam folder. There's been nothing. Of course, this has given Nathan Garland plenty of chances to sound off about "typical government incompetence", which annoys Topham. They're on the other side of politics from each other. It really annoys Topham when Nathan wears his campaign T-shirts around the railway.'

'Sometimes I think Nathan doesn't own any other sort of shirt.'

'Nathan says he's "shining a light on an important service", but Topham says he's exploiting the railway to make himself look good. The halo effect and all that. He says the railway should be free of politics.'

'Topham makes a good point.'

'He does. And I would agree with Topham even more if he hadn't taken the candidate from the other party on a tour of the railway with photos and quotes for the newsletter. It turns out Topham only doesn't like things being political if it's the opposite side of politics from what he agrees with.'

'Yeah, well. That kind of behaviour would probably annoy me more if Nathan Garland annoyed me less.'

It was 3.25am and Fleck and Alice were in the lounge room together. It was annoying that Alice was waking up for night feeds again. She should be sleeping the whole night through. On the other hand, Fleck kind of loved this secret middle-of-the-night time with Alice. It was just the two of them. The house was quiet. And Alice seemed to save up all of her most charming behaviours for their late-night sessions. The maternal and child health nurse had suggested night feeds should be 'strictly business'. No eye contact and definitely no play. But *come on*. You would have to be made of stone to resist interacting with this luminous little child.

While Fleck fed Alice on the right side, she continued her investigation using a family history app. (She wasn't supposed to use screens during night feeds either. Fleck was a night-feed rebel.) She set the name, location and date range, then she sifted through the results.

It didn't take long to find what she was looking for: a wedding announcement in *The Sun News-Pictorial.* Sydney Tozer was to marry Juliet Fitzgerald at St Andrews Methodist Church. Juliet Fitzgerald. That was her name. Fleck sent a text message to herself so she wouldn't forget in the morning.

Alice finished on the right side. Fleck sang an illegal song and gave illegal kisses as she burped Alice and changed her nappy. Alice chattered and giggled and gazed lovingly up at Fleck. So much for 'strictly business'!

As Fleck gave Alice the left side, she continued her search for Quinn's crowdfunding page. She had broadened her search to smaller crowdfunding sites and searched using different parameters and variations of his name and Reddit handles.

The breastfeeding hormones were kicking in and Fleck was finding it hard to keep her eyes open. She almost missed the post on payit4ward.com. She yawned and tapped the fundraiser. Then her eyes widened. She sat up straight in the armchair. Alice pulled off and gave her a quizzical look. Fleck blinked and looked at her baby. She spoke in an excited whisper. 'Mummy's worked it out, Alice! Mummy knows what's going on!'

Fleck was stationed at Quinn's workbench. If anyone asked, she could tell them she was waiting to meet Quinn so that she could interview him for her feature article. In fact, she had an entirely different conversation planned for Quinn, but that was a minor detail people didn't need to know.

All the pieces were in place for the Great Scrapbook Heist. Marian was watching the children at the playground. From Quinn's workbench, Fleck could peer through the grimy window in the door and watch Ruby at her desk. Ruby hadn't been sitting there when Fleck arrived, so it was possible she didn't realise Fleck was there at all. At any rate, Ruby seemed so absorbed in what she was doing, she mightn't have been aware anyway.

The only reason Fleck could identify the light-purple-coloured object in Ruby's hand was that Fleck had bought the exact same model for herself from Kmart a couple of months ago. It looked like a stumpy hair dryer, but it was actually a clothes steamer. Fleck had hoped that she would never need to iron her clothes again. The device had exhaled its steamy breath all over her crushed linen dress, but the crushed linen dress had remained determinedly *crushed.* Now it sat in the bathroom cupboard with the dodgy hair straightener and the trimmer Matthew had used back when he had a beard. But what was Ruby doing with a clothes steamer?

It was rather clever, really. Ruby was systematically steaming the stamps and address labels off a pile of envelopes. She put the labels and stamps to one side and set the envelopes on a little file rack to dry. Did she collect stamps? But then, why steam the labels off the envelopes as well?

Fleck soon had her answer. Ruby put the steamer away. She took one of the envelopes off the rack. Fleck watched as Ruby picked up a sheet of plain printer paper. She placed an assortment of little plastic wrappers on top of the paper. They could have been muesli-bar wrappers, or the wrappers from sweets. Small and crinkly. Then she folded the paper in thirds, like a business letter, so that it contained the mess, and placed the 'letter' into the envelope. Once she had sealed it, she affixed a stamp and address label and moved it to the side. The next envelope received a similar treatment, except this one had a piece of paper folded around a small pile of sequins and fine glitter. A third was filled with what looked like condiment sachets.

Fleck was so entranced watching Ruby create these strange packages that she almost forgot the whole reason she was there. Then Trixie appeared and began talking with Ruby. She was looking very smart in her vintage suit. Fleck knew that she planned to pose as an official from the grants office. She would ask Ruby to show her the building site.

Sure enough, Ruby and Trixie were soon leaving the engine sheds. Fleck waited a few more moments just to be sure, then she emerged from the work room. She extracted the large scrapbook out of its bag and placed it carefully on the table. It had a hard cover and spiral binding. When it was open, it took up the whole of Ruby's small desk. Inside were decorated lists, sketches, measurements and plans. There were all sorts of things – magazine clippings, photographs, stickers – pasted into the book as well. Fleck carefully took photos of each page as she turned them. There was Ruby's schedule for the month ahead: the double-page spread had been carefully divided into boxes with ruled lines, the name of the month splashed across the top in inky curlicues. Ruby had also created colourful divider tabs along the sides of the pages. There were sections for 'Ruby Ringtail', 'Miniatures', 'Railway Village', 'Local History' and 'Future Plans'.

And there, at the back, there was a section titled 'Retribution'.

Fleck couldn't resist. As soon as she had photographed the pages of the 'Railway Village' section, she flipped to 'Retribution'.

Fleck wasn't sure exactly what she was looking at. Like the other pages, it was part-collage. The double-page spread looked a little like a board game, with a winding path traversing the pages from one side to the other. Fleck looked at the 'start' section, on the left-hand side. Here were what looked like comments from YouTube, possibly made in response to a Ruby Ringtail video. Printed, carefully trimmed and pasted into the book, the comments were all from the same user. @MeOwDangIt47 had written:

> What is this? This is the most boring thing I've ever watched!
> Ruby Possum needs to lay off the possum snacks lol
> I don't get it. Fatso Possum is sad and alone and everyone thinks this is five-star content? What am I missing?

Following the path along the double-page spread, a new section showed Ruby's research of @MeOwDangIt47 and their other online profiles, including an email address and a Facebook profile in the name of Katz Pajammus. The final section of the spread showed a comment from Katz on the Facebook page of the Church of the Enlightened Brethren:

> I don't know why you think I'm interested in joining your church. Please stop sending me your newsletter. Please stop writing me messages.

This was followed by a polite message explaining that the church's newsletter was run on a strictly opt-in basis. In this case, Katz had apparently selected the maximum 'daily dose' level of contact. Katz had also requested to be contacted regularly by their team of spiritual accountability partners.

There was another comment below this – could it have been Ruby in disguise? It said:

> The Lord worketh in mysterious ways! Perhaps this was a small miracle? Praise BE!

Fleck flipped through the other pages in the 'Retribution' section. Some of the comments at the start were more graphic and upsetting than @MeOwDangIt47's, but the methodology remained the same. Beginning with a trollish user, Ruby documented attempts to uncover their identity, then she showed the ways in which she planned to make their life difficult, and sometimes she provided evidence of the results. It was almost frightening how well Ruby was able to cross-reference social media accounts and analyse their posts and photographs to uncover a home address.

Fleck took photos of each page. One of the pages had a comment at the end from the targeted troll to a video on the official Parks Victoria YouTube channel:

> If you care so much about the environment, why do you keep sending me packets of mayonnaise in the mail?

Comments such as this were all printed out, neatly trimmed and pasted in. But Ruby had also embellished them, sometimes with frames or starbursts. There were also many illustrations surrounding the comments and linking them together. A line of prim girls walking with books balanced on their heads, rendered in black ink and watercolours, connected the ragey comments from @furious_george to Ruby's unveiling of his identity as Derek Hill and his job as an assistant manager for the accounts department at a small packaging company in Des Moines, Iowa.

Ruby appeared to have arranged for Derek Hill to be sent prospectuses from deportment schools in England, Australia, India,

Switzerland, China and Botswana. Most of these prospectuses were large, glossy booklets and required a fee to be sent out, which Ruby had cheerfully paid. Ruby included pictures of some receipts and used illustrations to dramatise her process. The brochures, all fourteen of them, would be sent to Derek Hill's office address.

The last page in the 'Retribution' section was only half finished. So far, only the left-hand side of the double-page spread was filled in. This one was not for a troll, but a clone account. With the same name but slightly different capitalisation, 'Ruby ringtail' copied and reposted all of Ruby's videos. Ruby's impassioned requests to have the videos taken down were met with upbeat 'Thanks for your interest in our video' messages that looked like they had been written with AI.

It seemed like the clone account was one of thousands being run by a company called PMB Entertainment. Ruby had written 'PMB Entertainment' in bold letters. Tiny, coloured screenshots were pasted in the book, providing the screens to the circle of illustrated televisions surrounding the word. Every television was connected to 'PMB Entertainment' with a bounding arrow. This was as far as the little path on the page went. There were some plans written in flowing handwriting that followed the curve of the illustrated path:

Check company register (?), List of Board of Directors, Annual Report? Investigate office.

There was a sound outside. Fleck's phone bleeped with a message from Trixie.

On our way back!!

Fleck took a photo of the final page and closed the book. She could hear Trixie talking loudly outside, and Ruby's more subdued responses. Fleck carefully slid the book back into the bag and zipped it closed. Then, a document in the box of paper recycling by Ruby's desk caught Fleck's eye. She spotted the name 'Matthew Flanagan'. The doorknob rattled; Fleck could hear Trixie laughing and saying, 'Is there a trick to this door? I can't quite get it to …' Fleck grabbed the document out of the recycling bin and dashed back to Quinn's workbench. She was inside with the door closed just as Ruby and Trixie entered the shed.

She looked down at the letter in her hand. What was Ruby doing with Matthew's mail?

CHAPTER FOURTEEN

'Um. Hello. Did you need some help with something?' Quinn looked surprised as he stepped into the room to find Fleck sitting at his workbench.

Fleck shoved the letter into her bag and looked up at Quinn. 'Your girlfriend is a catfish and you need to stop sending her money.' She probably should have thought of a more gentle way to break this news to him, but she was nervous and it was making her babble. Quinn sat across from her now at his workbench, looking not unlike a fish himself as he opened and closed his mouth.

'I uncovered some alarming facts when I was doing background research for my feature article. And I found your crowdfunding page for this dog.' Fleck showed Quinn the website on her phone.

'All of your work. The extra jobs. The stuff you were selling online. That's what all this extra work has been for, hasn't it?'

Quinn was staring at Fleck. 'I don't understand. How do you know any of this? I barely know you.'

Fleck had started now and she wouldn't stop. 'Gwendoline says her dog needs emergency surgery? I saw the fundraising page you set up for her. It's harrowing what that poor dog is going through. And the pictures you included of this beautiful woman with her dog are heartwarming.'

'If Hugo doesn't get the surgery, he'll die. He's only got weeks to live without it.' Quinn's voice was barely more than a whisper.

'And he needs twenty thousand dollars to live?' said Fleck.

'Yes. Vet bills are expensive.'

'I mean, they are, but I don't think there's any surgical procedure that is *that* expensive.'

'Well, I guess he'll need therapy afterwards and stuff. I don't know. Or maybe he needs more than one operation. But if he doesn't get help soon he will definitely die.' Quinn looked imploringly at Fleck.

Fleck exhaled. 'He's a cute dog. I like the picture you included of him with your girlfriend on the fundraising page. The pictures were the clues, actually. The one of your girlfriend eating breakfast with the dog on her lap? You can see a newspaper in the shot.' Fleck passed her phone over to show Quinn the photo. 'See the ad for the German supermarket? They're multinational, but we don't have them in Australia. Of course, this picture might have been taken when she was on holiday overseas, but she had her dog with her. It's unusual to travel overseas with a dog. Especially one as big as Hugo.'

'What are you talking about?' said Quinn. 'Gwendoline is from Swan Hill. That photo is from Swan Hill. Hugo hates travelling. He won't even go in the car. That's why Gwen hasn't come to Melbourne. Beagles hate travelling.'

'That was another thing. I wanted to find out what breed of dog Hugo is.'

'Isn't he a beagle?' Quinn looked confused.

'I thought so too at first, but he looks too big to be a beagle. I found an app that lets you identify a breed of dog from a photo. I thought the app was going to tell me that he was a really large beagle, but it said he's a Hamilton hound.'

After trying and failing to do a reverse image search, Fleck had tried out a bunch of different search terms on Google: 'Pretty brunette breakfast freckles Hamilton hound'. Including 'Hamilton hound' cluttered up her search results with photos of the Broadway musical, so Fleck had experimented with the non-Anglicised 'Hamiltonstövare' and had more success. She decided to leave these steps out of her explanation to Quinn, though. She needed to get to the point.

'So, I did some searches and eventually, buried several pages back in the search results, I found a photo of a woman who looked a lot like Gwendoline. And that led me to this Instagram profile.'

Fleck handed her phone to Quinn, so he could look at the grid of a small-time Swedish influencer named Linnea and her dog, Gulleplutt.

Quinn shook his head. 'But these are all Gwendoline's photos. Why has she stolen all of Gwendoline's …'

Quinn trailed off. Fleck waited. Quinn looked some more.

Carefully, he tapped one of the photos on the grid to enlarge it. Linnea/Gwendoline stood next to a sign of directions, pointing at it with a wry smile. Her dog was jumping up on her, causing her to tilt sideways a little. But that wasn't what Quinn was looking at. It was the sign itself.

The words on the sign were all in Swedish.

He looked up at Fleck. Then he looked back down at the screen. 'I'm going to need a minute, I think.'

'Take all the time you need.'

Quinn continued to pore over the photos in silence. Through the door's window, Fleck could see Ruby packing up her things.

Quinn handed Fleck her phone. 'So you think my girlfriend is a con artist?'

Fleck grimaced. 'I don't think she's really your girlfriend.'

Quinn nodded slowly. 'I guess not.' He fidgeted with a small piece of metal – some sort of screw or bolt or rivet. 'I think I knew that already, but I didn't want to know. I didn't want it to be true.' He tapped the end of the metal bit against the table. 'When I come home from work or uni or whatever, I don't talk to anybody. I just go straight to my room. I don't have anyone who asks me how my day was. Gwen would always ask me how my day was. I don't know. I didn't want it to be true that she wasn't my girlfriend. I didn't want it to be true that I was some loser who's twenty years old and has never even had a girlfriend. I guess that's why I didn't ask too many questions, you know? I really wanted it to be true. I needed it to be true.'

'And that's why you took on all that extra work? And sold your gaming console?'

Quinn didn't answer.

Fleck tried again. 'Why didn't you talk to someone about it?'

'Gwen was the only person I could talk to about anything. I couldn't talk to Liam anymore.'

'What about your uncle?'

'If I spoke to Nathan about it, it might get back to Mum, and she has enough to worry about.' Quinn rubbed his hand over his face. 'But really, I think I was worried that Nathan would tell me Gwendoline wasn't real and I wasn't ready to hear that.'

Fleck drew a breath. It was time for the hard questions. 'So you were getting pretty desperate to raise the money for Gwen's dog.'

Quinn nodded, but continued staring straight ahead.

Fleck placed both her hands on the table in front of her. 'Random supplies from the railway have been going missing. And the Thomas the Tank Engine livery has disappeared. If you were desperate for money …'

Quinn looked at her in confusion. 'What? Do you think I stole stuff from the railway?'

Fleck raised her eyebrows. 'Lots of things have gone missing. If you were that desperate, maybe …'

Quinn barked a humourless laugh. 'I was desperate for money. But I didn't steal anything. Anyway, give me some credit. If I were to steal something, I wouldn't steal random supplies. And why would I want the Thomas gear?' He shook his head, then looked up, as if struck by an idea. 'I'll show you what I would do if I wanted to steal something.'

He led Fleck out of the office to the section of the shed where the engines were stored. Twelve long sections of track led to twelve small doors. The engines that were in use had been driven out, but there were many more still in the shed. Fleck followed Quinn down the steps. The floor around the engine tracks was sunken, putting the engines at shoulder height and allowing easy access to the undercarriages. Quinn pulled a dust cover labelled 'Pioneer Zephyr' off the engine at the near end of the track they were standing beside. Underneath was a sleek silver engine in a vintage design. The word 'Burlington' was stamped along the side in art deco capitals.

'This engine doesn't belong to the railway. It's privately owned. There are a few engines kept here that people are working on that the railway doesn't own. But nobody is working on this one. It's almost like the owner has forgotten about it. I could sell it. I could easily make forty thousand dollars. Maybe more. Or I could strip it and sell the parts separately. And I could put a dummy under the dust cover and nobody would know. That's what I would do if I wanted money.' Quinn looked at his hands and drew a long breath. 'Except that I wouldn't do it. I would never steal from the railway. The railway saved me.'

When Fleck got home, she fished various items of school uniform out from under Sam's bed and took them to the laundry. After she had set off a load, she set to work on her investigation wall. There were more notes up now, and they were better organised. She had added 'Juliet Fitzgerald' to Topham's section, mapped out her plan for accessing Ruby's scrapbook, connected Nathan to Quinn, and included all of the information around Quinn's crowdfund post. She had a lot more information to add after today's efforts.

Matthew came into the laundry with Alice on his hip and a handful of baby clothes. 'Any room in that wash for these jumpsuits?'

Fleck lifted the lid and Matthew tossed the clothes into the swirling drum. She closed the lid and they both turned to look at the wall with the sticky notes. 'How's it coming along?' Matthew asked.

Fleck frowned. 'I've found out a lot, but it seems to have only led to more questions. I don't feel like I'm ever going to get to the bottom of it.'

Matthew smiled. 'So everything is progressing as normal, by the sounds of it. You'll get there,'

Fleck jumped. 'Wait! I just remembered.' She pulled the letter out of her jacket pocket and handed it to Matthew.

Matthew stared at it. 'What? Where did you get this?'

'It was in Ruby's recycling bin.'

Matthew was reading over the letter. 'We've been accepted to the next stage of the grant application. How did this end up in the bin? How did this end up in *Ruby's* bin?'

Fleck shook her head. 'You see what I mean about more questions than answers?' She glared at the wall as if she was trying to stare through the plaster and sticky notes to something beyond. 'And something Quinn said today is bothering me. I can't quite … I can't put my finger on it.'

‘I still can’t believe you found this letter in the bin.’ Matthew shook his head and gently extricated Alice’s fingers from his nostrils. ‘I’ve got things covered with the kids if you want to continue staring at the wall for a bit.’ He hoisted Alice a little higher on his hip.

‘Quinn said that he didn’t steal the supplies.’

Matthew nodded. ‘Okay.’

Fleck shook her head. ‘But then, he said if he was going to steal something, it wouldn’t be random supplies. There were more valuable things he could steal. Why would he steal fertiliser when he could steal an engine that nobody checks on?’

Matthew opened his mouth to respond, but Fleck held up a finger and shook her head. He closed his mouth.

‘So I was thinking,’ Fleck continued. ‘What ties all of these things together? Random supplies, the Thomas livery … It’s not that it’s valuable to the person stealing it. It all needs *replacing*. It all costs the railway money to replace. Plus there’s the missing letter from the grants office …’ She grabbed the pad of sticky notes and a marker from the laundry shelf. She wrote on it and pressed the note to the wall.

The note was a single word, written in capitals.

SABOTAGE?

CHAPTER FIFTEEN

On Monday, Fleck walked up Peppercorn Street to Many Hands. She had parked her car next to the little playground on Highett Road, safe under the benevolent gaze of Nathan Garland's glossy, oversized head.

There was a large SUV parked in the one-hour spot outside the craft store. It was an unusual colour for a car. Fleck was still noticing car colours, even though she had solved the case with the purple car paint. This SUV was a solid pale blue, with a hint of green, like a robin's egg. Scrawled across the side, in white curling font, was the GelVita logo. When Fleck was a single shop's distance away, the door opened and Lynette jumped out. Had she been sitting there the whole time, waiting for Fleck?

'Oh hello! Hold on, just let me lock the car …' Lynette pulled out a set of keys with a large glossy GelVita-branded keyring. The shining SUV bleeped and whirred. 'Isn't it just gorgeous?'

'The colour definitely stands out,' Fleck said.

'Yes! I'm obsessed with it. It looks like a Tiffany's box. You know, Tiffany's jewellery? It looks like a Tiffany's box, like the gift box. And the logo is like the ribbon. I could drive it all day. I got it as a reward for my work with GelVita. I love being a consultant. The perks are phenomenal. *Phenomenal.*'

Fleck couldn't imagine Lynette would be driving a big GelVita-branded car for any other reason. She was pretty sure you couldn't just walk into a car dealership and ask for a GelVita-branded car just to pay homage as a fan. But she nodded, feigning mild interest.

'I've become a Lapis Lazuli–tier consultant, so that's why I qualify for the car. It's so good. You should see how much boot space there is. It makes it so much easier to do all of my deliveries. And you should see the dashboard. It looks like a spaceship!'

Fleck nodded. She didn't say anything.

Lynette ploughed on. It was as if she had planned a set number of topics to discuss and she wanted to do a thorough job of it. 'I really want to go to the Consultants' Cruise in January. I'm saving up to go. There are, like, all these seminars and you get to meet lots of Tourmaline-tier consultants and learn from them, and there are games and prizes, and there's a dinner dance on the second night. It's gonna be so much fun.'

Fleck attempted a bright smile as she turned to open the shop door. She hoped the sound of the shop bell would signify the end of what could become an extensive lecture on the many benefits of the GelVita lifestyle.

Bev, solid and dependable, was standing behind the shop counter, calmly stitching her patchwork.

'Bev! It's good to see you! What are you working on?' Fleck rushed to the counter, suddenly desperate to greet Bev.

Bev met Fleck's almost manic enthusiasm with equanimity. She pulled the thread through the patch, frowned, and inserted the needle into the next point along the seam before answering. 'It's the same rug I was working on last week, Felicity,' she said, pulling the thread tight again. 'I'm not such a fast worker that I finish a whole play rug in a week.'

'Of course. Of course. And you are making it for …?'

'Still making it for the refugee centre.' Bev did not look up from her work.

'Oh, yes. I remember now,' said Fleck. 'Hey, Bev, you remember Lynette? You should tell her about your, um, your stitching! Tell her about all your stitching!'

Bev shot Fleck a suspicious glance as Fleck quickly ducked behind the curtain into the back room.

Trixie was finishing telling a funny story and Kerryn was laughing so that her whole body shook. Trixie smiled in greeting. 'Fleck! It might just be the three of us today. Jo and Dima can't make it and I haven't heard back from Lynette.'

'Oh, Lynette's here too. She's just having a chat with Bev.' Was it Fleck's imagination, or did Kerryn's face fall when Fleck confirmed this?

'Okay then,' said Trixie. 'If you grab her, Fleck, we can get started. We've got a lot to cover today.'

Fleck stuck her head back through the curtains. Lynette was deep in conversation with Bev. 'So, depending on your downlines and uplines, you might be a Rose Quartz, or a Tanzanite, or a Peridot-tier consultant. Or if you're like me, you might get to Lapis Lazuli tier and qualify for a car. It's actually really easy …'

Bev turned and looked directly at Fleck. Her expression conveyed multitudes. Fleck hastened to interrupt. 'Lynette! We're just about to get started. Come on back!'

Lynette hesitated, then handed Bev a business card (a *business* card!) and followed Fleck into the back room. Fleck waved her phone and a charger at Trixie. 'All right if I charge my phone here? It's almost dead.'

'Go for it,' Trixie replied. 'We're just doing bring-your-own and basic crafts today because we've got a lot of planning to do.' Trixie gestured to the pile of basic craft supplies in the middle of the table. Fleck reached under the table to plug her charger and phone into the power board, then grabbed a ball of yarn and a crochet hook. Lynette took a colour-in bookmark and a pile of textas. Kerryn was already busy with the collection of earring hooks and jump rings that she'd brought with her.

The whiteboard on the wall beside the stairwell was covered with notes from the latest board meeting. Trixie wiped it clean. 'Sorry, Douglas!' she muttered gleefully. She uncapped a pen.

'So you know we've been making some big changes to the store. The Featured Maker shelf has been a great success. The store's social media presence is steadily growing. And Kerryn has been instrumental in helping us to devise short- and long-term strategies to make the store more accessible to disabled customers.'

Lynette frowned in confusion. 'Are you a disability expert?' she asked Kerryn.

Kerryn grinned. 'Well, I guess you could say that.'

'But is that your job?' Lynette persisted.

Kerryn shook her head. 'My job is making ridiculous earrings and brooches. I'm an expert at disabled customers because I *am* a disabled customer.'

Lynette's face clouded with confusion. She tilted her head sideways, as if checking that Kerryn did indeed have legs. '*You're* disabled? But you don't use a wheelchair!'

Kerryn smiled patiently. 'Well, I do, actually. I just don't have it with me just now. I'm an ambulatory wheelchair user. But that's not the point. Disability can be chronic or dynamic and it comes in many forms. And you can't always tell just by looking.'

Lynette looked at Kerryn appraisingly. 'Do you know what *you* need?' Her tone said, *You don't know, but I'm about to tell you. You're welcome.*

Kerryn nodded. 'Yes, I do, actually. I need greater accessibility and tailored accommodations in all public spaces.'

Lynette blinked. 'No, but do you know what would be really good for you especially?'

Kerryn lifted her chin. 'Increased representation of disabled people in the media and decision-making bodies nationwide?'

Lynette shook her head 'No, I'm not talking about any of that. What I mean is—'

Kerryn shrugged. 'Well, failing either of those things, a block of Lindt ninety-five per cent would be nice.'

Lynette screwed up her face in confusion. 'I don't know what that is, but I'll tell you what you really need. GelVita is just miraculous. If you became a consultant—'

'NOPE.' This was Trixie, cutting Lynette off loudly. 'I know what none of us needs, and that's unsolicited health advice and aggressive sales pitches. Now,' switching her tone, she addressed the whole group, 'we are talking about changes to the accessibility of the store. To begin with, we have the basics of adjusting shelf height and store layout, and getting a ramp to place over the front step. This has all been done. There are more long-term changes that would also be helpful that I'm looking into getting council grants for.'

'So we've got the new store layout and accessibility changes, and the Featured Maker shelf and social media,' said Kerryn. 'What was the other thing we're going to be launching?' Kerryn seemed to be talking quickly, with one eye on Lynette. Fleck suspected she wanted to move the conversation on quickly without giving Lynette another opening.

'The other thing we're celebrating is the new workshops program,' said Trixie. 'Beginners classes, social crafting and crafting for a cause. A lot of the things we do anyway, but we're formalising it so that people know when they can turn up and get started.'

'So where are we up to with the relaunch party? What's it going to look like?' Fleck asked. She already knew the answer, but she didn't want the conversation to get hijacked again.

Trixie shot her a grateful smile. 'Well, that's the exciting thing. We can have it right here in the store. The new shelves are on wheels, which means we can transform the store into a function space. We can have it in the evening after the shop is closed.'

'That's fantastic!' said Kerryn. 'You could even think about hiring the shop out after hours for exhibitions and book launches and things.'

'Yes. But we're getting ahead of ourselves. Let's focus on the relaunch party. Dima has promised a cake and we'll have sparkling drinks as well. If we can manage a liquor licence, we can have wine; otherwise, sparkling apple juice or lime mocktails or something. Actually, we'll have those even if we do get the licence. It's good to have options.'

'I can bring food!' Lynette was sitting up straighter in her chair. 'I can do sweet and savoury mini muffins. I can make three big trays!'

'Oh, that's super generous of you, Lynette!' Trixie's tone was appreciative and apologetic at the same time. 'But, do you know, I've been reading up on this and they say the best plan is to keep the catering as simple and streamlined as possible. You don't want the food to become a distraction. So we've got a couple of cheese boards, cake and wine. Plus some everything-free options. Anything beyond that is more than we can manage I think. So thank you, but no. Don't bring anything, please.'

Lynette blinked, her expression neutral. Fleck noticed that she gave no indication that she acknowledged what Trixie had said. Trixie pressed on. 'There is a possibility that we may have a jazz trio perform for us. Douglas's son-in-law plays the double bass and is keen to help out. And we need to think of advertising and invites. We'll invite the other Peppercorn Street traders, of course, and all of the volunteers of the Society.'

'Maybe we can put the word out to other craft groups and the local library?' said Kerryn. 'Maybe the local neighbourhood house?'

'Good idea,' said Trixie

'Could we look at getting a spot in the local paper?' Fleck suggested. 'Does anyone know how to go about getting an article in the paper? Is there a reporter we could contact, or …?'

'I've had an article published in the local paper before,' Lynette piped up unexpectedly.

'Oh!' Trixie sounded genuinely surprised. 'That's actually really helpful. Thank you, Lynette.'

Lynette was searching through her phone. Then she said, 'Here we are,' and showed the screen to the others.

The article showed Lynette in a blue GelVita-branded blazer. She stood smiling with her arms stretched expansively behind a table stocked with GelVita goods. The headline read 'Climbing the Ladder to Business Success'.

> Local businesswoman Lynette Chester is fast making a name for herself as a successful 'mumpreneur'. 'I'm a total girlboss and I don't apologise for it …'

The article outlined Lynette's success in building her GelVita profile.

> 'I started out wanting to make a little extra pocket money for treats. I had no idea I would soon be able to treat my family to lavish overseas holidays!'

The article ended with a 'for more information' direction to Lynette's email.

'It's a pity they interviewed me before I qualified for the Kia Sportage. That would have been a great fact to include,' Lynette said.

Trixie was looking at Lynette's phone. She hesitated before talking, still reading over the article. 'So you spoke to a reporter for this?'

Lynette nodded. 'Yes, it was all done over the phone. She was lovely – the journalist, I mean. She made it feel just like a nice chat.'

Trixie was nodding, still looking at the phone. 'And … did you need to pay them money for it?'

Lynette smiled. 'Of course. I got a medium news report. I considered getting a full-pager, but …' she drifted off. 'The paper emailed me their rates. I can see if I've still got the email. It was a bit expensive, but definitely worth it.'

Kerryn passed her phone to Trixie. 'I found their rates on their website.'

Trixie looked at the phone and drew in a breath. 'That's not in our budget. That's more than our entire drinks and catering budget combined!'

Fleck frowned. 'Okay, but what if it's just a news report? Like, not an ad, just local news? How do you let them know about something newsworthy happening in the community?'

Lynette wasn't following. 'I told you, you choose what level of news report you want and put in your order …'

'No, but what if you want an unpaid report? Just, like, news?' Fleck said.

Lynette shook her head, eyes wide. 'I don't think that's something they do.'

Fleck should have put her car keys underneath her charging phone. That way she couldn't have left without it. Now, she needed to swing by Many Hands to get her phone on the way to pick the kids up from kinder and school. At least Matthew was working from home today, so she could leave Alice with him.

There was nobody at the counter when she entered the shop. 'I'm just getting my phone!' she sang out as she slipped through to the back room. The back door was ajar and the table was pushed up against the wall. Fleck peeked underneath. Her phone was there, on the floor, still plugged into the charger. She crawled under the table. How she'd missed her phone!

Fleck heard Trixie come in the back door and charge through to the shop. She began talking to a customer who had just entered.

Fleck often bemoaned her diminutive height, but it had its advantages. She now sat cross-legged underneath the table, her back against the wall. She unplugged her fully charged phone and pulled the charger out from the wall. Her phone was full of notifications. Why did Facebook think it was important to let her know that some nobody she used to work with had uploaded a photo? Since when did that count as news?

'We can talk in here. I don't think I'll be getting any more customers in the next ten minutes anyway.' It was Trixie's voice. And it was in *this room*. Fleck froze.

Somebody sat at the table, right in the spot where Fleck had crawled under. Was that Kerryn? Trixie sat in the next chair. The laces on Trixie's magenta Converse sneakers were coming undone. There were now two people blocking Fleck's exit.

The woman started speaking. It *was* Kerryn. 'Here's the thing. I love what you're doing here. I love the shop, I love talking about crafting, I love that it's a not-for-profit and helping other women. I just—' There was silence as she broke off. Fleck imagined her searching for the words. 'I'm keen to come to the relaunch party, but I'm thinking of taking a bit of a break from the workshop sessions.'

Fleck felt mortified. Should she crawl out? Surely the window of acceptable time to do so had expired. Was there ever an acceptable time to come crawling out from under a table when you're a grown woman who should know better?

Kerryn spoke again. 'It's not anything you've done. You've been wonderful. It's just, I don't feel like I have the energy to deal with … some of the conversation is …'

'It's Lynette, isn't it.' Trixie's voice sounded dull.

Kerryn sighed. 'Yeah. It's nothing personal. I'm just struggling with the constant diet talk and casual ableism. I work hard to keep a healthy mindset and she's messing with it. Plus she messages me all of the time. She wants to know more about my condition. She thinks she can "heal" me. She wants to know about my financial situation. She wants to recruit me for her multilevel marketing thing. She says I would have a whole lot of people I could recruit in the disability community. She's so intense. I just don't have the spoons to deal with her most days.'

Fleck had heard of spoon theory before, and knew it had to do with Kerryn's health and how she rationed her energy. She had no idea that Lynette had been messaging Kerryn outside of the workshops, too. But wait! She really shouldn't be listening in to this private conversation! Should she block her ears? Should she hum? No, wait. She should definitely not hum.

The chair scraped as Kerryn stood up. 'I just wanted to let you know, so that when I stop coming to workshops you know that it's not your fault. It's just something I needed to do for me.'

Trixie's choked 'Okay' was barely audible, yet it seemed so intensely forlorn. She remained sitting at the table. She was very still.

Fleck's bottom was getting sore from sitting on the hard floor. It sounded like Kerryn had left through the back door, but she couldn't be sure. Should she wriggle out and confess to Trixie she'd been under the table the whole time? She shifted a little. Then she heard Helen's voice. She shifted back. Fleck was going nowhere.

'Trixie. What's wrong?' If you didn't know Helen, you might think she was being brusque. You had to listen to hear the compassion in her tone.

Trixie stood up and Fleck heard her moving to the sink and fussing with the dishes. Helen moved towards her and spoke again. 'Trixie?'

Trixie paused before she spoke. 'Kerryn just told me she wants to stop coming to the workshops.' Fleck's heart squeezed at that vulnerable little crack in Trixie's voice. 'And another participant, Lynette – she's starting to take over and influence the whole culture of the group.'

Trixie told Helen about Lynette's multilevel marketing agenda and her dominance over the group. If this conversation didn't wrap up soon, Fleck was going to be late for kinder pick-up.

'I just don't know what to do. It's not just that Lynette gets on my nerves. I feel like she's undermining everything. I worry that it's all going to fall apart because of her.' If Fleck had to guess, she would say she and Helen were washing and drying the dishes – she could hear the movement of water and clattering of dishes – which would mean they'd have their backs to her. Could Fleck edge out unnoticed?

'But I can't just ban her from the shop,' Trixie continued. 'Not if I want to promote a culture of inclusiveness. It's impossible.'

Helen's legs appeared beside the table. She might have been wiping it. 'You're going to need to deal with people you don't like. It's the nature of volunteer groups. I know I've needed to manage that over the years.'

Trixie moved beside her. 'But it's more than that. Have you needed to deal with someone who seemed to threaten the entire foundation of what you're trying to do?'

'Well, yes.' Helen's tone was reasonable, as if the answer should be obvious. Fleck saw her body turn to face Trixie.

Trixie's legs were angled to face Helen. 'Wait. You mean me?'

Helen remained still for a moment, then returned to wipe the table. 'Yes. To me, you were the oncoming storm, the destroying fire. I lost a lot of sleep when you first joined the Society. A *lot* of sleep.'

Trixie huffed out a little laugh. 'I guess I was a bit full-on. I never thought of things from your point of view.'

Helen returned to the sink. 'Yes. Well.'

Trixie's legs disappeared as well. 'But that doesn't tell me what I should do next. Going by your method, I should first have her arrested and then give her a job. I'm not sure that's a plan that works for everyone.' Fleck imagined them sharing a smile. They continued to work in silence for a while.

Fleck heard the dishwater drain. Then Helen spoke. 'You said she's in one of those direct sales businesses. Like Amway or Avon?'

'Yeah. She gets rewarded for taking on new recruits. I actually think that's the whole reason she joined here. She's trying to expand her reach.'

'Hmmm,' Helen said. Then it sounded like she strode across to the foot of the stairs. 'Ranveer! Would you come down here for a minute?'

Good gravy. Was everyone going to turn up? Fleck could hear footsteps coming down the stairs. Maybe she should text the kinder. But what would she say? *I'm running late. I'm trapped under a laminex table while* Guess Who's Coming to Dinner? *plays out all around me.*

Ranveer was talking to Helen. 'I'm all done now. I just wanted to finish those projections.' He stopped moving. Fleck wondered if he'd caught sight of Trixie's tearstained face.

Helen zipped her handbag and picked it up. 'Ranveer, Trixie needs your help. What's the name of the party-plan company?'

Trixie cleared her throat, but her voice was still husky. 'They don't do parties, but they're called GelVita.'

'Help Trixie investigate the business practices of this GelVita crowd,' said Helen. 'See if there's anything they could be reported for.' Her footsteps moved towards the back door and Fleck heard her open it. 'Thank you for your help today. I'm off.'

Trixie seemed to be hesitating. 'Thanks, Ranveer, but you don't have to …'

Ranveer, however, was already sitting at the table. Fleck heard the chime of his laptop starting up. 'It's my privilege to help. Let's get started.' Then he paused. Fleck heard Trixie make a little sob. Ranveer stood up. There was silence, as though he was hesitating. Then he pulled out the chair beside his. 'You don't need to cry. Sit down. We can do this together.'

They sat. Fleck finally shuffled out from under the table. 'Sorry to ruin this magic moment, guys, but I really gotta pick up the kids!'

CHAPTER SIXTEEN

'So what did Matthew make of it?'

'He was completely thrown.' Fleck frowned as she gazed at the Paradise Lake playground. She and Trixie sat on the bench as Sam and Joseph ran their own burger shop business from the inside of the climbing frame. Norah paced around the outside of the frame, eyeing her brother and his friend covetously. Alice snoozed in the pusher.

'He had never seen the letter before. And it's not like he would have read it and forgotten about it. It was really important – he'd been looking out for it.'

'Because it said that his project for the railway had reached the next stage in the grants submission?'

'Yes, and he's supposed to submit some more information.'

'I don't understand why it was a letter. Don't they do things by email these days?'

'That's what I thought. So I asked Matthew for the login details for the railway's email address. It's no big secret, many of the volunteers use it,' said Fleck. 'The whole thing is a bit of a hodgepodge of folders and messages. I got into the settings and there were a bunch of rules for sending emails to different folders.'

'Rules?'

'Yeah – you can set it so if an email comes from a particular address, it's forwarded to a particular folder. Like, if an email comes from a newsletter address, it goes straight to your newsletter folder.'

'Oh, I get it. Nah, I don't even use folders for my email. My inbox is a pit of despair. I think I might have 2000 unread emails!'

'Yeah, I'm like you. I keep meaning to set up the rules. I could have all of the school emails in a school folder and all of the kinder ones in a kinder folder. But I think if it's not right in front of me I'll miss something important.'

'So instead it all goes into a big soup and you miss something important anyway?'

'Exactly! But the railway has it all organised, of course. It's like a signal box sending all the emails off in different directions,' Fleck said. 'There are still plenty of emails that just turn up in the inbox, but if you go into settings, you can see this long list of rules. I was looking through it, and I discovered that someone had made it so that any email from the grants people wouldn't go into the inbox. They would be sent to another folder. It was called something like 2023/24 Financial Year. And when I looked in that folder, it was empty.'

'So what happened, do you think?'

'I want to know if someone funnelled the emails to a folder where Matthew and Topham wouldn't see them, and then deleted them.'

'Did you check the bin?'

'Of course. It was empty. But that's suspicious, don't you think? It means someone must have emptied the bin recently.'

Trixie nodded slowly. 'So somebody doesn't want the railway to get that grant.'

'Yes. And that got me thinking. What if the person stealing the supplies isn't doing it for their own personal gain? What if they are trying to *sabotage* the railway?'

Joseph was balancing pieces of tanbark and stone into stacks, presumably these were the burgers. Sam dropped a small pile of leaves in front of him. 'I got some lettuce. That can be some lettuce. Do you think we should have chips? I think we should make some chips too. Chips and burgers!'

Norah, meanwhile, peered at them through a gap in the play frame, eyes narrowed.

'I'm still not sure why Ruby was bothering to steam open all of those envelopes,' Fleck continued. 'Was it an environmental thing? Some sort of zero waste challenge? It just seems like a lot of effort to me.'

'But wasn't she also taking envelopes from Margaret? Were they special envelopes? Did they have the logo of the historical society on them or something?' Trixie asked.

'No idea. I wasn't close enough to see. But maybe,' Fleck said. She looked across at the miniature village from the bench vantage point. Fleck knew, from the photograph she took of Ruby's schedule in her scrapbook, that Ruby was supposed to be at the railway this afternoon. So far there was no sign of her.

Trixie stretched her long legs in front of her. 'And she was using these envelopes to be a nuisance to her enemies?'

Fleck nodded. 'Yeah. She was sending them rubbish and glitter and packets of mayonnaise.'

'So she was going postal on them?'

'Please stop.'

Norah had finally decided to strike. Pushing herself through the base of the Eiffel-tower-shaped climbing frame she kicked over the boys' neat stacks of tanbark and ran away. Fleck readied herself to intervene, but watched first for the boys' reaction. After the initial shock of Norah's attack, Sam leaned in to Joseph. 'Let's make it that she's the robber and we need to catch her!'

Fleck relaxed back into her seat as the play developed into a laughing chase game. 'That could have been a disaster. I think Joseph's a good influence on Sam. He doesn't arc up as much when he's here.' She looked at Alice, who was still dozing in her pusher. 'Did I tell you I figured out Topham's ex's name? Marian had it wrong. It wasn't Julie or Julia. It was Juliet. Juliet Fitzgerald. I had a look on Facebook. There were a few Juliet Fitzgeralds, but only a couple who looked like they were in the right age bracket. I sent them both messages.'

Sam and Joseph had tired of chasing Norah. They returned to the climbing frame. Norah was still running and squealing.

There was movement over at the site of the miniature village. 'That looks like Ruby,' said Trixie. 'You should catch her now.'

As she approached, Fleck observed the frames for the miniature buildings which had now all been erected. The small version of Paradise Lost Manor House was almost complete. Fleck looked from the shoulder-high miniature to the real-life manor house on the hill. 'That's amazing, Ruby. I can't believe how realistic it looks.'

Ruby looked up with a start. 'Oh! I was so wrapped up in what I was doing I didn't notice you were there.'

Fleck smiled. 'I'm sorry to break your concentration.'

Ruby stretched her neck. 'No, it's good for me. I don't mind talking about the village. It would be good for me.'

'What does Margaret think of the manor house?' Fleck said. 'She must be impressed. It's so realistic!'

Ruby shook her head. 'Oh no. Margaret hasn't seen it. We meet at the local history society now. She doesn't want to meet here anymore. She doesn't like it.'

'Oh?' Fleck raised her eyebrows.

'Yeah. She says it's because she doesn't like Musbrook Highway, but I think it's because she doesn't like Mr Tozer.' Ruby looked quickly behind her, as if making absolutely sure that Topham wasn't about to pop up suddenly nearby and overhear their conversation.

'Why is that?'

'I don't know. But she was really firm about it. She was insistent,' Ruby said.

Fleck mused. 'I did notice that she seemed to frown at him when she saw him last.'

'Yeah. And after that she asked me all about how often he was here. And when I said he was here all the time, she said she'd rather meet at the historical society. She didn't want to meet here anymore at all.'

They chatted a little bit about the kids, the park, the nice weather. Then Fleck took a deep breath. 'I wanted to talk to you about a letter I saw in your bin.' Fleck fished the grant letter out of her pocket and handed it to Ruby.

Ruby frowned. 'I don't understand. Did you say it was in my bin? Then it must be an old letter. It would have been headed for the shredder.'

'But why did you have a letter for Matthew in *your* bin?'

Ruby hesitated. 'It would have been rubbish. It would have just been some rubbish I had. I—'

But Fleck was already there. It was almost as if asking the question out loud gave her the answer. 'Was it the envelope? Were you using the envelope? What was the deal with that? Why couldn't you just use plain ones?'

Ruby shook her head. 'I don't know what you—'

Fleck looked at her. 'Yes, you do. The envelopes you were steaming. The one you took from Margaret's folder. What's the deal with the envelopes?'

Ruby's eyes widened. 'What?'

Fleck's brain was still working. 'Is it that you didn't want to use a generic envelope? They might not open it if it were a plain envelope from an unknown sender. And if they didn't trust the envelope, then all that glitter would go to waste. You wanted the letter to look official. You wanted to disguise the sender. That's *clever*.'

Ruby's mouth was open. 'Wait. How did you ...?'

Fleck pursed her lips in concentration. 'But why did you take mail before it had even been opened? That was an important letter! If Matthew and Topham had missed that they wouldn't have been able to get to the next stage of their grant application.'

Ruby shook her head. 'Of course I didn't just steal people's mail! That envelope was in the bin. It was going to be shredded. I *told* you.'

Fleck peered at Ruby. 'How do you know it was going to be shredded? Was there someone shredding it? Did you see somebody?'

'Yes. There was a pile of papers being shredded, and some envelopes in a shoebox. He was shredding all of them. But I grabbed the shoebox for myself because I could see it had envelopes in it that could be useful.'

'Who was shredding them?'

'Um, that guy? What's his name? He took a call on his phone and left the room, so I grabbed the shoebox and took it to my desk. It's still there now. You can have it if you like.'

They headed off to the engine sheds together. Fleck waved across at Trixie and pointed at the shed. Trixie gave a thumbs up. Then Fleck walked alongside Ruby, who immediately started talking about her letter-writing campaign.

'I know people say you shouldn't care about criticism and you shouldn't read the comments, but I can't help it. Art shouldn't be a one-way conversation. I need to know what people are saying about my work, how they are receiving it, you know?' They walked over the little bridge that crossed the narrow part of the ornamental pond. 'But some of these critics are so relentless. They don't ever stop. They get inside my head. It's not enough to just block them or delete their comments. It won't stop them thinking what they're thinking. I deserve a right of reply. When I send these letters out, it's like I can draw a line under the conversation. I don't know. It's like a mic-drop moment. And then I can move on.'

They reached the engine sheds. Ruby opened the door and they walked through. Under her desk was a brown shoebox. She handed it to Fleck. 'Here's the box that had all the envelopes in it.'

Fleck took the box. It was plain, with no branding; unbleached cardboard with a fitted lid. 'Thank you. But who did this belong to? Who was doing the shredding?'

Ruby frowned. 'What's his name? I keep forgetting his name. You know. He's big and kind of noisy. I think he might be a politician maybe?'

Fleck looked up. 'Nathan Garland?'

It was Sunday morning. Fleck walked with Matthew, Marian and the kids down the path towards the railway. Marian pointed to the space beside the station, where a coffee van was parked and flags and banners were being set up.

'The coffee van is here!' she said. 'I tell you what. How about you two sneak away and have a coffee together while I watch the kids? Go on! My purse is here somewhere. Just let me …' Marian fumbled in her coat pocket.

'Mum. Mum, stop,' Matthew said. 'Firstly, that's a great idea, thanks. But secondly, you don't need to pay for our coffee. It's enough that you're watching the kids while we drink it. Seriously, Mum.'

'Too late. It's already happening.' Marian bustled ahead, purse in hand. She did a funny little run down the hill.

'What do you think?' Matthew said to Norah, who was holding his hand. 'Should we catch Nanna?'

Fleck watched as Matthew ran with Norah and Sam towards the coffee van. They were still standing around the van chatting with the barista when Fleck approached with the pusher.

'Who won the battle?' Fleck asked.

'Neither of us!' Matthew grinned. 'It's free coffee! I got us large ones.'

The barista smiled. 'Courtesy of Nathan Garland. Enjoy!' she said.

By the time Fleck and Matthew were sitting on the clubhouse veranda overlooking the railway, a full catastrophe of Nathan Garland for Ashthorn campaigners had arrived, including Nathan Garland himself in his Nathan Garland car. At least, Fleck presumed he was the one who had parked it in the car park.

'What's happening?' Fleck said.

'Oh you didn't hear, did you?' said Matthew. 'I was talking to the coffee lady about it. Nathan Garland has donated a full set of Thomas the Tank Engine livery to the railway! We'll be able to have Thomas at the night train festival after all. It's so good!'

'I didn't realise you cared so much about the Thomas stuff. I thought you said you preferred the look of the classic engines.'

'But you don't understand,' said Matthew. 'Nathan knew that we were going to have to purchase a new set for the night train festival. He knew about the trouble we'd been having getting the grants, and that buying this livery would set us back even more. This donation might mean we have enough cash that we can still go ahead with our plans for the new outer loop.' Matthew beamed.

'Yes, but you were having trouble with grants *because* he was sabotaging your efforts. He's been deleting the emails and shredding the letters.'

'I'm still not convinced it was him who did that. He seems sincere in his regard for the railway. Why else would he have made such a generous donation?'

'I don't know,' said Fleck, unconvinced. 'You see a nice man who has given the railway a present. I see a man who has hijacked a community organisation for a feel-good photo shoot.' Fleck looked around. 'Where is he, anyway? His face is everywhere I look, and yet I can't find him.'

Matthew frowned. 'Maybe he went with Topham to the engine sheds. They're probably putting the livery on one of the engines to see how it looks.'

They sipped their coffees and looked out over the scene. It was lovely up here: you could see so much. The tracks wound past the station below through trees and bushland. A pair of scarlet rosellas flashed past as they flew towards the creek. Young people in brightly coloured campaign T-shirts busied themselves setting up banners that said *FREE coffee!*

Fleck wrapped her hands around her cup. 'What do you love most about the railway?'

Matthew considered. He often took his time before answering a question. Eventually, he said, 'The signals.' He slowly rotated his cup in his hands. 'I love the way there is a whole tangle of tracks, but the signalling system brings order to the chaos. I love how several trains can run at once without getting in each other's way. It's orderly and efficient.'

Fleck nodded. 'Does it bother you that our family isn't like that? Our household doesn't run like an orderly train system. Do you find the chaos hard?'

Matthew paused to consider again. 'There are times when it gets to me,' he said eventually. 'But I wouldn't trade it for anything. Plus, I'm well trained in chaos. You've met my family. Can you imagine what we were like as kids?'

Fleck smiled and looked across to the engine sheds. She saw a flicker of movement. It was Topham. He was coming out the side door, walking towards the clubhouse.

Then, one of the berth doors opened and a train emerged. It looked exactly like Thomas the Tank Engine. Fleck could see that the man driving it was Nathan Garland. Wearing an old-fashioned engineer's hat that looked almost cartoonish, Nathan beamed and waved and sounded the horn.

'That's not right,' murmured Matthew beside her. 'He doesn't have his licence yet.'

Further up the line, a small crowd of people in Nathan Garland campaign T-shirts crowded along the sides of the track. They were holding up their phones, ready to take footage of Nathan driving the train.

'Geez. He's a bit of a speed demon. He's going too fast. He shouldn't be driving that thing.'

Nathan did slow down as he approached the gamut of campaign volunteers. He waved and smiled as they snapped their phones. Then he sped up again.

'What's going on out here?' Topham had joined them on the veranda. By now Matthew and Fleck were standing, so that they could watch over the railing. 'Wait! Who is driving that engine? The trains aren't supposed to be running until eleven!'

'It's Nathan,' said Matthew. 'He doesn't have a licence yet, does he? I know he hasn't done the signals test yet.'

'What is Nathan doing driving that engine? I specifically told him not to. He doesn't have a licence!' Topham's voice was booming even louder than normal. A few more volunteers came out onto the veranda to see what the fuss was about.

'Slow down, mate. You need to slow down,' Matthew was muttering under his breath as if hoping to communicate telepathically with Nathan. 'Read the signal. There's a curve coming up. Slow down.' His muttering was becoming slowly louder as he watched Nathan merrily speeding along. Everyone followed the veranda around the corner to watch Nathan's progress. Matthew leaned against the railing and shouted. 'Oi! Nathan! MIND THE CURVE!'

Nathan beamed and nodded. Then he accelerated into the curved track.

When a miniature train crashes, it doesn't look as dramatic as you might think. The whole thing was not so much explosive as, well, *wobbly.* As Thomas the Tank Engine hit the turn, he teetered wildly, then tumbled off the tracks and rolled down the embankment. Nathan jumped off as Thomas derailed. He landed awkwardly, overbalanced and slipped down after Thomas into the creek.

Fleck and Matthew rushed down the stairs with everyone else who had been in the clubroom. They darted across to the creek. Nathan was standing beside the train, calf-deep in running water. Thomas looked unperturbed. He just smiled brightly even as the buttery brown creek washed his face.

Trixie arrived at the park with Joseph soon after. Fleck ran to meet them, arriving by their sides while they were still taking their bike helmets off.

'What? So he just drove a train into the creek?' Trixie cackled. 'Sorry, I know I should be asking if he's okay, but that's just the funniest thing.'

'He's okay. Pretty much,' said Fleck. 'I think he might have strained his wrist, but it's not the hand he shakes with so he should be fine.'

'He didn't injure his baby-kissin' lips?'

'As far as I'm aware, his baby-kissin' lips remain intact and ready for kissing.'

'Poor babies.'

They walked back to join the small crowd that had gathered around the crash site. Nathan and Topham were arguing loudly.

'I don't know what shed *you* were in, *mate*, but I clearly heard you give me the go-ahead to drive the train.' Nathan was white-faced with fury.

'I did no such thing! You don't even have your licence!' Topham was pompous and outraged.

Nathan's hair and clothes were wet and dripping all down his right side. His left side remained dry. He looked like an angry swamp creature. 'You were *there*, mate! This is a bloody stitch-up! You were *there*!'

The wheels on the engine were still spinning lazily. A group of volunteers were coordinating efforts to retrieve it from the creek. Fleck cast her eyes along the track. They fell upon the curve of track near where the train had derailed. She called across to Matthew. He came over to join her.

'That's not normal, is it?' Fleck pointed to the track at the switch point.

Matthew's eyes widened. 'That is definitely not normal.'

Trixie tried to look at what Fleck was pointing at. 'I don't see it. What are we looking at?'

Matthew pointed at the tracks. 'This is the point where the track can switch from one route to the other. There's a little motor in that box there. It's actually the motor from a windscreen wiper, but they are perfect for our points because they also switch between two positions.' Matthew demonstrated with his two hands the way the section of track could switch from one option to the other at the point where the track split. It was very much like a windscreen wiper.

'And that's not one of the two positions, is it?' said Fleck.

'That is not.' Matthew pointed to a large stone wedged between the switch track and the main track. 'That stone should not be there. It's jammed things up.'

'Where is Sam?' This was Joseph, bouncing on his toes and craning his neck.

'He's over at the playground with his nanna. We can go there next,' Fleck said. Then she turned back to Matthew. 'Does that happen a lot?' Fleck asked. She took a photo of the section of track.

'Well, no, because we're very vigilant about it,' said Matthew. 'We always do track checks before running our train and I saw the Mother Sucker being driven around just half an hour ago. This shouldn't have happened.'

'Do you think this is what caused—' Fleck began, but Trixie interrupted her.

'I'm sorry, but did you say "mother sucker"?'

Matthew smiled. 'Oh yeah. That's a specially designed engine we have that clears the tracks of leaves and debris before we run the trains.' He turned to Fleck. 'I think Nathan probably wouldn't have crashed if he hadn't been driving like a maniac, but this break in the track would definitely have contributed to the derailment.'

After a while, the crowd began to dissipate. Topham had stormed off to the ticket sales booths. Trixie was taking Joseph across to the playground. The errant engine had been placed back on the tracks by a team of volunteers and was now being checked for damage. Nathan's campaign volunteers surrounded him like a pit crew, offering bottled water, a towel and a clean T-shirt.

She looked back to Matthew. 'In your opinion, what is the likelihood that this stone was knocked into the point by accident?'

Matthew frowned. 'Given that the track was already checked this morning, I would say very low. It would be close to impossible.'

CHAPTER SEVENTEEN

Fleck and Trixie were in Fleck's laundry, assessing the sticky-note situation. Nathan Garland's section of the wall included a lot more notes now.

Trixie peered at them. 'Did he end up giving an excuse for just running off with the train?'

Fleck frowned. 'No. He remained convinced that he had been given the go-ahead by Topham. But Topham maintained that he gave Nathan the go-ahead to put the livery on the train, not to drive it.'

'The livery?' Trixie looked confused.

'The Thomas dress-up.'

'Ah.'

'So you would think it was just a mix-up,' Fleck said. 'Just Nathan Garland being impetuous and a doofus. That's definitely what I would *like* to think.'

'But?'

Fleck sighed. 'But I just can't get it to sit right. Topham was in the sheds with Nathan. Even if he wasn't in the same room, he would have heard the engine leaving the shed. He didn't try to stop Nathan.

It was only when Topham got to the clubhouse that he asked why there was a train out, and acted all surprised that it was Nathan.' Fleck ran her thumb over her pad of sticky notes, riffling them. 'And that was another weird thing. Topham never called out to Nathan to stop, but he was being really noisy, getting everyone to come out to the veranda to see what the fuss was about. It was almost as if he knew what was going to happen. And then there was the problem with the switch point.'

'That was the bit of tracks with the stone jamming it up?'

'Yeah. Matthew said it was most likely vandalism. He said that happens sometimes. But I can't get past the idea that this particular part of track was vandalised right before Nathan drove on it.'

Trixie nodded. 'Do you think Topham set Nathan up?'

Fleck pursed her lips. 'I'm not ruling out that possibility. I think I need to talk to Nathan Garland.'

They paused for a moment. Then Fleck said, 'Anyway. Speaking of difficult personalities – how are things going with Lynette?'

Trixie groaned. 'I tried to have a conversation with her. I told her that our Monday workshops were not a place for her to be selling her MLM crap.'

'Good! That must have been a difficult conversation to have. How did she take it?'

'She agreed with me! She's like Teflon. "Oh, I couldn't agree with you *more*, Trixie. I *definitely* won't be trying to sell GelVita at the workshops. But do you know, that's the best thing about GelVita. I don't even have to sell it. The product just *sells itself*." So I said, "Just so long as it doesn't sell itself when you are at Many Hands," and left it at that. But I don't know if any of it actually got through to her.'

'I don't think the problem is only about her trying to sell the product; she's trying to sell *herself*. Her lifestyle,' Fleck observed. 'It's like she's running a press conference, not having a conversation. She wants to recruit people to sell the product for her. She cares more about that than people actually buying the gels.'

'Ugh. You're right. But what can I say? "Please stop talking about how good your life is?" "Nobody wants your laxative cupcakes, Lynette"?'

'She messages me all the time,' Fleck said. 'Half the time it's just memes or "thinking of you" sorts of things. But she sometimes wants to let me know about special deals or tells me that it's the best possible time to sign up as a consultant because they have bonus starter packs this month or something. I don't know how to say "unsubscribe" without hurting her feelings.'

Trixie smiled, eyes on her phone. 'Imagine if you could do that. I would unsubscribe from all droning mansplainers right away. Oh look! Speaking of which, Nathan Garland's coming to our school!'

'What?'

'Yeah. It says here, he's coming to Our Holy Redeemer on Thursday. He's going to be helping the Grade Sixes with their mock parliament.'

'Where are you getting that from?'

'It's in the "What's on" section of Nathan's website. Of course, if either of us read the school newsletter, we would probably already know all this.'

'Yes, but we're allergic to reading the school newsletter, remember?'

'Oh yeah.'

When Thursday came around, Fleck was ready and waiting outside the school gym to catch Nathan at the end of his visit. When he emerged, Nathan stretched his mouth into his broadest, toothiest Charming

Candidate smile, which slackened only slightly as he recognised who she was.

Fleck fell into step beside him as he walked to the school office. 'I don't want to talk about the crash. I want to talk to you about grant applications.'

Nathan pinned his smile back in place, reassured. 'That's something I can definitely give advice on. What are you applying for?'

Fleck shook her head. 'I want to talk to you about the grants the railway was applying for.'

Nathan nodded. 'Absolutely. Off the top of my head we applied for the Building Better Communities grant, the Healthy Outdoor Spaces grant, and we're preparing to apply for Active Volunteers, Active Tomorrow. So far we've had crickets from the first two, but I wouldn't expect anything less from our current government. Hopeless, the lot of them.'

Fleck looked across at him as they walked. 'That's interesting. I suppose it makes you look good when the government fails to deliver.'

Nathan grinned. 'To be honest, it really does! It's been so frustrating dealing with them. I mean, would it be that hard to send a basic response saying "Your application has been received and we're considering it"? I don't know what kind of turkeys they have running this operation, but a simple email would have been enough.'

They rounded the corner and walked down the stairs towards the school office. 'That's the interesting thing,' she said. 'It turns out the grants office did respond to the application. Somebody using the railway address has been deleting the emails before anyone else had a chance to see them.'

Nathan's step faltered as they pushed through the main door. He looked at Fleck. 'Surely not. Why would someone even do that?'

Fleck shrugged. 'Oh, I don't know. Perhaps an aspiring politician who wants to make the government look bad and appear like an attractive alternative?' Fleck didn't know for sure that the emails had been deleted, but it was a pretty sound hypothesis, and she wanted to check Nathan's reaction.

Nathan stopped walking and turned to face Fleck. He gave an astonished chuckle. 'Wait, do you think I've been deleting the emails? Why would I waste my own time like that?'

Fleck raised an eyebrow. 'That's what I'd like to know.'

Nathan shook his head. He seemed both baffled and amused as he returned his visitor's lanyard to the school office. 'No, but think about it. It wouldn't make sense for me to sabotage the grant efforts. That wouldn't be a win for me. If I help the railway get money to expand their branch line, I look good to a lot of people. That's a win. If the railway misses out, maybe the government looks bad to a handful of people. But I don't look like I've done anything. That's not a win. It's not in my interest to get in the way of the grants.'

They fell back into step as they headed outside. 'In that case, why were you trying to shred letters from the grants office before they had been read?' Fleck asked.

Nathan frowned, but continued to stride towards the visitors car park. 'I'm not sure what you're talking about.' He paused to think, but continued to walk. 'I *was* shredding documents last week—'

'Why? Why were you shredding documents? What was that even about? You don't think that seems suspicious at all?' Fleck had to skip a little to keep up with Nathan's long quick strides.

Nathan shook his head. 'Nah, I was just helping out. I was at the railway waiting for Quinn to finish. I thought I'd make myself useful. I'm going to visit the Lost Dogs' Home this week and they always need shredded paper.'

'Where did you get the papers from?' Fleck asked.

'Everywhere. There is a "to shred" pile in the admin corner of the clubhouse. And I went around to all the workshops and sheds to see if anyone else had any contributions. And while I was sitting at the shredder, a couple of people came by to use it and I told them to just add their papers to the pile and I'd shred them.' He had stopped walking now. They stood hovering beside the visitors car park.

'Somebody had a bunch of envelopes in a brown shoebox,' Fleck said. 'Can you remember who that was?'

'I think I remember a shoebox. I couldn't tell you who gave it to me. I was in the zone. I was one with the shredder. I would have started shredding table napkins if I'd run out of documents.' Nathan grinned.

Fleck frowned, thinking. 'I know I said I didn't want to talk about the train crash—'

Nathan groaned loudly.

'—but I think it would really help if I heard the story from your side.'

Nathan shook his head. 'I honestly don't see the point. It's my word against Topham's and everyone is inclined to believe Topham. Quite frankly, it's embarrassing. The whole business. Topham says I should stop volunteering there—' He broke off, shaking his head. He looked anguished.

'But you say that Topham told you it was okay,' Fleck prompted.

Nathan shook his head. He wasn't saying 'no' to Fleck's question; he was saying 'no' to the whole situation. 'Topham was a completely different person inside those sheds. He told me I should drive the train. He said I was close enough to getting my licence and I'd earned it, just this once. He gave me directions and …' He trailed off and looked away.

'He gave you directions?' Fleck repeated.

Nathan put his hands over his face and sighed through his fingers.

When he spoke, it seemed to be causing him actual pain. 'I'm not like my nephew. I never studied physics at school. I—' He looked away, and shook his head. Then he tried again. 'Topham gave me advice on how to best handle the train. He said it would stall if I ran it too slowly. He said I needed to be careful on the turns. He said – he said it was counterintuitive, but it was important to speed up on the curves so that the wheels could grip the track.' Nathan covered his face again. 'How could I not know such a basic thing? I can't believe I just took his word for it. He completely set me up.'

'Why do you think he did that?' Fleck asked.

'He doesn't like me hanging around,' Nathan said simply. 'There's an election coming up and Topham wants the other guys to win. He was sabotaging my campaign. And now he wants me off the railway. It's not fair. I love the railway. That organisation does far more for men's mental health than any hospital or foundation. Everyone has a role to play. It is beautifully managed. It's democratic. And it's far more efficient than any public transport system in the country.' He pressed a button on his keys to open the boot of his campaign car.

'And you think Topham did this to damage your campaign?' Fleck shook her head. 'I don't like politics. Just a bunch of men big-noting themselves and stabbing each other in the back. No offence.'

'Some taken,' said Nathan. He smiled, but this smile wasn't his usual campaign beam. It held a glint of challenge. After a pause, he spoke again. 'I get pretty impatient with people who act like politics is something that's beneath them. There are plenty of places you can live in the world where you don't have to bother about such lowbrow things as campaign speeches or elections. You can have all the convenience of a dictatorship where all the politicians are beyond reproach, at least according to the press. You don't have to agree with me or agree with my policies. If you don't like any of the politicians, you can put yourself forward.'

‘Is that why you’re running? Because you don’t like any of the others?’

‘I run because I don’t feel like I can criticise others in the role unless I’m willing to give it a go myself. And I get involved at the party level because people have to. People have to get involved – to represent real issues and keep the total megalomaniacs out.’ He caught her look, rolled his eyes and smiled. ‘To keep the *other* megalomaniacs out, then.’

He slipped his bag off his shoulder. ‘I may be a sleazy politician,’ he said, ‘but I’m not the bad guy.’

As he put his bag and suit jacket into the car, something else in the boot caught Fleck’s attention.

‘You have Margaret’s books.’ Fleck pointed to *Grand Homes of Melbourne* and *History Along the Yarra* spilling from a canvas bag, beside an umbrella and a first-aid kit.

‘Oh yeah. I wanted to read up on local history. Have you read them? They’re interesting, but the writing can be a little dense and hard to get through.’

Fleck’s eyes were still on the books peeking out the opening of the bag. She knew there was something important there. It was tickling the edge of her brain. What was it?

She couldn’t help herself. ‘Actually, could I take a look at them real quick?’

Nathan gestured to the bag. ‘Help yourself.’

Fleck pulled *Grand Homes of Melbourne* out of the bag. It was right there on the cover. She knew there was a reason the name had seemed vaguely familiar.

Grand Homes of Melbourne had two authors: Margaret O’Dowd and Juliet Fitzgerald.

CHAPTER EIGHTEEN

The Paradise Heights Local History Association met every month in the little meeting room inside the library from 10.30 to 11.30am. Fleck planned to talk to Margaret just after the meeting finished. For now, she was attempting a library visit with Norah and Alice. She had already grabbed some Andy and Terry Treehouse books for Sam, along with a *Guinness World Records*. Now she wanted to see if she could find some theory books on detective work.

So far, she was having very little luck. Fleck knew she could ask a librarian, but she also knew that this would mean sitting at the information desk and attempting an adult conversation. Norah would seize this opportunity of maternal distraction to pull a pile of large-print books off their shelves or investigate the cables under the computer table or steal some other kid's drink bottle. Norah seemed convinced that all drink bottles were a public convenience to be shared communally. It was gross.

The catalogue wasn't much help. The results were all mixed up with crime fiction, and even when she filtered by non-fiction results, she ended up with lots of books on how to write crime fiction, or books called *The Healthy Food Detective: Deciphering Ingredient Lists and Additive Codes.* Were there no books that taught you how to be a detective?

Alice wanted to be let out of the pusher. She wrestled with her straps and grunted. Fleck ignored the implied request. It was hard enough having one troublemaker on the loose without Alice speed-crawling into places she shouldn't be. Fleck gave her a toy that was supposed to stimulate her brain with colour and sound. A stimulated brain was great, but really, Fleck just liked the way it distracted her from wailing sometimes.

Fleck gave up on her pursuit of detective theory. She picked up a book about solving crosswords by David Astle and put it in her bag. That was as close as she would get. The meeting would be finishing soon. She turned to look at the fiction paperbacks while keeping an eye on the meeting room door.

The library had complicated turning stands for its featured paperbacks. Each was a pillar with four rotating carousels, which could be turned around independently of each other, but were connected on a frame. There was one for 'Fiction A–K', another for 'Fiction L–Z' and a third for 'Romance'. In the middle of each pillar, surrounded by the turning shelves, was a Norah-sized space. Norah was obsessed with trying to climb through and stand in the middle of them. Did it make Fleck a bad mother that she was more concerned about getting told off by the safety-conscious shelf-stacker than the threat of her small child getting permanently mashed by the spinning shelves? It had actually been a good set-up before the shelf police found out. Norah would stand, happily caged, while Fleck browsed the A–K paperbacks in relative peace.

Fleck was once again extracting Norah from the carousel shelves, taking the opportunity to also grab a Sandie Docker book for herself, when she saw the meeting was breaking up. She lifted Norah onto her hip and prepared to approach Margaret as she followed the others out of the meeting room.

'Hello Margaret,' she said. 'I'm not sure if you remember me. I'm Fleck Parker. I was wondering if I could ask you a few questions about the Paradise Lost Manor House?'

Margaret frowned and then nodded. 'I only have about ten minutes, but I'm happy to talk.'

They moved to a nearby table and sat down. Fleck pulled some crayons and colouring pages out of her bag for Norah. Alice arched her back and grunted, but then settled and watched Norah take the crayons out of the pencil case.

Fleck pulled out a pen and paper for herself, more so that she could look official and writerly than anything else. 'So the park started out as private property? It was just somebody's house and farm? When did it become a park?'

Margaret slipped easily into professor mode. 'To be clear, if we are going to talk about how things started out, the park has always been Wurundjeri land. When we talk about things such as real estate and ownership, we are looking at only the last few moments in a vast history. But in that sense, you are right. It moved from private ownership to parkland in 1979. That's when the Board of Works purchased the property from the Neeson family. As the land falls in a riparian zone, it cannot be subdivided, so parkland was the most sensible option going forward.'

'And so the manor house used to just be a family home?' Fleck asked

'That's right.'

Norah held the crayons in her hands and was making them talk to each other. It looked like the green one was bossing the others around. Alice pointed and babbled.

Fleck turned back to Margaret. 'I heard there was a group of people who wanted to restore the house. Were you part of that drive to turn it into a cafe and art gallery?'

Margaret smiled faintly. 'Yes, and I can tell you, I wasn't too popular for it. There were some bureaucrats within the Board of Works who wanted to keep the manor house as a perk for them to use as they pleased. But Juliet and I had plans. An art gallery showcasing local Indigenous artworks and a coffee shop. It would have been a wonderful use of the space.' She sighed.

'So the Juliet who was helping you, was that Juliet Fitzgerald, your co-author?'

Margaret nodded. 'Yes. It was her idea, actually, to open the house up to the public. It made sense, really, rather than having it mouldering away up there, like it is now.'

'Are you still in touch with Juliet? I was hoping to talk to her about the manor house.'

Margaret sighed. 'No, I'm afraid I lost touch with Juliet years ago.'

Fleck bit her lip. 'Is it true that she is Sydney Tozer's ex-wife?'

Margaret's lips contracted slightly. 'That is correct.'

'Is it true that she left him because he was so obsessed with the railway?'

'Ha!' Her laugh, a single syllable, came out like a scornful bark. 'Is that what Sydney tells people? Oh, poor Sydney, so community-minded! So misunderstood!' She lapsed into a contemptuous silence.

Norah's pink crayon was having stern words with bossy Green. The orange crayon was crying. Fleck let Margaret's pause linger, then tried again. 'So it wasn't the railway that came between them?'

Margaret shook her head firmly. 'Sydney Tozer did not care one jot for that railway until *after* his wife disappeared. He'd had nothing to do with it. Then all of a sudden, he was there every day. Like one moment he is obsessed with controlling his wife. Then his new obsession is controlling a bunch of little trains.'

Fleck raised her eyebrows. 'Did you say he was a controlling husband?'

Margaret hesitated. She adjusted the handbag on her lap. Norah, meanwhile, slid off her chair, leaving her crayons on the table. She raced over to the Romance paperbacks carousel and gave the closest shelf an experimental twirl. Fleck looked back to Margaret. She wondered if she was going to answer at all. Margaret remained quiet for another moment, but then something seemed to bend inside her. She looked at Fleck. 'I can't say that for sure. It was just my understanding of things. There were times when she seemed … But then, she was timid by nature so it might just have been …' Margaret sighed and shrugged. 'I couldn't say for sure.'

'But you were her friend?' Fleck darted a look at Norah. She was still standing at the carousel rack, inspecting the books.

Margaret made a motion that might have been a shrug. 'I was the closest thing she had to a friend, but we weren't that close. She was incredibly shy, you must understand. She didn't have any friends really. At the time, I didn't think there was anything amiss. If there was something going on, she wouldn't have told me.'

'What made you think something might be going on?' Fleck asked. Norah had squeezed herself into the middle of the carousel tower. A paperback with a broad-chested man on the cover bounced onto the carpet.

Margaret opened her mouth and then closed it again. 'There was nothing really. She had a habit of dressing modestly. Long sleeves. High necklines. Later I wondered if … I mean, if something was going on it wasn't unusual in those days. But that was only later I thought that maybe …' She drifted off and looked at the crayons on the table. Then she spoke again. 'I just felt like Sydney was a controlling husband. Juliet was a skilled historian and an excellent researcher. But Sydney wouldn't let her get on with it. He seemed to resent her work. He would call the office and ask to speak to her. He was constantly interrupting us with trivial things. Or if we were in the library, he would call there and have her paged. This was in the days before mobile phones, you understand. He would turn up and whisk her away for some reason or other. And she just went along with it. She was very timid, I suppose.'

'And then she left him?'

'Yes.' Margaret paused again. Norah was sitting in her little cage, happy in her self-imposed imprisonment. Alice was arching her back again. Margaret looked at her hands. 'It was the way she left that confirmed it for me. No warning. No negotiations. No forwarding address. Just up and left.' She looked at Fleck. 'That's the way it often happens in those situations. It's like they don't feel safe to stay and talk about it.'

'Do you know where she went?' Fleck asked. None of the staff had noticed what Norah was doing yet, and Fleck did not want to abandon this conversation.

'I think I heard somewhere that she went to Western Australia. I know she went interstate. But I lost contact with her. People lost touch in those days. It was normal. I know these days it's a lot easier to track down an old friend. In the eighties, you just accepted that some friends dropped out of your life. It was sad, but it happened.' She inspected the zip on her handbag. 'I did think of tracking her down for the anniversary celebrations. We put an advertisement in the newspaper and I'd hoped she might see it and come. I asked around to see if anyone was still in touch with her. I even asked Sydney when nobody else could tell me anything. He was highly offended. He said she had changed her name and he didn't know where she was anymore. Good on her, I say. Good on her for escaping. But still, I was sad she missed it. Just like I was sad that she couldn't be there for her own book launch. I mean, it was only tea and cake in the community centre, but still. She'd worked hard on that book. She deserved to be there.'

Margaret stood, and Fleck stood up beside her. 'I should be going,' Margaret said. But then she hesitated as if she had one last thing to say. Fleck waited. Then Margaret spoke again. 'These days people talk about gaslighting. We didn't have a word for it back then. But do you know what is telling? A couple of years ago I read an article describing what is meant by gaslighting. It talked about how sometimes people play mind games on their spouse. How they cause them to doubt their own perception of things and undermine their self-confidence. And as I was reading it, the people I pictured as being in a gaslighting relationship were Juliet and Sydney. I hadn't seen either of them in decades, and yet that's exactly where my mind went.

'The men all saw him as a great bloke,' she continued. 'They still do. Men never have a sense for these things. He was a pillar of the community even back then. So if there were a few women who had a bad feeling about him we learned not to trust our gut. He might make the hairs stand up on the back of my neck, but he's president of the tennis club and chairman of the church council.' She heaved a large sigh. 'I'm sorry I've gone off topic. I need to go now, but I'm happy to answer any more questions you have about the manor house another time.' She hurried to the door.

Fleck's phone pinged with a text from Trixie.

> Shopping mission tomorrow? We can go after the school run <3

Fleck looked up. An older woman, a fellow library patron, was *right there*, accosting her. 'Excuse me. Are you so oblivious that you don't even realise that your own child is *trapped* over there in the paperbacks?' she huffed. 'Too busy looking at your phone to supervise? Typical! You really ought to be paying better attention.'

CHAPTER NINETEEN

Norah was having a try. Which was good. Fleck needed to encourage her to use the toilet. Norah hovered over the too-big hole in the toilet seat. Fleck hovered over Norah, ready to catch her if she fell in. It was good that Norah was showing initiative to use the toilet like a big girl.

Or it would be, if she didn't insist on doing it when Fleck's friends were over.

Fleck was missing the entire conversation. They were having an interesting chat and she could hear it but not contribute. It was maddening.

Norah swung her legs and looked up at Fleck. 'I'm a big girl, Mummy.'

Fleck smiled. 'You are a big girl, Norah. Such a clever big girl!'

They had been researching GelVita. Ranveer was sure there was something illegal about the company's business model. He was almost certain it was a pyramid scheme. But he wasn't sure there was enough evidence to approach the Australian Competition and Consumer Commission. Fleck could hear him talking at her kitchen table. 'It's difficult, because there are product sales involved. A true pyramid scheme involves recruiting and sending money upline, but doesn't include product sales. A pure pyramid scheme is illegal in Australia. It gets complicated when it's multilevel marketing. But I think there is enough here to argue that product sales are incidental to the true nature of the business. It's near impossible for consultants on the bottom two levels to make any money at all from the business. The only way the business works is if you are getting income from your downline – that is, from the people you recruit.'

Trixie spoke. 'But Lynette must be doing all right. She's got a car from it at least.'

Fleck looked at Norah. 'All done? That was a good try, big girl! What a good try!'

Norah blinked and shook her head. 'I'm still trying.'

Ranveer was talking again. 'The cars are rentals; they are provided to the consultants at commercial rates.'

'What? She has to pay for it? I thought it was a perk.' Trixie sounded surprised.

'No,' said Ranveer, 'although it's true that you have to reach a certain level of sales to qualify to lease one.'

Trixie made a scoffing noise. 'What a rip-off! I suppose it's helpful to have. It definitely makes her look successful. And it's easier to introduce GelVita into conversations when you're driving a massive, noticeable car. I see that car everywhere. But she definitely made it seem like that car was an expensive gift from the company.'

'From what I can see, the margins at the lower levels aren't enough to cover costs,' Ranveer continued. 'They aren't purchasing the product wholesale. It's a minor discount. The discount improves a little as they recruit more workers and move to higher levels, but even at Lynette's level the business model seems highly unsustainable. The other place they could be tripped up is with the Therapeutic Goods Administration,' he said. 'I'm certain it's not legal to make some of the claims they do about the efficacy of those gels.'

Trixie made a sound of agreement. 'You're right. Sometimes Lynette talks about them like they're medication. If it's actual medicine, you shouldn't be able to buy it out the back of some lady's car boot.'

Fleck wanted to agree. She wanted to join in the conversation. She did not want to be trapped forever in this tiny room with this adorable three-year-old, waiting for a bowel movement.

By the time Norah had given up on the toilet experiment and they had carefully washed their hands after flushing the (empty) toilet, Ranveer and Trixie were chatting about an adventure they'd had on the car trip over. Fleck joined them at the table. Norah ran outside to find Joseph and Sam. Alice had fallen asleep in her highchair.

'So we see Lynette's car up ahead on the road, and I go to Ranveer, "Why don't we tail her? Why don't we see where she goes?"'

Ranveer smiled. 'It's such a conspicuous car. It wasn't hard to follow it.'

Trixie nodded, then turned back to Fleck. 'We almost lost her a few times. But Ranveer kept on her trail.'

Fleck laughed. 'Did you find out where she went?'

'We did!' said Trixie, 'We successfully tailed her.'

'All the way to the Aldi underground car park,' added Ranveer.

Trixie laughed. 'It was a bit of a wild goose chase.'

Ranveer smiled. 'I didn't mind. It was fun. It's like we're Maxwell Smart and Ninety-Nine!'

'Who are they?' Trixie asked.

'Are you kidding me? Have you never seen *Get Smart*?' Ranveer seemed astonished.

'Oh, I think I've heard of that show, but I never saw it.' Trixie said.

'I can't believe you haven't seen it. I used to love that show. Have you, Fleck?'

Fleck nodded. 'Of course, but when it came to reruns, I was more of a *MacGyver* fan.' She turned to Trixie. 'Don't you remember? The opening credit had him going through a lot of opening doors and the closing credits were all the doors closing.'

Trixie shook her head.

Ranveer feigned shock. 'I think *Get Smart* might have been my favourite show when I was a kid. Or at least in the top five. Maxwell Smart and Ninety-Nine were two spies. They worked to fight against the agents of KAOS.'

Trixie raised a single eyebrow. 'Ranveer, you've spent time with me and Fleck. Are you certain we're the good guys and not the agents of chaos?'

Trixie was moving slowly around the room, checking the seats, the microphones, the side table with the food. She was wearing a vintage evening gown, covered in beads in what looked to be an art deco design. Her turquoise hair was piled high on her head and held in place with ornate combs. She looked stunning. Fleck was wearing her favourite green velvet cocktail dress and strappy heels. Her feet hurt already, but she could find a seat when the speeches started.

'Knock knock! Did somebody order a cake?'

Dima walked into the shop bearing a large white box. She was looking quite beautiful, with dramatic make-up, a golden-brown dress and a shimmery beaded headscarf. There was a flurry of fuss around cake stands and positioning. When Dima pulled the box away, Fleck sucked in a breath.

They had all enjoyed eating Dima's cake scraps around the workshop table, and Fleck had seen pictures of Dima's cakes on Instagram, but she had never seen one in real life before. It was magnificent.

Fleck didn't want to say 'That cake is a work of art' because it would sound trite. But there seemed no other way to describe it. How else could such simplicity command such attention?

The cake was tall and white. Carefully arranged along the side and top of the cake were sturdy magnolia stems with delicate plum-coloured blooms and dark-olive buds. On closer inspection, Fleck noticed that the smooth white icing had the occasional vein running along the side in shining gold.

The three of them stood smiling at it for a moment. Then Dima clapped her hands together. 'We need to get ready. What still needs doing?'

Trixie smiled and shook her head. 'We're just about set. The AV stuff is working. The seats are all in place. I got a text from Kenneth – he's the son-in-law of one of our board members – that our jazz trio is five minutes away. The food is where it should be and Fleck and I have just finished putting the programs out. The main thing to remember is …' Trixie paused. Ranveer had just stepped into the shop. He was wearing a tailored dinner suit. Dima looked at Trixie. Trixie closed her mouth, then continued. 'The main thing to remember is to highlight the work of the Society. That's the whole reason the shop exists. Hello, Ranveer.'

Ranveer flashed a small smile as he joined their circle. 'I was going to help set up the drinks table, but it looks like everything's ready. Are you nervous, Trixie?'

Trixie swallowed. 'Sorry, what?'

Ranveer was adjusting his silver cufflinks. 'Are you nervous? About your speech?'

Trixie shook her head. 'Not really. I just need to focus on the message I'm getting across and not think about where to put my hands. I care about the message.'

'Did you manage to convince Helen?' Ranveer asked.

'Helen?' Fleck lowered herself into a seat. She stretched her legs in front of her and rotated her feet. When had she last worn heels? It had been a while. She was out of practice.

Trixie turned back to Fleck and gave a wry smile. 'Helen was worried about exploiting me. Except she didn't say that at first. She just said, "No you're not doing it." Which made me arc up and say, "Yes I am! Try to stop me," and then we had a classic blow-up about all of it. When Bev calmed us down, it came out that Helen didn't want to exploit any of the women who are assisted by the Society, and that includes me. I could respect her point of view. But I'm not doing this because I feel obligated. I'm doing this because I really do care about the Society and I know that telling my story can help. Helen still wasn't sure, but I said "Nothing about us without us, Helen" and that shut her up.'

Later, after half an hour of mingling and chatting to the sound of live jazz music, the small crowd gathered to listen as Helen formally welcomed them. Then the door opened and Lynette walked in. She was looking resplendent in a stylish blue suit with a diamante brooch in the shape of the GelVita logo and an oversized designer handbag. Helen hesitated briefly, smiled at Lynette and continued.

As Helen started talking about the new microfinance program, Lynette produced a plastic container and started offering the contents around. She was outlining the health benefits of her GelVita-infused baked goods in a stage whisper as Helen continued to show slides and talk about financial inclusion.

Trixie glared at Lynette and held a long finger to her lips. Lynette shrugged and turned back to face Helen. As Helen continued to talk, Fleck looked across to see what Lynette was doing. She caught her breath and winced. Lynette had moved over to the food table. Dima's cake stood tall and elegant on a flat gold platter. It was very striking. Or it would be, if Lynette wasn't busily crowding the platter with mini muffins, emptying her plastic container as she placed the little brown cupcakes all around the base of the cake. It was horrific.

Relieved of her load, Lynette turned back to listen to Helen as she described the work of the Society and the women they assisted. Thankfully, Lynette had stopped whispering to her neighbours about her business. In fact, she looked fascinated by what Helen had to say and listened in transfixed silence.

Helen finished her speech and handed over to Trixie. Fleck noticed Jo discreetly moving to the food table, holding a plate from the kitchen.

But once Trixie started talking, all thoughts of cake crime flew from Fleck's head. Fleck felt captivated as Trixie talked about her life.

Trixie didn't usually talk much about her past. She would say it's because she liked to live in the moment, but Fleck suspected she found it too painful to go there. Trixie's husband died when Joseph was a toddler. Trixie found herself widowed, grieving, in a state of dire mental health, unable to work, and homeless.

'Looking back, I see that there were services I could have accessed. There were people who could have helped me. But it's like I was drowning and couldn't see the shore. I didn't make appointments with the maternal and child health nurse. I didn't go to the GP. I was afraid they would judge me. I was just trying to get through each day and survive. I was so desperate. I wasn't thinking straight.'

From her position at the side, Fleck could see the faces of the crowd as well as Trixie. Everybody was engaged and watching Trixie as she spoke. Lynette in particular was watching her with animation, mouth agape. She turned to the person next to her and started muttering responses to Trixie's words. Trixie hesitated and continued to talk, describing her first encounter with the Many Hands Society and their housing program. Lynette, meanwhile, seemed to be warming to her theme. Her muttering was becoming louder, more distinct and enthusiastic.

'The housing solutions that the Society arranged for me and Joseph were the turning point for us. Honestly? It felt like I could breathe again. It was only when I had that stability and safety that I was able to seek the help that I needed. I'm sorry. Lynette, is there a problem? Was there something you wanted to say?'

There was nothing in Trixie's tone that could be mistaken as a genuine invitation. It was intended as a polite rebuke of Lynette's muttering-turned-chattering, and yet, here was Lynette, standing up and approaching Trixie. She neatly wrenched the microphone from Trixie's hand and addressed the crowd.

'Thank you, Trixie. Yes, there is something I want to say. I just felt compelled. I felt *compelled* to say something. This is a spirit moment. I feel compelled. I was listening to these stories about the women in need and I was listening to Trixie's story. Such a powerful story, thank you Trixie.' She put her hands together in what would have been a 'prayer' position if they weren't still also grasping the microphone, and gave a pious little bow. Then she turned back to the audience, smiling broadly. 'I want to announce a partnership. I want to help these women.' She paused for a moment's anticipation, then launched into her announcement. 'I am going to be their business mentor. I am going to train them to be GelVita consultants and pull themselves out of poverty. I've only just thought about this now, but I'm so excited. You have inspired me, Helen. You have inspired me, Trixie. I thought this was just a craft shop. I had no idea there were all these underprivileged women who needed help. I want to help them. I want to help them to look after their health and look after their families.' Lynette crossed her hands over her blue-suited breast and cast her eyes briefly at the ceiling. 'If you could just take me to them, I can show them what they need to do. I can mentor them. This is going to be big. I just know it. This is the next big thing. And, oh, just let me say one more thing. Just let me say one more thing, Trixie—' Trixie was leaning towards her with her hand outstretched, demanding the microphone. Lynette skipped sideways, closer to the food table, out of Trixie's reach. She pulled the microphone away protectively, jerking her elbow back. There was a terrible muffled *thunk.*

The tall white cake tipped over. Everybody froze for a moment in silence. It was almost majestic the way it teetered, toppled and fell.

CHAPTER TWENTY

The brown shoebox from Ruby's desk had *stuff* in it. Matthew had tidied the living room yesterday, and used the box to gather all of the 'orphans' – toys and items that belonged to sets and needed to be returned. The box was filled with Duplo pieces; little trains; Little People; yellow Shape-O shapes; cards from Uno, snap and Skip-Bo; magnet blocks; board game pieces; bright-coloured shoelaces from Norah's threading game; a magnifying glass from Sam's bug-catching kit; Jenga blocks; puzzle pieces; and velcro-backed rectangles from the fabric play calendar.

Alice and Norah were playing together on the rug. Well, they were together on the rug, and they were playing on the rug. They weren't exactly *playing together* on the rug. Norah was sitting with her bucket, consulting with her various Batman figurines. Alice was crawling around on her usual quest to locate something she definitely shouldn't put in her mouth.

Fleck should put the random items away. She needed to get the shoebox back. She wasn't done with it yet. But she hated this job. Keeping toys together felt like such a Sisyphean task. It never lasted. Whenever Fleck managed to get all the pieces together of a game, puzzle, set of blocks or fabric picnic set, she became overwhelmed by an irrational urge to lock the toy away. She fantasised about a toy cupboard with a large padlock on the door, where all the toys rested, safe in their complete sets, undisturbed by curious hands.

Fleck gazed at the collection of random items. Surely it wouldn't take that long to put them all away? Maybe if she set a stopwatch, she could see how long it actually took and then it wouldn't seem like such a mammoth task next time. She set the stopwatch.

She was only thirty seconds into the exercise when Norah came over to inspect what she was doing. 'Those are mine, Mummy. I want them. I want them please.'

Fleck hesitated. 'Oh, not these, Norah. I'm just putting these away.'

Norah's face clouded over. 'No. They are MINE. I need them! I need them all for Batman!'

Fleck held the box out to show Norah the contents. 'No, but look, Norah – it's just blocks and things. It's just things that need to be put away.'

'Thank you. Please thank you,' Norah said as she removed the box from Fleck's hands. She took it over to the spot on the rug where she had been sitting with her bucket of Batmen and tipped it over. Then she showed the Jenga block to her favourite Batman. Fleck sighed and flopped on the couch. She cancelled the stopwatch on her phone.

Alice crawled over to Norah to investigate this new development. She picked up a fabric rectangle that said 'December' and another that said 'Windy' and waved them around. Fleck watched them play. It wasn't actually so bad. Her main motivation to put the toys away was to empty the shoebox and the shoebox was now empty. She reached over and picked the box off the floor. It was still just a plain brown box. Fleck turned it over in her hands and looked inside. There was a mark on the inner wall of the box. At first, Fleck thought it was a smudge, but as she looked closer, she realised it was a label of sorts, stamped in fading ink.

Fleck grabbed Sam's magnifying glass off the little pile on the floor and took the box to the table, where there was better light. She pulled out her everything book and a pen. She took a moment to appreciate how very much like a detective she felt, what with the magnifying glass and all.

She could make out the faded print now. She copied it into her everything book.

Angus Brogues Tan S 12 D

Alice was giggling. Fleck looked up. Alice was reaching under the couch and kicking her legs in excitement. When she sat up, Fleck saw that she was now holding a green apple with brown and dusty bite marks. She babbled and shook the apple up and down. For somebody who'd had no interest in her little tray of cut-up fruit half an hour ago, Alice seemed entranced by this disgusting couch-apple. Fleck leapt across the room to intercept her just as she was about to shove it in her mouth.

'Can you find any size six? Or should I just go size seven and roll the cuffs up?'

'Do they have size seven? Or are they just even numbers?'

'What are you talking about? They have size seven. Of course they have size seven. We are in the boys size two to seven *area*.'

Fleck and Trixie were trawling the school uniform section of Big W in search of blue tracksuit pants with reinforced knees. The store was having a sale.

‘So now you think Topham is the thief?’ Trixie was pulling the waistband open on a pair of tracksuit pants, looking for the tag.

Fleck sighed. ‘It’s not that simple. He’s definitely suspicious, but I don’t have any footage of him taking objects out of either shed door in the timeframe when things were stolen. If he did it, how did he do it? Plus, he’s been so involved in chasing the grant money and planning for the branch line duplication. But I suppose that could just be his cover. Plus it would be easier for him to sabotage from the inside, I guess.’

‘And tell me again about the shoebox?’ Trixie made a face at Alice, who was sitting in the baby seat of the shopping trolley Fleck was pushing. Alice giggled.

‘So the shoebox was filled with a bunch of stuff, mostly junk mail, but it did include a letter from the grant office telling Matthew that they had reached the next stage of their application,’ said Fleck. ‘This box was rescued from the shredder by Ruby, but it was clear that whoever was using that shoebox fully intended to destroy the contents.’

‘And the shoebox didn’t have any branding on it?’ Trixie returned the tracksuit pants to the rack.

‘No. It was blank. But then I had a closer look,’ Fleck said. ‘There was something printed against the cardboard on the inside. I used the magnifying glass from Sam’s bug-catcher kit to look at it properly.’

‘Like a proper detective,’ said Trixie.

‘Exactly,’ said Fleck. ‘I should start keeping one in my back pocket. So I looked and the words said “Angus Brogues Tan S 12 D”.’

‘Brogues are a kind of shoe, aren’t they? I know that, but I don’t know exactly what they look like,’ Trixie said.

‘They’re leather lace-up shoes. Sometimes they have decorative little holes in them. Do you know what I mean?’

‘No. But I’ll take your word for it. And size twelve is fairly big? Would that be a tall man?’ Trixie asked.

'Yes. I looked up the design and got a picture of them,' Fleck said. 'It turns out I had seen this sort before. They are exactly the type of shoe Topham Tozer wears!'

Trixie whistled. 'Ohhh. Dodgy-dodgy!'

Fleck nodded. 'Definitely dodgy. By themselves, none of these things mean anything. Sure, Topham might be a nasty piece of work who lied about his original interest in the railway. That's not evidence. Sure, the shoebox that contained the letter to be shredded was for the same kind of shoe that Topham wears. That's also not evidence.'

'But they build a picture. I think you need to look more closely at Topham,' Trixie said.

'Yeah,' Fleck said. 'I also think that Big W needs to look more closely at making trousers with reinforced bottoms.'

'The cuffs, you mean?' Trixie had pulled another pair of trousers off and was checking the tag.

'No. The bottom. Where your bottom goes. The seat of the trousers,' Fleck said. 'Sam keeps getting holes in his. I think he's sliding down gravel slopes or something. I can cope with holes in the knees, but holes in the bottom is a different problem entirely.'

'We need to get Bev to give us a tutorial on patching.' Trixie put this new set of trousers in the trolley.

They wandered to the party section. Fleck wanted to see if they had any cheap glowsticks. They would be selling glowsticks at the festival on Sunday for some exorbitant amount. Sam and Norah would lose their tiny minds over having a glowstick of their very own. If Fleck could buy them in advance now, her life would be so much easier on Sunday.

'There's another thing about Topham,' Fleck said as she inspected a Mega Glow Party Pack. 'Margaret was suggesting he might have been an abusive husband. She said his wife didn't leave him, she *escaped* from him.'

'That's horrible!' Trixie said.

'I know. It doesn't paint Topham in a good light at all. But I only have Margaret's word for it so far, and she doesn't like Topham. I've been trying to track down Topham's ex-wife, but so far I haven't had any luck. I know her maiden name was Juliet Fitzgerald but I think she might have changed her name again, which is making things impossible.'

Trixie raised her eyebrows and shrugged.

Fleck yawned. 'Have you worked out what you're going to do about Lynette? I still can't get over what happened with Dima's cake. It still tasted good though.'

Trixie frowned. 'I don't know. I could ask her to leave and not come back, but what would I say? "The tribe has spoken"? "You no longer spark joy"? "I think we should be consciously uncoupled"? And it's not like she's a bad person, exactly. She's annoying and thoughtless, but I don't think she's bad at heart.'

Fleck nodded. 'She really did seem to think she would be doing a good thing for the community by signing people up to her business.'

'Can you imagine it though? "Hi there. I'm sorry you're escaping family violence. Here's a food hamper and a list of support agencies and a voucher for the op shop and a chance to slave away selling boxes of fake medicine for very little pay. You are so welcome."'

Fleck giggled. '"Hi there. I'm sorry you're escaping the horrors of war. Welcome to our country! There's nothing more Australian than debt. Here's our starter pack!"'

They were at the checkout now and their conversation lapsed as they bought their trousers and socks and glow sticks and random extra things.

Trixie was pushing the trolley now. As they trundled back to the car park, they walked past the supermarket. 'Ooooh. Can we swing by here?

I'm out of cheese slices.' Trixie pulled them all inside the automatic gate before Fleck had time to process.

You go on ahead. I'll wait in the car. That's what she should have said. *I'm fine for groceries. I'll meet you in the car. You go on ahead. I'm good.*

They walked through the fresh food section to the back of the store, where the chilled foods were kept in refrigerated displays. 'Where is the cheese?' Trixie asked as they walked past shelves of flavoured yoghurt and snack packs of smallgoods. The smell was stronger here. The artificial chill was more pronounced. Fleck's breathing was becoming shallow.

Trixie was ahead of her with the trolley, and Alice. 'Where's the home brand? They've only got the fancy stuff.'

Fleck couldn't control her breathing anymore. It was coming in little puffs. She tried to tell Trixie, but she couldn't get her voice to work.

Trixie was scrutinising a block of cheese. 'Maybe I should get this one and cut it myself. I know that ends up cheaper but I really couldn't be bothered. And I end up slicing it too thick anyway.'

From here at the back of the supermarket, it really did feel like the place had no exit. Fleck couldn't see out from here. There were no windows and no visible doors. There was no way out. There was no way out.

'Do you know I went through a whole phase of being obsessed with fake cheese?' Trixie said. 'You know, the wrapped singles? I didn't have them on sandwiches or anything. I just ate them by themselves. They were my fixation food. I knew they were processed and gross, but I couldn't help it. I loved the texture, I think. Then one day I just got over it and didn't want to eat them anymore. They went from being my favourite thing to totally gross in the space of about thirty seconds.'

Fleck hadn't been to the supermarket for a while now. Fleck had managed to avoid supermarkets ever since – ever since.

The smell really was quite strong. Fleck thought she might vomit, but it wasn't that exactly. Her entire gut, her entire digestive system, had transformed into a concrete block. Surely she couldn't puke up a concrete block?

'Fleck? Are you okay?' Trixie was looking at her with concern. Fleck stared back at her imploringly for a moment, then emitted a strange, strangled yelp and ran from the store.

She wasn't really looking where she was going. She just needed to get out. The entry gates were supposed to be one-way. If Fleck had been thinking, she would have pushed through the checkout area. But Fleck hadn't been thinking. She hadn't been thinking at all. She pushed through the one-way gate. It complained loudly with an alarm and red lights but Fleck didn't stop. Fleck didn't stop until she was standing outside the supermarket, drawing great breaths.

She could still smell it. It was still in her nose, but she was out of there. She was out of there. She could see a window. Fleck looked at the window and kept drawing breaths.

Trixie was quietly beside her. She steered Fleck to a free table and asked her to sit down. Fleck realised with a jolt that Trixie had Alice in the trolley with her. They sat in silence for a bit. The young man at the nearby donut shop called out names for coffee orders. Slowly the smell in Fleck's nose, that smell of industrial refrigeration, was replaced with the smell of fried dough and cinnamon.

Fleck looked up at Trixie. Then she looked down again. 'I find it hard. The fridge there. It's too much like …' She looked up at Trixie, whose face was flooding with comprehension.

Trixie clasped both of Fleck's hands in hers. 'Oh, Fleck, I'm so sorry.'

Fleck didn't like to think about what could have happened to her when she had been trapped in that coolroom. Most of the time she didn't think of it at all. It all came good in the end. There was a big bruise on her hip and a scratch on her leg but they had just about healed now. She should be fine. There was no reason why she should not be fine.

Fleck looked at Alice, who looked back at her with a curious expression. 'I can't believe I abandoned my own daughter.' Her voice was a flat monotone.

Trixie made a huffing noise. 'Oh, give me a break, Fleck. It was an emergency and you left your daughter temporarily in the care of a trusted friend. You didn't even leave the centre. Stop looking for ways to torture yourself.'

Trixie waited until Fleck looked at her again, then she held her gaze as she spoke. 'Fleck, you went through some pretty awful stuff in that coolroom. You were threatened with a gun. You thought you were going to die. Have you thought about seeing someone to talk it through?'

Fleck reached into her bag and pulled out her everything book. She opened it to the page with the pink duck sticky note. She peeled it off and handed it to Trixie. 'Do you remember how I met Max Roberts a few weeks ago?'

Trixie turned the pink note over in her hands. 'I remember he came into the shop. How is he?' She must have been wondering where Fleck was going with this.

Fleck nodded a few times. 'Good. He's good. He's grown his hair out. Well, you would have seen that, I guess. He looks all different.'

Trixie waited.

Fleck took the note back from Trixie and smoothed it back on her book. 'Max had given me the name of a psych. He said I should call her. He said she's really good. He said what we both went through in that coolroom – him and me – that it was important that I talk to someone after. And I planned to. I kept meaning to call her. I got this note to remind me to call her.'

Trixie frowned in confusion. 'But there isn't a phone number written on it.'

Fleck shrugged. 'I know. But I didn't really need the number. I could just google her name. I didn't want to write the number. That would make it real. That would make me feel like I was committing to doing it. And if Matthew saw the note with the phone number on it, he might ask me what it's about. He might encourage me to call the lady. I wasn't ready for that pressure.'

'But didn't he think it weird that you were just sticking a pink duck note with nothing on it about the place?'

'We've been married a long time. He's used to me doing strange things.'

They paused, each thinking their own thoughts. At the donut shop, the young man was talking to a customer who stood waiting with an empty trolley.

Then Trixie spoke again. 'So you were blocked? You couldn't call the psych and you couldn't go to the supermarket?'

Fleck nodded slowly. 'I guess I was. But I didn't realise it. I always *planned* to call the lady. I always *planned* to go to the supermarket. But the end of the day would come and I would have done nothing. It's silly. I just need to get over myself. What if I call the lady and she says I have no right to be calling her? I bet she has heaps of people who really need her. I just need to get over myself.'

Trixie gave a little smile. 'Are you having imposter syndrome over whether your trauma is traumatic enough?'

Fleck smiled and shrugged. 'I guess I don't want to be the sort of person who has to see a psychologist.'

Trixie rolled her eyes. 'So if you tear your calf muscle, would you hobble around and do nothing about it because there are people with worse injuries and you don't want to be the sort of person who has to see a physio?'

Fleck shook her head. 'I know I have to do it. It's just the thought of calling the place and talking to a receptionist and trying to look at my diary and think of all the variables while also talking to the receptionist and I don't know if it will be a mean receptionist and I don't know if I'll accidentally double-book myself. It's just super overwhelming.'

Trixie nodded grimly. 'I know. I hate phone calls. I hate making appointments.' She paused. 'Do you want me to make the call for you?'

Fleck drew a long breath. 'No. I think I can do it. Can you sit with me while I call?'

Trixie grinned. 'Pow! Do it now!'

In the end, Fleck's phone call was short and perfunctory. She wrote the date and time of her appointment in her everything book. 'I'm embarrassed by how easy that task was. I can't believe I put it off for so long.'

Trixie shook her head. 'That wasn't small at all. That was huge. You deserve a treat for that. I'm getting us both donuts.'

Trixie stood waiting behind the customer with the trolley. There was an awkward business as the young man attempted to pass a very large, flat box of donuts over the counter to the woman with the trolley. It seemed a little precarious. Trixie stepped back to make space. Another employee appeared at the front counter. Fleck suspected this woman was the young man's boss. 'Side door, Callum!' she barked. 'Catering orders always collect through the side door.'

A moment later, a door opened beside the counter, and Callum filled the trolley with boxes while his manager served Trixie two fresh cinnamon donuts.

Fleck stared at the tableau in front of her, the wheels in her head turning. The counter and the side door. The trolley full of goods. The counter. Handing big things over the counter. There was something there. She was so close. What was it?

Trixie walked back to the table with a paper bag. Fleck bounced to her feet. 'I know where I've been going wrong! I've know how he did it! I can't believe I missed it. It's so obvious! We need to take another look at the surveillance footage!'

CHAPTER TWENTY-ONE

'It was the donut shop that made me realise I had been looking at it all wrong.' Fleck had navigated her way out of the shopping centre car park and was now driving down Middleborough Road. They still had a little bit of time before school pick-up, so they'd be able to stop at Fleck's house for a cup of tea before they got the boys and Norah. 'The donut shop has a door at the side. That's the only place you'd really think of for how people get in and out of the shop.'

'Okay. The donut shop has a door at the side. So far you are blinding me with your startling insight,' Trixie said.

'Oh shush. There is a door, yeah? Just like the engine sheds have a door. That's the *official door*. But the donut shop also has a counter. You can also pass things in and out over the *counter*.'

'I feel like I'm getting a full briefing on donut store operations here, but I'm still not following,' Trixie deadpanned.

Fleck tried again. 'We kept looking at the *doors* into the engine sheds. The side door and the back door. But what about the trains? What if somebody loaded up a *train* with stolen goods and just drove it out of there?'

Trixie was silent for a moment. 'Of course. But where to? It's not like they can drive a train all the way home. And if he drove it to his car, we would have seen it in the car park footage.'

Fleck drummed her fingers on the steering wheel. 'All I know is we need to look at the footage again to see if we can see a train full of goods.'

They pulled up to a traffic light behind a line of cars. Ahead, cars turned onto their road from the intersecting Maroondah Highway. A familiar pale blue SUV followed the curve around.

'Hey look! Do you think that's Lynette?' Trixie sat up straighter in her seat.

The lights changed to green and Fleck started moving again. The Tiffany box of a car remained ahead in the distance as they drove along, dropping in and out of sight as it coasted over hills and slowed for intersections.

'You know, Ranveer and I tailed Lynette's car again. We've done it a few times now,' Trixie said, as if by way of conversation.

'Is that right?' Fleck changed lanes to avoid a parked car.

'Yeah. We haven't discovered anything yet, but Ranveer is getting really good at tailing.'

They kept driving in silence. A knot of traffic up ahead was bringing them closer to what they were now presuming to be Lynette's car.

'I think you'd be even better than Ranveer, though,' Trixie said. 'I think you'd be an expert.' Fleck could hear the request in Trixie's voice.

'We need to pick up the boys!'

'We still have time.'

'Hmmm.'

They continued on their route and, up ahead, so did Lynette. Then, 'Look!' said Trixie.

The pale blue SUV was in the right-hand lane with its blinker on. It waited there for half a minute and then turned into the car park of an industrial-looking building. As they approached, the signs on the side of the building became clearer. 'WE SELL BOXES!'

'It's the storage place! Oh, come on, Fleck! We *have* to see what she is up to!'

Fleck couldn't help herself. They had time. And she really did want to find out what Lynette was doing. They turned into the car park. Fleck could see where the blue car was parked and took care to park a distance away. She even executed a reverse park, so that they could sit inside the car and watch Lynette from there. It was pretty impressive, Fleck thought. She looked to see if Trixie was also impressed by her reverse park, but Trixie was carefully watching Lynette.

'She's stopping at that roller door. Number forty-seven,' said Trixie. 'Let's get out while she's distracted unlocking the door.'

By the time Fleck and Trixie had strapped Alice into the pusher and reached shed forty-seven, Lynette had rolled the door all the way up and had stepped inside. Fleck had no idea what they were going to say to her. Would they say anything at all? But before she had made up her mind on this, she was distracted by the sight of the inside of the storage shed.

There was hardly any room to move in there. They were stacked all the way to the ceiling. Boxes and boxes and *boxes* of GelVita. Surely this was more than one person could ever sell? Fleck and Trixie exchanged glances. What *was* this?

Lynette shuffled out of the storage shed, edging out sideways through the narrow gap between the piles of boxes. She was looking at the keys in her hands and didn't see Fleck and Trixie hovering at the door at first. When she did, her face fell.

'Hi Lynette.' Trixie said the words almost like an apology. 'What's going on?'

Lynette busied herself closing and locking the roller door. Only when this was done did she turn to face them. She summoned a bright smile, but her eyes remained startled. 'What are you doing here?'

Trixie didn't answer the question. Instead she said, 'That's a lot of GelVita stock you have there, Lynette. Is that a lifetime supply?'

Lynette attempted a breezy shrug. 'That's the nature of business at my level. You need to move a lot of product.' Her voice wobbled a little bit.

But it didn't look like that product was moving. It looked like it was standing still. And there was so much of it, stacked rows deep and up to the ceiling. 'Are you sure that's not more than you need? It kind of looks like you're stockpiling it.' Trixie gestured to the storage shed, now with its door closed.

Lynette swallowed, then shook her head firmly. 'No. I need all this. I'm Lapis Lazuli. I can definitely sell it.'

'But all this is on top of the stock you are storing in your house and garage. Surely you don't need a house full of product, plus two storage sheds?' It was the first time Fleck had spoken. Both Trixie and Lynette turned to look at her in surprise.

'I don't know what you mean.' Lynette was finding it harder to conceal her nervousness. 'Who said I had two sheds?'

Fleck calmly pointed to the keys in Lynette's hands. 'You have two of those little keys on your key ring. I'm guessing, given that you went to this shed first, that the other one is even more full than this one. Is this how you managed to get to Lapis Lazuli level? You just keep buying the stuff?'

Lynette shook her head. 'No. This is only temporary. This is a temporary situation. I used to have two consultants on my downline. Two women from my church. But they couldn't last the distance. They were quitters. I just need to sign up some more consultants. Some more consultants who aren't quitters. Once I've replaced them, it will be easier.'

Trixie looked horrified. 'Wait. Are you expected to keep buying stock for your consultants to sell even if they quit?'

Lynette hesitated. 'Not exactly. But I would lose my status. I would drop down to Ocean Pearl level. I would lose the car. I don't want to lose my status. I need to project success if I want to encourage people to join me.'

'That doesn't look like success to me.' Fleck nodded towards the storage shed. 'That looks like you're in trouble.'

Lynette shook her head. 'Nobody is supposed to know about that. That's private. That's a private part of the business.' She heaved a sigh. 'GelVita – it's the only thing I have going on in my life at the moment that's successful. I can't let that go. I can't lose my Lapis Lazuli. I've worked too hard. I go to the meetings and everyone treats me like I'm winning. There are all these little prizes and awards and you go up the front and everyone claps. They don't really care how much you sell. It's all about how many people you have under you and how much stock you buy. When I go to their meetings, I don't have to be the woman whose husband is spending all our money on SportsBet and sneaking around with the accounts manager at his work even though he thinks I don't know about it. I get to drive my car around and be this different person. I get to be the one who helps people.'

'But all of this stuff,' Trixie said. 'You can't possibly be making any money from this. You must be running at a terrible loss.'

Lynette examined her keys. 'But that's part of business. It's the stage I'm at. You have to spend money to make money. And in the meantime I get to be my own boss. I get to help people.'

Trixie shook her head. 'It's not helping people if you're just dragging them into the same pit you've fallen into. Like how you wanted to recruit the women from the Society's programs. These are women facing homelessness, women dealing with addiction and violence. How on earth can't you see? Getting them involved with your pyramid scheme will put them into a whole world of pain.'

Lynette shook her head. 'It's not like that. I genuinely want to help them. It could be really good. And I'm not in a pit. It's not a pit. Don't say that. It's just a stage. I just need—'

'One big win?' Fleck interrupted.

'Stop it! That's not what I meant. I'm not a gambler.' Lynette was looking distressed now. 'What I was trying to say is that I just need to get better at it. I've been doing the modules, I've been going to the training sessions. I just need to work on my pitches. I'm going to a seminar called "Pitching the GelVita Way" next month. I just need the right attitude. I need to work harder.'

'Or maybe you need to cut your losses,' said Trixie. 'Maybe you need to work out which way is the GelVita way and then go in the opposite direction.'

After their side quest, there was no time to stop home and check the footage. Instead, they went straight to Norah's kinder, then to school.

Once they were finally home to Fleck's they set the three older kids up outside with fruit and biscuits, and settled Alice down for a late nap. 'Let's take a look at the footage while they're eating,' Fleck said.

They sat in front of the laptop. It took a few tries to figure out which folder was the right one to show trains entering and leaving the engine sheds. Then they had to find the files in the folder that were in the correct timeframe.

It started to rain. Norah and Joseph came in from the backyard and then, after Fleck went out and called him, so did Sam. Fleck pulled out the big tub of wooden train tracks in the hope that it might be a suitable distraction. Then she sat back at the table with Trixie. When Norah saw that the laptop was open, she wanted to watch the movie too. She climbed onto Fleck's lap. Sam ignored the tub of wooden tracks and pulled out his coloured magnet blocks. Joseph joined him.

Because the first day they were looking at was a Saturday, there weren't too many trains in action over the course of the day. At various points in the morning, an engine without carriages attached left the engine sheds and returned twenty minutes later. There was another engine that left pulling a carriage filled with garden tools in the morning and returned in the afternoon with the same garden tools. It wasn't until later in the day, at 4.25pm, that a train with two carriages left the shed. Or perhaps the proper word wasn't 'carriage' but 'truck', because these weren't the sort to carry passengers, but goods. Both trucks were piled high with objects and covered with a tarp. It was hard to see who was driving the train.

'Not this one!' Norah pointed at the screen. 'No! Not this one! BLUEY!'

'Hold on, Norah. Do you want to play with the train track?' Fleck tried to make it sound like the most tempting prospect ever. *Train track? Oh yes please!*

Norah continued to point at the screen. 'Not this one,' she repeated. 'Bluey. Bluey, Mummy.'

Meanwhile, the (boring, black-and-white, non-animated) train on the surveillance footage did not appear again for ninety-seven minutes. Fleck scrubbed forward until there was movement again. At 6.02pm, the same engine trundled back to the engine sheds. Three things were immediately apparent. Firstly, Norah was about to drop her bundle. Secondly, the two trucks were now completely empty. Thirdly, the driver of the train was unmistakable. It was Sydney 'Topham' Tozer.

CHAPTER TWENTY-TWO

Fleck had a bit of time before picking Norah and Sam up, so she and Alice dropped in at Many Hands to see Trixie. The Featured Maker shelf was currently displaying crocheted Pokémon-style plushies from a popular Melbourne-based influencer who used chenille yarn to give his plushies a soft finish. The little creatures looked adorable clustered along the shelves. Trixie was very excited about it. 'He's already posted several times about the shop. He has 108,000 followers!'

'Has that affected your followers, do you think? Have you noticed an increase?' Fleck asked.

Trixie nodded. She had established @manyhandscraftstore a little while ago. As well as pictures of stock and information about sales and workshops, Trixie had taken a lot of video of Bev one quiet afternoon, and cut it into bite-sized snippets. As a result, #fridaybev was fast becoming a beloved feature, and Bev herself seemed to be gaining cult-figure status for her sincere, no-nonsense advice and brief craft-hack tutorials.

Fleck gathered their cups and took them back into the kitchenette. The shop bell tinkled loudly. Fleck peered through the curtain. Trixie jumped and put her phone away. Lynette had opened the door quite roughly and was now striding towards the counter. She looked incensed.

'You couldn't leave it alone, could you? Could you? What do you think I'm going to do now? You have wrecked everything! Everything!' She bumped the Featured Makers shelf roughly, sending adorable Bulbasaurs and Flareons and wide-eyed Pikachus bouncing across the floor.

Fleck held her breath. Trixie took an involuntary step back. 'I'm going to need some context, Lynette. What are we talking about here?'

'I have been prevented from selling GelVita products or recruiting GelVita consultants indefinitely while the company is under investigation after a series of anonymous reports. Who made those reports, I wonder? Oh! Hmmm! I wonder who it might be? Who has been against me from the start? Who has not wanted to see me grow my business, to build my downline, to live my best life? You have been a thorn in my side. A constant thorn in my side. Because you are not a winner. You do not have what it takes to be a GelVita pro, so you just want to bring everyone else down. I hate you. I hate you!'

Trixie bit her lip. 'I'm sorry, Lynette, but I don't know what you're talking about. It's true that I don't like GelVita, but I haven't reported them to anyone.'

'Do not lie to me, Trixie.' Lynette was leaning right over the counter and breathing hard. Trixie pressed her back to the wall, but Lynette was still only inches away.

Lynette was being so intense, it almost seemed like she might turn violent. Fleck was about to go upstairs for back-up when she saw Ranveer was already striding down towards her. Fleck stepped aside to let him through and he stepped into the shop. 'I think you need to calm down. Step back from the counter, and stop shouting.'

Lynette turned to Ranveer with a scornful look. 'You can keep your nose out of this, Mr Knight in Shining Armour. This has nothing to do with you. Everything has collapsed. Everything I worked so hard to build. And all because Miss Priss – green hair – Trixie – whatever you call yourself – decided it would be a good idea to throw GelVita under a bus.'

Ranveer spoke calmly in a voice that rang across the store. 'I can tell you for a fact that Trixie did not report GelVita to the Australian Competition and Consumer Commission or the Therapeutic Goods Association.'

Lynette gave him a withering look. 'How can you possibly know that for sure?'

Ranveer met her gaze without flinching. 'Because I did.'

Both Lynette and Trixie turned to stare at Ranveer. Fleck was surprised too. Ranveer continued. 'The more I researched the GelVita corporation, the more I realised what an unscrupulous operation they were running. They exploit their workers to profit the few executives at the top levels. The design of the company is unsustainable and predatory. Their medicinal claims are unethical and illegal. They should not be allowed to operate under Australian laws.'

Lynette shook her head. 'So you just went and dobbed on them? Have you any idea what you've done?'

Ranveer shook his head. 'It wasn't just my report that caused this. The company has been under investigation for several months now.'

Lynette gaped. 'What? They never told us that!'

'I'm pretty sure there are lots of things they never told you,' Trixie chimed in.

'There have been several elements of the GelVita's business model that takes it out of the multilevel marketing category and puts it in the category of pyramid scheme,' Ranveer said. 'As a result, it would not be legal for them to operate under federal laws here in Australia. You shouldn't blame Trixie for this. You should blame GelVita. They put you in this position. They are profiting from your pain.'

All of the bluster seemed to have drained from Lynette. She stood in the shop, limp and forlorn. 'But … but … what about all my stock? My car? How can I recruit more consultants?'

Fleck slipped through to the shop side of the curtain and traded looks with Trixie. Ranveer, who was standing alongside Trixie, cleared his throat. 'I don't know what the outcome of the investigation will be. There might be a class action you could join. In the meantime, well, you could always just eat the GelVita yourself …'

'Yuck! No thanks. It tastes like chocolate dish soap and makes me constipated.'

Trixie stifled a sudden giggle. This set Fleck off. Ranveer covered his mouth and shared an amused look with Trixie. Even Lynette gave a reluctant smile in spite of herself.

After a pause, Trixie spoke. 'Look, I don't want you recruiting at our workshops and going on and on about being a girlboss, but I think when you're not busy hustling, you're pretty good value. You'd be most welcome to keep coming along and crafting with us.'

Fleck nodded and spoke up for the first time. 'Absolutely. I agree. You'd be very welcome.'

Lynette laughed and it made a scoffing sound. 'Thanks, but no thanks. If I'm not going to be recruiting anymore, Many Hands is the first thing I'll stop doing. I can't stand crafting. I think it's a waste of time. No offence, but why spend forever working on something I could just buy from Kmart for five dollars?'

Trixie's mouth was open. She had no response.

'I'm going to get back into silent Zumba,' Lynette continued. 'I used to enjoy it but stopped going because there were no networking opportunities. Because you're not supposed to talk,' she added, by way of explanation.

‘Well, if you’re sure …’ Trixie’s voice was a little weak. Fleck swallowed and kept her eyes down. Her attack of the giggles was threatening to make a reprise.

‘Definitely. I have enough to be getting on with without playing around with yarn and buttons. Also, no offence, but you’re all a little weird. Socially, I mean. When it comes to friendships, I think I can do better.’

Lynette left the shop. Fleck’s giggle threat had fast evaporated. She stood, bewildered, with Trixie and Ranveer, looking at the door. After a moment, Trixie turned to Ranveer. ‘You really are a dark horse. That was a proper secret-agent move.’

Ranveer affected a Maxwell Smart accent. ‘Reporting unscrupulous operators to the relevant authorities? That’s the oldest trick in the book!’

Fleck giggled, but Trixie shook her head. ‘Are you quoting that old TV show again? You know I haven’t seen it. I’m going to shut the shop up now. It’s five minutes early, but I’m calling it.’

Ranveer grinned. ‘Good thinking, Ninety-Nine.’

CHAPTER TWENTY-THREE

Sunday was a clear autumn day. Fleck tried to convince Sam and Norah to have a lie down in the afternoon in anticipation of the late night ahead, but it was a lost cause. After an early dinner of nuggets and broccoli with Trixie and Joseph, they drove to Paradise Lake Park.

There was a small queue of cars at the Musbrook Highway entrance. Two men with white beards and high-vis vests used light-up sticks to direct them to an empty spot in the car park.

'Ohhh no! I forgot the glow sticks! I left them on the bench!' Fleck exclaimed.

'No, you didn't. I grabbed them,' said Trixie.

The railway was abuzz. It seemed every train was on the track. Many were lit up with fairy lights affixed along their frames. A fire engine was parked next to the station, offering children the chance to climb and explore and chat to the firefighters. The air was alive with the smell of coal fire and diesel fuel and fried onions and jam donuts. A long queue of excited, chattering people snaked out of the station and continued up the hill. Fleck used her phone to share her location with Matthew, and he came out to greet them. 'Mum's already here. She's over by the fire engine. I gave her a bunch of tickets so you don't have to line up for them.' His face was glowing with excitement in the cool air of the evening. 'The queue for the train looks long, but it's moving really fast. We have three platforms open and all hands on deck. Fireworks will be at 9.30pm. Do you reckon they can stay awake that long?'

'We'll see how we go. They haven't had a nap, but look at them! The question will be if I can stay awake that long. But you know I can't say no to fireworks. I love fireworks.'

It wasn't long before they were all settled on the long padded benches for the train ride. Matthew was right – the line had been long, but it had moved quickly. As they puffed around the little track, Fleck sat with her arms around Sam in front of her and took note of the railway course. The inner loop and the outer loop. Ruby's miniature village, complete and all lit up. The picnic areas, bridges and tunnels. And, at the far end of the outer loop, shrouded by bushes, a quiet railway siding.

Fleck craned her neck to look at the siding, that bit of track that ran off the main line, when she went for a second train ride, this time with Norah on her lap. She was almost certain this was the spot where Topham must have unloaded the goods. But where did he put them after that? There were garden sheds dotted around and there was the clubhouse, of course, but she knew Matthew had already checked all of these thoroughly. Where else could the stolen goods have gone?

Later, after they had spent a full half-hour simply standing at the crossing, waving at passing trains and admiring the engine that had been dressed up to look like Thomas, fresh from his swim in the creek, Trixie and Fleck sat with Marian at the bench by the playground. Joseph and Sam ran around in the dark. Norah snuggled into Marian, looking like she might drift off to sleep at any minute. Alice was already fast asleep, all rugged up in the pusher.

Fleck gazed at the queue of people still snaking down the path, past the brightly lit food trucks to the bustling station. Topham was striding the length of the queue, talking to the visitors. He was wearing a top hat and a suit with a cream waistcoat and black tailcoat. He really did look like the Fat Controller.

'I think I've found the spot where Topham parked the train full of stuff and unloaded it. It's sort of in the bushes. I tried to get a look when the train went past but it was hard to see,' Fleck said.

'What's this?' asked Marian. 'Is this part of your detective work?'

'Fleck's been helping Matthew work out who has been stealing things from the railway,' Trixie explained.

Marian beamed. 'I like that you have your detective work, Fleck. Everybody needs to have something. And that goes double for young mums. When Matthew was a baby, I was very active in the tennis club. Did you know that? I would often go for a hit with the Mothers Club. But anyway, how's it going? Do you have any suspects? What's your plan?'

'Right now, my chief suspect is Topham Tozer,' Fleck spoke in hushed excitement. 'I think he stole the items using one of the little trains, but I still need to figure out where he put them. I think I've worked out the place where he might have unloaded them, but I still don't know where he took them after that.'

'Do you want to go take a look now?' Trixie said.

Marian clapped her hands together. 'Oh, I think you should definitely go now. Take a moment while you can. You might find something. We've got things covered here, haven't we, Trixie?'

Fleck smiled at Marian. 'I don't know. I probably wouldn't be able to see anything at all in this light.'

Trixie pointed. 'Your leg is jiggling. I know you want to. Actually, I think you *need* to if you want to sleep at all tonight.'

Fleck looked down. Her leg *was* jiggling. She looked back up at Trixie.

Trixie gestured to the playground and to Marian. 'We've got this, Fleck. Off you go. Take your time.'

Fleck rolled her shoulders a few times and breathed in a lungful of cool night air. She probably wouldn't find anything, but it felt so good to be doing detective work all by herself. She felt giddy with the independence of it all. There was a garden path lit at either side by little tea lights that led her past the engine sheds and towards the miniature village. Fleck stepped around the large crowd admiring Ruby's intricate handiwork and continued on the path.

The path didn't lead all the way to where the siding was; rather, it curved around the clubhouse, back towards the station. Fleck would need to leave the path and cross the tracks.

She wasn't sure exactly what she was looking for in this bushy siding. Perhaps something had been dropped, but it was getting too shadowy to see the ground properly. She probably should abandon this quest and come back and investigate properly in the daytime. If she got no information out of this excursion, did this mean she was literally getting sidetracked? Fleck smiled broadly to herself in the darkening light.

There was a section of bushes on the far side, away from the railway, that were squashed down as if someone had beaten a path through them. Fleck followed the makeshift path to the simple wire fence that divided the railway from the park proper. She saw a section of fence missing, and an old, empty wheelbarrow. Fleck stepped through the bushes and out onto the grass. There was no road on this side of the railway. No car park. Fleck stood at the foot of the big hill. She looked across to the reedy lake. Then she looked up the hill. All of a sudden, she knew exactly where the stolen goods were hidden.

It was a steeper hill than she remembered, and the grass was slippery in places, but Fleck was committed now. The manor house was not lit from the inside, but there were floodlights illuminating it from the outside. Fleck paused halfway up and turned to look at the trains moving about with perfect efficiency. Then she continued up the hill.

The manor house seemed even more creepy in the fading light. Fleck peered into the bay window on the ground floor. She saw a room with no furniture and an empty fireplace. A set of wires dangled from the ceiling around the place where a light fitting should have been.

The front door was locked, of course, but it had been worth a try. Fleck slowly walked around the house, peering up at the doors and windows. How on earth was she supposed to break into this house? This was not her area of expertise. Should she have learnt how to pick a lock? If she'd actually managed to find a library book about being a detective, How to Pick a Lock would have been Chapter One.

It was as she was gazing back down the hill at the railway, lit up like a carnival, that the solution came to her. Of course. If her theory was correct, she wouldn't have to find a way to break into this house – the house would have already been broken into. There would be signs.

Her phone battery was on 2 per cent. She didn't want to use up the last of her battery life by using the torch. Then she remembered: she had a handful of glow sticks in her coat pocket! Cracking them, Fleck held the luminescent wands in front of her, sweeping them along the ground. What exactly was she looking for?

It wasn't long before she found it. It was definitely a wheel track.

And around the corner, the clump of agapanthus had a section that was quite flattened. Fleck moved over and stood on top of them, looking at the house. There were some large windows half-hidden behind the springy plants, which had become a little overgrown along the east side of the house. Wading through the floppy leaves, pushing aside the flower stalks and trying very hard not to think about snails, Fleck held the glow sticks against the large window. From there, she could see the latch. They weren't just windows, they were French doors. Fleck stepped a bit closer and fiddled with the latch. A narrow panel of window swung inwards. Success!

As Fleck straightened up on the other side of the window and brushed herself off, she looked around. It was hard to see much in the darkness, even with her luminescent lanterns. But she could tell this room was empty as well. Except, there by the window, a sturdy torch sat on the floor. Fleck picked it up. It shone brightly as soon as she switched it on. This was evidently a recent addition.

The door at the end of the room led into a much larger room. It would be generous, perhaps, to call it a ballroom, but it had that feeling about it. It was twice the size of a normal room and also twice the height. Dominating the room was a sweeping staircase. It curved around the far corner of the room, hugging the wall. The upstairs landing extended along three inner walls of the room, kind of like an indoor balcony. Was that what they called a gallery? Fleck couldn't remember. It was designed so that a person could be standing upstairs and leaning on the ornate railing to look into the ballroom below. Fleck had an immediate urge to climb the sweeping staircase. Not because of her investigation; because it was a really cool staircase. She was already halfway up before she realised it might have lost some of its structural integrity after decades of neglect. She kept climbing anyway. It seemed sturdy enough.

The gallery that jutted into the room from upstairs acted as a sort of one-sided corridor, with doors on the wall side, all the way around. Fleck opened the door to the closest room and shone the torch around. It was the size of a large bedroom, but unlike the other rooms she had seen so far, this room was not empty.

Fleck shone the torch around the inside of the room. It was stacked full of all manner of supplies: folding chairs and tables, mechanical parts, garden hoses, sections of railway track and other random items. Fleck noted the presence of several cans of diesel fuel, boxes of toilet paper and sacks of fertiliser. When her torch beam reached the middle of the room, she screamed and almost dropped her torch at the sight of the large, beaming face gazing back at her.

CHAPTER TWENTY-FOUR

'Bloody Thomas!' Fleck muttered. There were also the round faces of Percy and Gordon, as well as the coloured panels to affix to the sides of the engines. Fleck gazed at the stolen hoard. There were other things here, things Matthew hadn't even mentioned were missing.

So she had found the stolen things. And she had footage of Topham leaving the shed with them. Well, she had footage, at least, of Topham leaving the shed with a full train and returning with an empty one. What was she going to do next? Perhaps she should take photos of the set-up and show them to – who? The police? Matthew? Should she go back down the hill now and come back again during the day to have a proper look? But she should take photos now, at least. Just in case the stuff got moved away. She pulled out her phone. Drat it! The battery had completely drained!

The room suddenly filled with light, and Fleck could see it all at once, not just the range of her torch. It was as if someone had switched the light on in there, though Fleck knew that would be impossible. She turned around quickly. There in the doorway, his hand on the switch of a hanging camp lantern, was Sydney Tozer.

Fleck's mouth dropped open. Topham was still in his suit and tailcoat, but he was no longer wearing the top hat. He glared at her. 'What on earth do you think you are doing here?' he demanded.

Fleck assessed the situation. Topham was standing at the room's only door. She was alone and smaller than him. Was she in physical danger? While Topham was quite large, he was bulky rather than muscular. He didn't appear to be armed and he must be almost seventy years old. Still, he was blocking the exit and he looked very angry.

Fleck lifted her chin. 'I was just checking out your collection of stolen merchandise. It's impressive. How long have you been undermining the railway's resources in this way?'

The situation wasn't dire, but she should get out of here. If she charged towards him, she could put Topham off his guard and push past him through the door.

Topham's mouth turned into a snarl. 'I don't know what you think you are doing here, but you need to stop involving yourself in places you aren't wanted.'

Fleck's eyes darted to the space between Topham and the door. Once she pushed Topham aside, she was certain she could outrun him at least. Thank you, Paradise Lake parkrun!

She looked back at Topham. She would need to be quick. 'Some of this stuff has been here a while. How long have you been trying to sabotage the railway?'

'Sabotage? I don't know what you are talking about. Wait! What—'

Fleck had launched herself forwards in a dash for the door. But something went badly wrong. On her second bounding step, part of the floor collapsed beneath her foot. The wood must have been rotten right at that spot. Fleck stumbled over, her foot shooting right through the floor, halfway to her calf. Her other leg dropped to her knee in what felt like some bizarre genuflection. When she tried to draw her leg back out of the floor, she found it impossible. Large splinters of wood stabbed into her calf.

Topham's face broke into a wicked smile. 'Oh, you do need to be careful on this floor. There are parts of it on your side that have gone soft. That's why I only put things on the other side of the room. You need to stick to the beams when walking on old floorboards. Follow the nails. Didn't you know that?'

Fleck tried again, unsuccessfully, to pull her leg out of the floor. She was stuck fast.

Topham had a strange smile on his face. He was nodding. It was strange and off-putting, and the Island of Sodor cosplay only added to the effect. 'This is good. Yes. Yes. This makes sense. I can contain this whole situation. It's not too late.' He was nodding rapidly and began to pace. 'All of this can be contained. I can fix this. After all, it's dangerous for a woman to go off by herself at night. Anything could happen. Anything. You really ought to have been more careful.'

Fleck shook her head. 'What's going on? I need some help. My leg has gone through the floor ...'

But Topham wasn't listening. He was talking to himself. 'I saw the hooligans hanging around the manor house from the bottom of the hill. I suspected they were up to no good. When I went up to investigate, yes, when I went up to investigate they had already set the house on fire. I didn't see their faces as they ran away. I tried to stop them but I was too late. If I had known there was a woman trapped inside I would have tried harder. I would have done anything. But how could I have known? If only I'd got there sooner. If only I had caught sight of those vandals earlier.'

Fleck went cold. 'Topham, Topham – Sydney, listen to me ...'

Topham still wasn't listening. He continued to talk to himself, his words rapidly tripping. 'Yes. Yes. I saw the hooligans hanging around the manor house from the bottom of the hill. The bottom of the hill. When I went up to investigate – no. Wait. I suspected they were up to no good. When I went up to investigate, they had already—'

'SYDNEY.' Fleck spoke as loudly as she could, in her most commanding tone. Topham looked up in surprise. She continued, in a calm and coaxing manner. 'So I found out you've been stealing stuff from the railway. Big whoop. That's no reason to overreact. You don't need to murder me because word might get out that you're nicking toilet paper. Let's just calm down and sort this out.'

Topham looked at her, his eyes wide, an incongruous grin on his face. He shook his head at her. 'You're right. I wouldn't need to kill you because you know I've been stealing toilet paper. I would not. But it's more than that, isn't it? That's the problem. You've figured it all out, haven't you? You've figured out the reason I've been undermining the railway's finances. You've been sniffing around the outer loop track. You've figured it out. And that is a very dangerous thing indeed.'

Fleck shook her head and affected a bewildered tone. 'What makes you think I know anything?'

Topham took on the tone of voice he used when explaining a feature of the railway to an interested group of people. 'I've been concerned for a while, the way you have been nosing around, asking questions for your "feature article". It has altogether been rather too close for comfort. But more recently, I found you had been talking with Margaret O'Dowd. I found out you had been trying to track down my ex-wife. That, in itself, was concerning enough.'

'I didn't manage to track her down. I haven't spoken with her at all. You don't have to worry about that.' Was she laying it on too thick? Her voice was so high-pitched.

Topham frowned. 'Perhaps. But then I was walking along the queues of people waiting for the train and I overheard my name in conversation. This was only twenty minutes ago. It was two women, and I knew one of them was Matthew's mother. I heard them talking, then I stood on the pathway behind them to overhear the rest. They were talking about your investigation. One of them said she didn't know exactly what you knew, but that you'd had a breakthrough. It had something to do with Topham Tozer and the outer loop track. Then she mentioned that you were going to look at the siding at the back of the railway. That's when I knew things had gotten out of hand. That's when I knew I would need to put a stop to things.' He punctuated this statement with a nod, then walked to where a group of diesel cans stood in a line.

'You don't need to put a stop to anything, Sydney. Don't make things worse than they already are. You don't need to do anything rash.'

'I do, actually. I need to contain this. I've managed to keep it contained for thirty years. This is just a complication. I can get on top of it.' Then he tipped one diesel can on its side so that it spilled slowly out in a glug-glug-glug across the floor. He picked up another can and began liberally splashing around the room.

'Stop it!' Fleck tried to keep the note of terror from her voice. 'You're making a mistake!' But Topham had tuned her out. He had gone back to reciting his planned police statement: 'I saw the hooligans hanging around the manor house from the bottom of the hill … If I had known there was a woman trapped in the house …' He picked up two more diesel cans and left the room, closing the door behind him.

Fleck really had to get her leg up out of the floor. *Don't think about the pain.* She tried again. *No. No. No. Ow.* Trying to pull her leg out was only driving sharp pieces of wood further into her skin. She panted and looked across the room. Diesel fuel continued to spread out from the upset can. Maybe she should just grit her teeth and wrench it out. Just wrench it out really fast. *Three. Two. One.*

21

There is a Shakespeare festival in the park. You bring a picnic and watch Shakespeare. Fleck wants to go but it's too hard to bring a picnic. She keeps losing all her picnic things. Her plastic cups have actually grown little legs and are walking out of the cupboard. But she's here now anyway for some reason. Here in the park. There is a woman leaning out of one of the upper windows of the manor house. She's shouting 'Romeo' but she's doing it wrong. She's all in a panic.

Fleck looks around. Everyone else has brought a picnic dinner. Matthew has an entire watermelon with the top sliced off and he's eating it with a spoon. Maybe he'll share some with her?

But, no, the play. She's here to see the play. Juliet is hanging out the window shouting 'Romeo! Wherefore? Wherefore?' And Fleck is impressed because it sounds like this Juliet knows that 'wherefore' means 'why' and not 'where'. This is a very good start. But why is Juliet so distressed? Isn't she meant to be in love?

Fleck looks down to where Romeo should be standing. There he is, but he looks more like Richard III. Surely that's Richard III and not Romeo? He's all in black. He's old and stooped and he has the floppy hat. Are they doing a mash-up? Maybe this is some sort of avant-garde theatre company that likes to mess around with Shakespeare?

Everybody has a picnic except for her. Matthew is sitting with an enormous roast turkey on his lap and he has given drumsticks to the kids, so they're fed at least.

She looks back at the play. Is he Romeo or Richard III? Fleck doesn't remember much about Richard III except the play starts with a winter of discontent and ends with a dead body in a car park.

She wants to watch the play a bit longer. She needs to figure something out, but now Matthew is beside her. 'We need to go down to the railway,' he says. 'That's where it's happening.'

Fleck squints at Matthew. He is drinking coffee out of a thermos, but it smells like diesel fumes. 'But what about the corpse in the car park? It all ends in the car park.'

Matthew smiles and shakes his head. 'Not the car park. It's the outer loop. The outer loop.'

Fleck opened her eyes. She was back in the room, in the manor house.

Topham was back in the room too. He was grabbing another can of diesel. It took Fleck a moment to realise she was looking at Topham and not Richard III. She opened her mouth to speak. She needed to keep him in the room. Nothing good could happen once this man left the room. 'I know why you were worried about me.'

Topham didn't respond. He kept dragging the can. Fleck tried again. 'Topham! I know what it is now. I know why you were worried about me. I know why you're going to all this trouble. Topham! Hey! Topham!'

Topham looked at her.

Fleck continued. 'It was because I was looking at the tracks. The outer loop. It's all happening at the outer loop. That's what made you panic.'

Fleck no longer felt groggy. It was all becoming so clear now. The sabotage. The theft. This was what Topham didn't want her to find out. This was the secret he was willing to kill for.

Topham was watching her in silence. She had to get him talking. 'The outer loop track was built in nineteen eighty-seven. That was the same time your wife went missing, isn't that right?'

Topham shook his head. 'My wife left me. She did not go missing. There is a difference.'

Fleck nodded. 'Ah yes, but that's the thing. Nobody else ever heard from her again. I've been asking around. You're the only person who has supposedly heard from her since that day. She's missing. And after she went missing you joined the railway. And you've stayed there ever since.'

Topham set the diesel on the floor and straightened up. 'There's no crime in volunteering at a railway.'

Fleck held his gaze. 'There would have been a lot of digging around the time the original outer loop was built. The ground around the tracks would have been nice and soft. And I bet you made sure your first job at the railway was to plant a bunch of shrubs and put down plenty of smelly fertiliser.

'Is this where it happened?' Fleck looked around the room. 'Is this where you killed her? Is that why you keep coming back here? So thirty-eight years ago, Juliet was working here in the manor house. You turned up and interrupted her because you're a controlling tyrant. There was some sort of fight that escalated. I don't really need to know the details. But the end result was you murdered your wife. Maybe you didn't mean for it to go that far. Maybe you did. But you were stuck with a body. Lucky for you, there were construction works going on down the bottom of the hill. So you waited until the middle of the night and you buried your wife deep in the soft earth. You joined the railway to keep a close eye on things. You told everybody that Juliet left you and moved away. For thirty-eight years it looked like you were going to get away with it. Until one day Matthew said he wanted to dig everything up to duplicate the outer loop track.'

Topham shook his head. 'He would not let it go. I suggested other projects, but that man was so set on the second outer loop.'

Fleck kept talking. She tried to ignore the searing pain in her leg. 'So you decided to get behind it as well. You decided to champion the project from the outside while you sabotaged it from within. You joined the steering committee. I don't know. Maybe you thought you could steer things away from this project going ahead. But then you found quiet ways to sabotage and undermine the railway. You ran interference on the grants correspondence. You stole supplies so that there wouldn't be enough room in the budget for special projects. My friend Ranveer showed me how you over-purchased and never allowed the railway to make more than a certain amount of money.'

Topham turned back to pick up the diesel can. Fleck spoke fast. 'It wouldn't help at all if you killed me. I've already discussed my theories at length with Detective Max Roberts of the Australian Federal Police. I told him everything. It would work out very badly for you if I were to disappear under suspicious circumstances.'

Topham gave a scornful laugh. 'You're bluffing. If that were really the case, you would have mentioned it earlier. You're just trying to save your skin. But it's too late for that. This has already passed the point of no return. It needs to be contained.' He lifted the can and turned towards the door.

Fleck swallowed. She *had* been bluffing. She had told her theories to nobody. Her surge of energy and clarity had passed. Fleck was starting to feel woozy again, but she made her voice ring out clearly. 'I think you chose this manor house to hide the supplies because you are obsessed with this place.' Topham stopped walking, but he did not turn around. 'Your crime happened almost forty years ago and since then you've never really left this room. You don't travel. You don't rest.' Fleck drew in a shaky breath. 'I might have my leg caught in the floor, but you're the one who's stuck here.'

Topham turned and, for the first time, looked at her properly. His eyes were blazing with fury. He opened his mouth to talk and then closed it again. Then he strode out the door, slamming it behind him.

Fleck tried shouting after him, even though she knew it was useless. She yelled a bit longer, then stopped. Yelling was making her breathe in too many fumes. She had to get her leg out of the floor. But she mustn't allow herself to faint. Her leg felt like it was on fire with pain and her heart was beating very fast. The smell of the diesel fumes was becoming overpowering. She needed to get out of here. What was she going to do?

She could hear bangs and pops and a persistent rumbling sound. Fleck felt herself fall into a microsleep. No! She must stay awake! The room was feeling much warmer than before. There was another smell too. Was that smoke? She dozed again. She fell asleep.

And was jolted awake by the ground smashing beside her.

CHAPTER TWENTY-FIVE

Fleck's leg shook free as she was pulled from the wrecked floor. It was Matthew. Matthew was here. He had smashed the floor beside her leg with a metal side panel from the Thomas livery. 'We need to get out of here,' he said, pulling back from their embrace. 'Can you walk on that?'

'Yes. Yes. OW! No. Not really.' Fleck hopped away from the hole in the floor, from which smoke was floating into the room.

'Wait here a sec.' Bending double, Matthew darted over to the closed door and put his hand against it. 'Argh! Hot!' There was a loud prolonged crashing noise on the other side of the wall. 'I think the staircase and the landing have collapsed. It's going to have to be the window.'

Matthew crouch-ran across the room. One of the trestle tables was set up beside the window. Matthew shifted it aside to inspect the latch.

Fleck tried to hobble at a crouch towards the window, but quickly gave up and crawled there instead. 'Is the window jammed? Is it locked?' She looked at Matthew, who was looking at the window.

Matthew turned and looked at Fleck. 'There is a wrought-iron grille on the other side. It won't matter if I get it open. We can't get out.'

Fleck looked at Matthew in dismay. This was bad news. But there was something worse. Something in the careful way Matthew spoke. The way each breath had seemed to become a slow, deliberate choice and not a reflex action. 'Matthew,' Fleck said, 'do you have your inhaler with you?'

Matthew frowned. 'I'm fine,' he said. 'I just need to think.' So that was a no, then.

'Let's lie down to think.' said Fleck. 'We need to get out of the smoke.'

The floor was so warm. Their faces were inches apart. For a moment they just looked at each other. For a moment, Fleck allowed herself to feel the full depth of emotion she felt for this man. This man, this life that they had built, full of joy and chaos and mundanity and friendship and sacrifice and messiness and so much love. All of this time, she kept thinking of some future when things would be less hectic. But this was it. This had been the time.

Matthew gazed back at her steadily. He reached out a hand and brushed a curl back from her face. She could see it in his eyes. Those deep brown eyes with the crinkles in the corners. He thought they were going to die.

Eyes, look your last. Fleck didn't know why this line floated into her head. She must have Shakespeare on the brain. Matthew opened his mouth to speak.

'No,' said Fleck. She stood up, putting all of her weight on her good leg. She didn't care that she was ruining what would have been a tender moment. She would not allow them to die in this house.

'What are you doing?' said Matthew.

'I don't know,' said Fleck. 'But I'm going to MacGyver us both out of here.'

Fleck pulled a bogie out from a tangle of equipment beside them.

Then she placed this little running board with wheels on the trestle table near the window and shifted the table closer to the window frame. Matthew was up now too. 'Get down,' said Fleck. 'I've got this. You need to stay out of the smoke.'

'What I need is to get out of this house. Learn to accept help, Fleck.'

He rolled the bogie along the table. 'If you are going to use that to ram the window, it will need some more weight on it to give it momentum and heft.'

Fleck felt a perverse shot of annoyance. Matthew was interfering in her moment of brilliant initiative. She was even more annoyed that he was right. The next few moments were spent quickly building and consulting. They needed to work fast.

'I'm going to lay these tracks along the table to run the bogie along.'

'What if we grab that other table to make it a longer run?'

'Is that steady? It doesn't need to be steady for long but it can't fall over before it gets to the window.'

They had fashioned a makeshift battering ram out of a bogie, some rope, a few sacks of fertiliser and a long metal panel that was designed to be Gordon's left side. Matthew laid tracks along the two trestle tables leading to the window. It was a hastily cobbled-together situation, but they had no time. The patch of broken floor where Fleck had been stuck suddenly caved in and became a much larger hole. Flames started reaching through from the room downstairs. The heat and smoke were becoming unbearable.

'We're only going to get one shot at this,' said Matthew. Something crashed loudly outside the room and the floor shook.

This was not ideal, what with Fleck's wonky leg and Matthew's wonky windpipe. But they had to try. Fleck looked at Matthew. 'Let's go!'

They ran either side of Bernard the Battering Ram. Fleck's leg gave out under her after a few steps and she stumbled over, but Matthew kept going, gathering speed, pushing the contraption along the tracks until it crashed into the window.

Fleck looked up just in time to see the impact. The glass didn't shatter like she expected. Instead, the surrounding wood crumbled and the entire window popped out: frame, grille, glass and all. The battering ram rolled out after it, following the window down the roof, and toppling onto the ground below.

The flames in the room flared up angrily as Matthew pulled Fleck through the gap where the window had been. He peered over the edge of the roof. Fleck watched his chest in concern. She could see he was labouring for breath, but trying hard to keep it under control. He needed his puffer.

Matthew stepped back from the edge. 'It's not a clean drop,' he said, 'We're going to need to jump clear of the house.' He looked at Fleck's leg and then looked into her eyes.

It was as if they might start slow-dancing right there on the slanted roof. Matthew wrapped his arms around Fleck, and she pressed the side of her face to his chest. 'I'm going to need to do the running,' he said. 'Just keep your head tucked in. One. Two. Three.' It was not a slow dance. Matthew ran down the roof, his arms wrapped around Fleck, and flung them both off the edge just as flames engulfed the room with a roar.

They were gathering speed. Over and over they tumbled. Matthew's arms protected Fleck's head. Fleck could hear the roar of the burning house. And there was another sound too. High-pitched and whining. Then a distant gunshot. Another high-pitched whine. Then a loud crackle. The ground beneath them seemed to be becoming less steep, but they were still hurtling along. Then there was no ground beneath them.

And then everything went ice cold.

21

Fleck sat up among the reeds. Cold water was seeping into her socks and underpants. The pain in her leg was slightly better, but that was perhaps because it was too cold to feel it. She was sitting in the lake.

'Fleck! Are you okay?' Matthew was beside her. He looked a little dazed.

The whining noise sounded again with a pop. Fleck looked up. The sky was decorated with coloured sparks. 'Fireworks,' she mumbled.

Matthew pointed to the manor house, fully ablaze. It suddenly flared up in what looked like an explosion. Then part of the house collapsed.

'I think that was the upstairs room catching fire,' said Fleck. 'But are you hurt? Are you injured? You're the one who copped the brunt of our fall.'

Matthew attempted a rueful smile. 'I think that agapanthus copped the brunt of our fall more than anything. I'll live.' But his voice was strange and controlled. Like Fleck, he was out of breath, but unlike Fleck, he seemed to be struggling to get air into his lungs.

It gradually dawned on Fleck that there was another light show going on. As well as the fireworks in the sky, the carnival lights of the railway and the raging fire of the manor house, the lake around her was now flashing red and blue. Two people were approaching them. They were moving fast while also looking supremely relaxed in that peculiar manner of paramedics.

'Hello. We're from the ambulance. I'm Eli and this is Orrin. Can you tell us what happened here?'

'He's having an asthma attack! He doesn't have his puffer! He needs ventolin!' Fleck attempted to stand up in the lake, but accidentally put weight on her bad leg and collapsed again.

Matthew stood up and helped Fleck to her feet. 'I'm fine, it's just some mild asthma. You should look at Fleck first.'

Fleck shook her head at him. 'Learn to accept help, Matthew.'

The other paramedic, Orrin, was standing right at the bank. 'Are you in any pain? Are you able to get yourselves out of the water? How about you come sit on the grass here and we can look at you.'

The way the paramedics were talking, it seemed like there was no fire, no homicidal Fat Controller. It felt like they were all just sitting on the park bench beside the lake, chatting about ducks. Eli was carrying a red bag and had already produced a puffer with a spacer attached by the time Matthew reached the shore.

Fleck flopped on the grassy bank. Her head was still spinning a little from the tumble down the hill and, well, everything else. Then she sat up in alarm. 'No. Not an ambulance. We need police. We need police to stop him. We need to stop him. He killed her. He killed his wife!'

'All right. Let's calm down. It's all good. We've got the whole gang here tonight. The firies and the police have gone with the other ambulance to the top of the hill. When we saw you rolling away, we decided to follow you and see if you needed help. Your mate here is getting his asthma meds. The whole situation is under control.'

Fleck said, 'Oh. Okay. Good.' Then she fainted.

EPILOGUE

'I still can't believe you've never seen *Get Smart*,' Fleck said as she put the first disc from Ranveer's box set into her DVD player. 'They used to play the reruns on Sunday nights. The show always makes me think of toasted cheese jaffles.'

'Oooh! Maybe we can have toasted cheese jaffles at intermission,' said Trixie. 'But meanwhile, I have popcorn.'

Fleck returned to the couch, settling beside Trixie. Ranveer, on Trixie's other side, pressed 'play'.

'I still can't work out how it happened, with Topham,' Trixie said. 'Surely he didn't light the fire while he was in the house.'

'No, he was definitely out of the house,' said Fleck. 'The police say the accelerant went all the way out the front door. Their theory is that he tried to go back inside after the house was alight.'

'Why would he do that?' said Trixie.

'It's possible he saw Matthew go in and wanted to stop him. But then, when he went up the staircase, it collapsed under him and, well, he was trapped.' Fleck cast a look at Sam and Joseph. They were building magnet towers on the floor with Norah and paying no attention to the conversation.

'And another thing,' said Trixie. 'How did Matthew know where to find you?'

Ranveer pressed 'pause'.

Fleck stretched her leg out. 'He looked at the ceiling of the first room he got inside and saw my leg poking through. He told me that he's a big fan of my legs, so he recognised it immediately.'

'They are great legs,' Trixie observed.

'Thank you. What they lack in length, they make up for in legginess,' Fleck said.

Ranveer looked confused. 'Doesn't "legginess" mean "length"?'

Fleck shook her head and scoffed. 'No. "Length" means "length". "Legginess" means "like legs" and my legs are *definitely* like legs.'

'You're not wrong. Hey, why aren't we watching this?' said Trixie. 'Press play, Ranveer.'

Ranveer pressed 'play'.

'And the police found … they found Juliet?' Trixie asked.

Ranveer pressed 'pause'.

Fleck nodded. 'Yes. They conducted a search and – yeah. They found some, um, some historic remains.'

Trixie sighed. 'That's awful.' After a pause, she added, 'Did I tell you that Ruby has signed up to do workshops at Many Hands? And Kerryn's back on board now too.'

'That's fantastic. Matthew was telling me that Ruby and Quinn have become good friends over the past few weeks as well. They've been hard at work at something. I think she might be helping him track down his catfisher.'

'Is there any more chatting that we need to do before I press play?' Ranveer asked. 'Let's get it all out of the way now.'

Trixie laughed and leaned her head playfully on Ranveer's shoulder. 'I'm sorry! We'll be good now. I promise!'

Ranveer pressed 'play'. Maxwell Smart, the Chief and Nintety-Nine were sitting around a table with a birthday cake. Ninety-Nine took off her earring so that the Chief could use it to read the hidden birthday message written in invisible icing.

'Spy earrings!' exclaimed Trixie, sitting up straight. 'Oh, Fleck! We need to get you some detective spy earrings like that. How cool would that be? I wonder if you can buy them online?'

'Trixie ...' said Ranveer.

'Oops, sorry, Ranveer,' said Trixie, relaxing back into the couch. 'I'm sorry. I forgot. We can buy *you* some spy earrings too.'

Today's workshop was on basic mending. Bev sat at the head of the table and showed them how to repair seams, darn holes, fix hems and sew patches. Trixie had set up her phone on a tripod to record the session for more #fridaybev shorts. Trixie, Fleck, Jo, Dima, Kerryn and Ruby sat around working on various garments and toys that needed repairing.

'Oh, Fleck. You could go to Adelaide on that thread! It does not need to be that long!' Bev tutted at Fleck as she watched her thread her needle.

Fleck continued doggedly with her small corduroy overalls and too-long thread and turned to Ruby. 'So, what's the latest on the catfish situation?'

Ruby smiled. 'Oh, didn't I tell you? They caught her. It turns out she had a lot of victims, mostly older women like herself. I suppose she knew how to tell them what they wanted to hear. Anyway, the police have her now. But Quinn and I sent her one last glitter packet in the mail. I don't do that anymore, so I used up the rest of my stock. Glitter, tiny cows, mayonnaise, the works!'

'You've stopped sending out your packages?'

Ruby nodded. 'I realised that I was spending all of my energy on the haters. There were people saying really nice things on my page and I wasn't even responding to their comments because I was so busy tracking down trolls. I don't want to be like that.' She sifted through the tin of buttons on the table. 'Anyway, I don't have time anymore. I've been helping Quinn launch his YouTube channel. It's already got quite a lot of followers. It's all about Melbourne trains.'

'Oh, mine's gone all wrong!' Dima held up the skirt she was mending. The seam had a tangle of thread all bunched together.

'You see?' Bev was pointing at Dima but looking at Fleck. 'You need to keep the thread short and taut.'

Fleck groaned. 'But I don't want to have to thread another needle. I just want to keep using this one.'

'Hey, Fleck, do you have a new case yet?' Jo was perched at the corner of the table, darning a sock that was patterned with fairy wrens.

Fleck shook her head. 'I'm going to take a little break. But I want you all to keep an eye out for me. It won't be long before I'll be wanting another case to work on. I just love untangling things.'

'Well, isn't that a good thing?' said Bev, pointing. Fleck looked down. Her extra-long thread had tangled into a massive knot.

Because of the sticky note situation, Trixie was convinced the pink duck psychologist should be named Pinky Duckworth or Rose Dux or maybe Redmond Drake. But her name was Ramesha Khan and she had a little office within a podiatrist's practice in Blackburn.

The first thing that Fleck noticed about Ramesha's office was the books. The room was filled with books – more than could fit on the shelves. There were neat little stacks of books and audiobook CDs on the desk too. 'It's my living lending library,' she explained to Fleck as they walked in. Fleck sat in a very normal-looking chair and Ramesha settled behind her desk.

She had certificates on the wall: forensic psychologist, clinical psychologist and neuro psychologist qualifications, as well as some awards. These certificates were the only thing that told Fleck that this was a psychologist's practice and not the office of an overworked English teacher who really wanted to help you get through Year 12.

They talked about family life, Many Hands and the joy Fleck found in detective work. They even talked about parkrun. Eventually, Fleck landed on the topic she'd been circling. She had almost died. She had almost died twice. And she couldn't bear being inside a supermarket.

'The weird thing is I'm more stressed about the effect of all this on my state of mind than the fact that I was almost killed twice. And the thought of giving up detective work sends me into a panic as well. I love it. It lights me up inside. But what good is that if I lose my mind or lose my life?'

Ramesha paused to think before she answered. 'If you told me that you had taken up skateboarding and that it gave you a lot of joy, even though there were risks, I would say go for it. But if you told me you had taken up skateboarding without a helmet, because you thought it was weak to wear one, I would have some concerns. I journey with a lot of detectives and police workers. Regular therapy is part of the vocation. It comes with the territory. There is nothing weak or strange about it.'

'So you're my safety helmet?'

Ramesha smiled. 'I'm perhaps the *strap* of your safety helmet. There are plenty of other things we need to make sure are in place as well, but I'm getting ahead of myself. It sounds like you are mostly in a good place. You have good family support, and excellent friendships.

You are taking time to pursue your passions. But let's talk about the supermarket situation.'

'I'm so embarrassed. I just need to get better at it. I'm being such a baby. I just need to tough it out. It will get better.' Fleck felt her face getting hot.

'Have you thought about online shopping?' Ramesha said.

'No!' Fleck shook her head firmly. 'I should be able to do a proper shop. Online shopping is expensive. I'm a stay-at-home mum. I'm not earning an income, but I can help save the family money by doing a proper shop.'

'It sounds like you are going to "should" yourself to death.' Ramesha smiled. 'Let's deal with reality. Not with "should". You have worth far beyond whatever money you might save for the family by getting all the specials. Being able to tolerate supermarkets is something we can work on in the future, but in the meantime you deserve to have food in your cupboard.' Ramesha was writing directions down on a piece of paper as she spoke. 'When we finish this session, before you even go home, I want you to sit in your car and order ten things to be delivered. I don't want you to do a full shop. I don't want it to be a perfect shop where you don't forget anything. Just order ten things. Pay the delivery cost. And make sure one of those things is your favourite treat.'

At the end of their session, Ramesha handed Fleck some books and articles to read and gave her a 'prescription'. 'I want you to keep buying groceries in the way that works for you, I want you to keep going to parkrun, I want you to keep going to your friend's craft workshops, and I want you to keep solving mysteries in a way that is safe. And I want you to keep coming here to process it all. Do we have a deal?'

Afterwards, Fleck sat in her car with her phone. She ordered unscented wipes in the blue packet, roast sesame dressing that was non-spicy, peanut butter, regular butter, bin liners, muesli bars, Weet-Bix, nappies, chicken nuggets and a packet of sour lollies to hide in the car. She didn't stop until she had put in all her details, booked a delivery slot and paid for the order. It actually wasn't too expensive.

Then she sat for a moment looking out the car window. A Japanese maple hung over the fence in a glory of red and orange leaves. The sky above was blue, with puffy clouds. Fleck smiled. It was time to go home.

ACKNOWLEDGEMENTS

So many people have helped me with this book. Here are just a few of them.

I used the Diamond Valley Railway in Eltham as the inspiration for the Paradise Lake Miniature Railway. Pat Minihan gave me a behind-the-scenes tour of the Diamond Valley Railway and tirelessly answered all my questions afterwards. All mistakes are my own.

Agnes Mary Hanna is a brilliant clinical psychologist who helped me to understand what Ramesha Khan's session with Fleck might involve.

My parents and siblings have a message thread going, separate from the regular family thread, and it's for advice. I can't tell you how often I bombard it with random writing-related questions. They always come up with the goods. For this, and for so much more, thank you to Alan and Kathleen Walter, Daniel and Danielle Walter, Emily Walter and Luke Neill, James Walter and Kathy Giordamnis, Michael Walter and Sarah Cosgrave, and Felicity and Michael Neeson. I also want to thank Aileen Moriarty.

James Solly watched many train videos with me and helped me discover the best creators. One of these is Taitset, AKA Martin Bennet, who very kindly responded to my emails and helped me to find interesting things for Quinn to talk about.

Bob and Nola Solly provided advice and encouragement and a nice quiet house to write in! Grace Solly teased me a lot, but she also read my book and told me it was good.

My wonderful publisher, Kelly Doust, has treated me with kindness and patience, and has given me excellent writing advice at the times when I needed it most. Thank you also to my editor Zoe Sorensen, who helped me so much in shaping the manuscript. And many thanks to everyone at Affirm Press, especially Kevin O'Brien, Dana Anderson, Alistair Trapnell, Brooke Lyons, Andrea Dobbin, and Susie Kennewell.

I know I've said that Julian Sargeant is not George, and he isn't. But the spirit of Julian's Kitchen is what I most tried to capture in its fictional counterpart. It breaks my heart that by the time this book is published, Julian will have moved back to Europe with his family and the cornerside community hub he built will be no more. Thank you for many years of coffee, conversation and a table to write at.

Rose Solly was so patient with me when I was busy writing and couldn't do all the things. And she read my other book and told me it was good!

Jack Heath helped me in many ways throughout the writing of this novel, but I am particularly grateful for the phone conversation where we thrashed our way out of a burning house. Thank you for your generosity, expertise and insight.

Eli Solly helped me to understand how the paramedics would behave and what language they would use. Michael Solly helped me to untangle many plot problems while I taught him to drive.

Emily Solly is human sunshine. Thank you for your encouragement and warm hugs.

Chat 10 Looks 3 is a podcast, a Facebook community, and a class-3 certified cult. I am so grateful to this kind place on the internet for their cheerleading, support and help with random questions. There is a spin-off to this group for chatters who are ADHD or otherwise neurodivergent. It is called 'Chat 10 Look…what's that over there?' This group has helped me immensely. There are so many ways in which my ADHD helps me to be a great writer, but there are also days when it's really difficult. This group helped me on the hard days and celebrated with me when things went well.

I wrote this novel using free software from novlr.org and I really recommend it. There is a Discord server attached to the Novlr community full of writers around the world who did sprints with me. Thank you, team!

When I needed a quiet set of days free of distractions to write, Tarrawarra Abbey looked after me in beautiful, prayerful surroundings and with delicious, nourishing meals. I'm so grateful for their hospitality.

Thank you to Kerryn Mayne, Emma Grey and Sandie Docker for all of their writerly support.

Thank you to Siang Lu and Kristy Diffey for all of the bizarre shenanigans.

Sally Waller is the generous donor who even outbid her husband to win the silent auction prize to name a character in my book. As a result, Coco Waller-Hunt appears in these pages as an energetic six-year-old. Thank you, Sally!

The Aussie writing community is a beautifully supportive place. There are too many wonderful people to name here. Plus, it feels like name-dropping and showing off! So I'll thank you as a group. I hope that's not a cop-out!

There is too much to thank David Solly for. I hope he already knows. But specifically, he patiently talked me through the mechanics of bashing a window out of an old house. It's more than that. It's everything. But the window advice was really helpful.

There are so many people who have sent me an affirming message that always seemed to arrive just at the right time. I can't name you all. I hope that you know who you are, and I hope that you know what it means to me. Thank you.

BOOK CLUB QUESTIONS

1. Have you had any experience with miniature railways like the one depicted in this book? Do you know or love any train nerds?
2. 'It didn't feel like passion. It didn't have the same texture. It was desperation.' How does Lynette's insistence on selling GelVita erode the culture of the Many Hands workshop community? Have you had to deal with difficult personalities in groups before?
3. Would you class this book as a 'cosy mystery'? Are darker themes managed in a way that maintains a cosy atmosphere, or is there too much harsh reality in the crime?
4. Ranveer says that before he met Fleck and Trixie 'all of my days looked the same'. How has this changed?
5. Would you rather watch a Ruby Ringtail video, eat one of Dima's cakes or browse the shop at Many Hands?
6. Trixie insists that hobbies are a means of fighting the patriarchy. Do you agree?
7. In the first Paradise Heights novel, Fleck is trying to discover what she's passionate about. In this novel, Fleck knows that she loves detective work, but she's trying to figure out what that looks like in her life. What have your experiences been of trying to make room for creative interests in your life?
8. Is Fleck actually a good detective? What skills does she bring to the role?
9. Three-year-old Norah can sometimes be a polarising character. Do you find her charming or insufferable?
10. Do you think that Fleck and Matthew have a healthy relationship? Why or why not?

ALSO BY KATE SOLLY

Fleck Parker loves a good puzzle. She spends most of her time feeling invisible, caring for three small children, and that's fine, really. But it does make her brain itch occasionally. When Trixie, fellow school-mum and avid crafter, is accused of stealing money from a women's crafts charity, Fleck feels compelled to investigate and clear Trixie's name.

READ THE FIRST CHAPTER OF *THE PARADISE HEIGHTS CRAFT STORE STITCH-UP*

CHAPTER ONE

They were going to be on time today. Fleck just knew it. She finally had a system. Sam's school uniform and Norah's kinder clothes had been laid out the night before. They were both awake and eating breakfast. Sam's hair was brushed. Alice was also awake and painting herself with toast fingers in her highchair. Library bags were packed and she had even remembered to clean both the lunch boxes.

It was when she was tying Norah's hair into two neat plaits that things started to go wrong.

'I can't find my other shoe,' said Sam.

'I'm sure it's there. We laid it out, remember?'

'It's not here.'

'It's not a shoe.' This was Norah chiming in.

'Check under the couch.'

'Nope.'

'Are you sure it's not there? Did you check all around?'

'Yep.'

'It's not a shoe.' Norah again.

'Well, did you move it?'

'Nope.'

'Well, where can it be?'

'Are you cross, Mummy?'

'No. No, I'm not cross. I'm just confused. Why did the shoe decide to go off on a holiday by itself?'

'You're funny, Mummy.'

'Okay, Norah, that's your hair done. I'm going to put the lunches together. Sam, you keep looking for your shoe.'

'*It's not a shoe!*'

Fleck began loading the two lunch boxes with sandwiches and snacks. The fruit bowl was bare, despite having been full yesterday, but Fleck had a backup plan: she reached into the pantry, took out a Vita-Weat box and shook out two mandarins.

Norah's eyes lit up at the sight of the two pieces of fruit. 'I want a mandy!'

'No, Norah. We need these for kinder and school. You can have one for your fruit break.'

'I want a mandy NOW!'

'These are the only ones left. They need to go in the lunch boxes.'

'You go to the fruit shop.'

'There's no time. I'll get some more later, but we have to go to school soon.' Why was she having this conversation? Why was she negotiating fruit shortages with a three-year-old?

Alice, sitting happily in the highchair, made a noise that could only mean one thing.

'Sounds like it's nappy-change time for you, young lady!'

Fleck had just finished applying the nappy cream when she heard a colossal crash from the family room. She quickly placed Alice in the cot for safekeeping and rushed to the scene of the crime. It wasn't as bad as it had sounded. Sam, while vigorously searching for his lost shoe, had toppled a basket of clean washing over the floor. Matthew's business shirts and Alice's bunny-rugs lay unfurled across the floorboards. It was a mess, but that wasn't the main problem.

'*Norah!*'

A picture of innocence, the small child sat primly at the table in her favourite Batman t-shirt. She gazed back at her mother with her enormous brown eyes, blinked her impossibly long lashes and continued to clumsily peel one of the mandarins. 'I'm hungry,' she said, stone-faced.

'No.' Fleck lifted Norah out of her chair and placed her at her original place at the table in front of her half-finished breakfast. 'If you're hungry, you can finish your toast.'

'NOOOOOOO!' Norah stormed out of the room.

Fleck gazed forlornly at the half-peeled mandarin. There was already a small bite mark in one of the segments. Now what was she going to pack for fruit break? Did she have time to cut carrot sticks? Norah wouldn't eat them, but at least Fleck would look like she'd made an effort.

'Mummy!' Sam said. 'I still can't find my shoe! It isn't anywhere!'

Fleck opened the fridge and peered into the veggie drawer. 'Just keep looking.'

The carrots in the fridge were pretty sad. But what if she finished peeling the mandarin and broke it up? She could put the unbitten segments in one of those little containers from the plastics cupboard. Done!

She was on her hands and knees digging into the back of the cupboard when it struck her: things were a little too quiet. All she could hear was Alice babbling and giggling in the next room. Where was Norah?

'I can't go to school with no shoes on!' Sam stood in her path, bouncing from foot to foot.

Fleck stepped quickly around him. 'Hold on a minute.'

Norah and Alice were sitting side by side in Alice's cot. Alice's skin was white as snow. She gazed haughtily up at her mother like some tiny French aristocrat while Norah *continued to apply zinc cream to her chubby arms and legs*. Norah, meanwhile, had at some point liberated her plaits from their restraints. She doggedly persisted in her costume design pursuits beneath a frenzied halo of red hair.

'*Norah!*'

Norah shot her a defiant glare. 'Alice is Mr Freeze.'

Fleck cocked an eyebrow. 'Naughty step.'

They were already running behind. Three minutes on the naughty step for Norah would throw them out even more, but it had to be done.

Alice, who had been enjoying her stint as the Crown Prince of Chilblains, did not take kindly to the warm face washer. Fleck soon discovered that lotions designed to repel moisture were near impossible to wash off. It was 8.49am. Fleck hunted for a long-sleeved onesie in the laundry, the nappy bag and the upstairs chest of drawers, then zipped Alice's still mostly white limbs into it. Nobody needed to know.

Sam stood at the door, looking to be near tears. 'I don't have any more places to look. I can't find my shoe!'

Fleck looked at her son. Something clicked into place. 'It's not a shoe,' she murmured under her breath.

'What?'

'Hang on a minute, Sam.' With Alice on her hip, Fleck strode across to the step where Norah was perched. She crouched down to look her in the eye, ignoring the loud popping sound her left knee made.

'Norah, where is Sam's shoe?'

'You can't talk to me. I'm on the naughty step.'

'Is it not a shoe?'

'Not. A. Shoe,' Norah repeated emphatically.

'Then what is it?'

'Batmobile.'

'Batmobile?'

Norah gave a firm nod. Fleck stood up and walked to the toy box. Inside it was Sam's shoe. Inside Sam's shoe was Batman, looking coolly impressed with himself in his new black leather vehicle.

It was 8.58am – well past time to go.

Technically, having a coffee at George's Kitchen was supposed to be her reward for a successfully executed school run. Fleck often set up systems of reminders and rewards to coax her brain to focus on boring things. But it didn't always work. On mornings like today, when they'd stumbled in after the bell with Sam before dropping Norah off late at kinder, her hair in a messy bun, Fleck still went to the cafe. The thing was, she *needed* the coffee more on the mornings when she'd failed. And it all came down to how she defined success, really. Were all three children alive? Yes? Were they naked? No? Job done. Strong latte, please.

George was busy with some takeaway orders as Fleck slipped into the cafe and set Alice's capsule down at her favourite corner table. While she waited, she got out her exercise book, in which she'd been nutting out her morning routine. Fleck carried an exercise book around with her for to-do lists and meal plans and drafts of notes and random thoughts. She called it her 'everything book'. She examined her nightly to-do list now. Having clothes laid out the night before had worked well, but next time she should put the shoes out of reach. And the zinc cream out of reach. And the rare lunch-box items out of reach.

George placed Fleck's coffee on the table. 'I've got one for you.'

'Ooh! What is it?'

'There are four countries in the world that have only one vowel. Can you name them all?'

'Ooh, that's a tough one,' Fleck said. Then, 'Chad!'

'Chad is one. Can you name the rest?'

'Give me a minute.'

She flipped the page over and started scratching out answers to the riddle. This was far more interesting than the morning routine. As she scoured her memory, made lists and turned the problem around in her head, she felt her brain slip into that sweet spot. This was a good puzzle.

If there was one thing that Fleck Parker loved, it was a puzzle to solve. She wasn't fussy. Sometimes it was the codebreaker in the Sunday paper. Sometimes it was the Friday cryptic. Sometimes she even pulled out a maths textbook and brushed up on logarithmic functions. But it was never the word finds or sudokus, or the one where you had to guess the song from all the little sound bites. Okay, maybe she *was* fussy.

'This is hard,' Fleck announced. George had returned to the counter and was making his own morning coffee. 'Niue has only four letters but three of them are vowels!'

'Niue's not a country!'

A new knot of patrons arrived. George always maintained that making himself a coffee was like a rain dance for attracting customers. As he took their orders, Fleck continued to play with the problem. She stayed away from South America. They all seemed to have vowel-heavy names. Was it some obscure Caribbean country like Saint Kitts and Nevis? She'd be in trouble if it was.

'Egypt!' Fleck exclaimed.

'Egypt is another,' George said as he passed a tray of takeaway cups to a portly man in a suit.

Alice stirred in her capsule but slept on. Fleck continued to scribble in the margin of the page. 'Does "Czech" count? As in "Czech Republic"?'

'Have you ever heard anyone call that country "Czech" by itself? No. Czech Republic does not count. I think it's Czechia now anyway.'

'Ugh.' This was hard. It was delicious, but it was hard. Of course, her phone was right there. She could easily just google a list of the world's countries. But she didn't want to. She knew she could solve this herself, even if it took some time. But she would take a break from it for now. She stored it carefully away in her mind to play with later. Then she grabbed the newspaper from another table.

This was definitely the best table in the small cafe. In this seat, with her back to the wall, Fleck could chat to George and easily look out both windows. On her right was busy Highett Road, with its trucks, buses and occasional tram, and straight ahead was the smaller Peppercorn Street – with its collection of shops, their racks out on the footpath – which real estate agents loved to describe as having a 'village feel'.

Fleck flipped forward to the puzzles page of the paper. She snapped a photo of the crosswords and brainteasers to look at later. They weren't the supreme Friday crossword, but they were still worth a look. Sometimes she would get obsessed with a particular type – acrostics or nonograms, say – and spend every spare moment on it until she had completely mastered the form, after which it was too easy and she became sick of it. Then she would abandon it entirely for a new obsession.

It was like her brain was constantly itching for the perfect problem to solve, when her brain clicked into rhythm. She became completely absorbed, investigating, turning things over. The perfect problem was rare, but it was *wonderful*.

She flipped back to the front of the paper and started reading the news. The second wave of takeaway orders dwindled away. Fleck was now the only customer in the cafe.

'Quiz?' George called.

'Quiz!' Fleck rifled through the pages to find today's twenty-five questions.

Doing the quiz was another rain dance for making customers arrive, but today they managed to make it through the one-point and two-point sections without interruption. Fleck was preparing to read out the first of the three-point questions ('Which Australian capital city was once known as Palmerston?') when George narrowed his eyes and squinted across the road – the big road, that was – at the new cafe.

'What is their story?' he muttered. He strode out from behind the counter to get a better look through the window. Fleck followed his gaze.

'Five staff on and zero customers. Look: there are five! And they've had a full roster since seven! Who puts all their staff on that early? I do not understand their logic.'

It was true. The cafe across Highett Road was bustling, but not with customers. Staff in aprons straightened signs, dusted counters and paced around empty tables. Meanwhile, Fleck knew the answer to the question. It was Darwin.

George shook his head slowly. 'They are a textbook case on how not to run a cafe. I really feel like I should go over and give them some advice. And they should have gone with a different name. "Espresso 312"? Not very creative!'

'Well, the other cafe is *too* creative.' Fleck gestured at the large cafe on the other side of Peppercorn Street. 'It's like they went through a multi-step process to arrive at "dangermouse". Step one – find an obscure nostalgic reference. Step two – make it all one word. Step three – remove any capital letters. Step four – open your brand-new edgy cafe.'

George chuckled and shook his head. 'Yes, because opening a cafe is definitely that simple. I'm going to think up some new names for them. Stay tuned.' He walked back to take a tray of croissants off the counter and slotted them into the display fridge. He shot another look at the cafe across the road as he straightened. 'But look at them! I definitely want to give those new guys some advice. It's driving me crazy watching them make such simple mistakes.'

Fleck laughed. 'Don't give them advice! They're the competition! You're too nice, George.' Palmerston changed its name to Darwin in – when was it? 1911? 1912? – after Federation, anyway. It was when the Northern Territory was transferred to the Commonwealth. Before that, it was all part of South Australia. They needed to get back to the quiz so that she could show off.

George smiled. 'I'm not stressed about their competition just yet. Yesterday they didn't open until ten. And they left their deliveries just sitting there on the doorstep for almost an hour! That's very unprofessional.'

George put his hands on his hips. He was a large man with a neatly trimmed beard. His black hair was not yet turning grey, even though he must have been in his fifties. 'You'd think, with that many people on, they could get someone to fix that graffiti. That's been there all week!' He gestured to the side of the cafe where a large tag in a dull purple scrawl defaced the bricks. 'I'm going to call the council on them. You can't leave graffiti up. You have to nip it in the butt.'

Bud, Fleck thought. *You nip things in the bud. Like flowers on a basil plant.* Fleck only ever corrected people's grammar in her mind. This was the best policy for maintaining friendships. Anyway, 'nip in the butt' was funnier. She pictured George in his apron, with massive lobster claws instead of arms, chasing a hapless graffiti artist who was covering his backside in fear.

The bell jangled. More customers! Fleck sighed. No more quiz today. At least they'd made it through most of the questions. Plus, it was time she got going. She packed up her things and carried her cup over to the counter. George rang up her purchase.

Fleck tapped her card on the side of the reader. It beeped. 'Cyprus!' she exclaimed.

George beamed. 'Cyprus,' he confirmed. 'I'll see you soon.'